John T. Sladek was born in Iowa in 1937. He was educated at the University of Minnesota where he studied mechanical engineering and English Literature. He lived for a time in New York, travelled on the continent, and settled in London in the 1960s. Now he has returned to Minnesota, where he works as a technical writer. He has one daughter. His first novel, *The Reproductive System*, was published to enormous critical acclaim and his fertile, inventive fiction, as well as his humorous cast of mind, have been likened to Kurt Vonnegut at his best.

D1240380

By the same author

JOHN SLADEK

Bugs

PALADIN
GRAFTON BOOKS

A Division of the Collins Publishing Group

LONDON GLASGOW
TORONTO SYDNEY AUCKLAND

Paladin
Grafton Books
A Division of the Collins Publishing Group
8 Grafton Street, London W1X 3LA

Published in Paladin Books 1991
9 8 7 6 5 4 3 2 1

First published in Great Britain by
Macmillan London Ltd 1989

ISBN 0-586-09023-1

Printed and bound in Great Britain by
Collins, Glasgow

Set in Palatino

Chapter One

The televised naturalist looked a bit like Susan. She kept a fixed smile as she demonstrated how to use some sort of beetle to clean an animal skull.

'We start with something like this badger head, for example. After skinning and boiling it, I cut away most of the meat. Then all I have to do is drop it in this box. My little darlings do the rest.'

The camera looked down into the box at a seething mass of pale beetles crawling over bones, into eye-sockets.

'I put a few things in here yesterday. Let's see how they're doing.'

The gleaming white object she lifted from the box was a small human skull. It matched her own fixed smile.

'Like little piranhas, they are. Clean as a whistle. Now, let's see what else we have.'

She dipped her hand into the box again, as into a bran-tub for some prize. The smile held for a moment, then vanished. Her hand seemed somehow to be stuck in the box.

'Help me, Fred!'

Fred reached out and took Susan's other hand, but he couldn't pull her back. She was not just stuck, but being slowly pulled into the machine. Susan screamed and screamed, but her voice never rose above the loud hissing of the hungry bugs.

Fred woke to find he was the last passenger on the Minneapolis Rapid Transit city bus. He retrieved his book, a paperback of *The Time Machine*, which had fallen to the floor.

The bus, full of sleep-inducing fumes, lurched off the freeway into a concrete lay-by and hissed to a stop.

'This is it,' said the driver, looking pleased. After a brief hesitation, he added: 'Sir.'

'Doesn't this bus go all the way to Paradise Valley?'

'Nope.' The driver was positively gleeful now. 'That's eight more miles, sir. You need the extension bus.'

'The extension bus. All right. When does the next one leave?'

'Only one a day, at five-twenty P.M.' By now the driver seemed ready slap his knee and fall out of his seat. 'Sir.'

Fred looked at the watch he'd bought from a man in the street in New York City: 9.10 A.M. Fred had twenty more minutes to get to his job interview at VIMNUT Industries.

'Only one bus a day? I can't wait here all day. I – '

The bus driver waited until Fred had stumbled down the steps. 'Don't wait. It don't stop here anyways.'

'Sorry?'

'Nothin' to be sorry about. You gotta go back downtown to catch it. So long, *sir*,' said the driver cheerfully, as he closed the door and drove off.

Fred looked around. He seemed to be on a round elevated platform, a kind of saucer of smooth concrete that jutted out from the side of the freeway and flew over a wild forest. There were no buildings below, no sign of civilization unless you counted the spray-painted graffiti on the parapet, most of which was illegible. *THE CONdUMS*, he read. A street-gang? A rock band? Or some cryptic general observation, like 'the pits'? Life in this here modern American gheddo is just the condoms. He leaned over the parapet and gazed upon translucent green aspen leaves. There was nothing to be seen through their translucency but other green aspen leaves, round and shuddering.

His full name was Manfred Evelyn Jones. A month ago he had been at home in Britain, thinking of himself as a promising young novelist. All right, a promising novelist.

Now he was desperately scrambling for a technical writing job in a strange disturbing land. *The pits*, he thought.

It was mainly from television that he knew how Americans went about defining this or that as *the pits*. Aside from sport, the main function of British television now seemed Americology – the detailed study of Yank culture and idiom. And the only way Britain could keep up was to import more and more American television: cop dramas, soap operas, chat shows, comedies and family sagas. When any genre began to pall, all you had to do was combine it with another: family comedies, cop operas, soap sagas. It was the way Americans liked to combine all the things they loved: cookies in ice-cream, maple syrup in sausages. If only a family crisis during an exciting car chase could somehow be combined with an American pro football game . . .

The British could not get enough of all this. The worst intellectual fast foods America could develop were eagerly devoured in Britain: programmes like 'All My Cops' were beginning to rival football or show jumping in popularity. For that matter, British kids now wanted to grow up to play American football – the kind that requires fifty pounds of padding and still causes crippling injuries in every game.

'All My Cops' was the formula cop drama that combined violence with elements of soap opera. The producers took pains to balance the number of drawn guns with an equal number of tearful, hugful family reconciliations. The show featured policemen and policewomen of all known races, gays and lesbians, good junkies and (for contrast) an occasional bad junkie. Thus it reached all audiences. Mum might take an interest in the sergeant's blind wife, the lieutenant's alcoholic father, or the captain's homosexual son. Dad meanwhile could identify with danger and duty – the need to 'blow away a few scumbags' every week. For the kids, there was up-to-date slang, detectives in fashionable clothes, and car chases.

After a time, Fred found the stairway and descended. Below the trees was a Tarmac road, Roman-straight, leading

7

nowhere discernible in two directions. Endless. No footpath, nor anything like a phone-box or a taxi-rank.

Fred wasn't sure he could have afforded a Minneapolis taxi anyway. He had gathered some idea of their prices from the signs they carried, depicting the credit cards they would accept – Mr Card, Vice Charge, Americana Excess, Gourmandcard – with the implication that, for passengers going *all* the way across the city, a bank loan might be arranged. There was nothing in the credit-card class that Fred could really afford. That was why he dined only at McIntosh's. That was one of the reasons he desperately needed this job at VIMNUT Industries.

The main reason was to save his marriage. Money, Fred believed was the secret ingredient of successful marriages. At least, a marriage could not last unless both partners had mutual cash for each other. He knew that if he could heap up a pile of wealth, and fly back to Britain on Concorde, it would at least make Susan pause and pay attention. Money could heal a marriage. Money could do anything in America.

If only Susan believed that.

It was the lack of money that had brought them to America. His American agent had asked Fred to come over and meet publishers. He'd promised a big breakthrough, swearing that 'British novels are in'. Fred and Susan had scraped together the air fare (standby passengers on Air Zambezi) and arrived in New York with rather high hopes. If they could make it there, as the song went . . .

Not only hadn't they made it there; they had been destroyed by it. New York had turned out to be noisy, dirty, dangerous, expensive, and crammed with obnoxious people who got on each other's nerves. Within days, he and Susan had also begun to get on each other's nerves. She'd gone back to London – leaving him, as she put it, to enjoy the city of cockroach motels.

He'd sat in an Irish 'pub' and said: 'My marriage was eaten

by cockroaches.' An Irishman had told him to bugger off out of Northern Ireland.

'No, but listen. My marriage – '

'Why don't you Brits just bugger off?'

Buggering off seemed like a reasonable idea. He'd buggered off to La Guardia, and from La Guardia to the high technopolis of Minneapolis. He'd arrived only yesterday, and he now calculated that his money would last two more weeks. By then, Fred had to be VIMNUT's technical writer.

Fred found Minneapolis exciting and disturbing, especially its sky. Here the sky was huge, a living presence forcing itself upon the attention of the Cro-Magnons below, showing them that there was room for One God Only. No wonder the people here all trooped round on Sundays to their churches (designed by Finns who were obsessed with 'natural' wood and askew spires) to pay homage – they'd better. Even the atheists here glanced at the sky and hurried off to their Unitarian temples to ponder questions of sociology, Third World politics, and the birth of the blues.

He compared this great brooding presence to London's miserable patch of civilized grey. Even when blue, London's sky was about as prepossessing as a faded soiled Cambridge sweatshirt. No one looked up in London; there was nothing to behold.

Growing up in London, Fred had been five years old before he managed to catch a glimpse of a rainbow. It was not at all like the illustration in his book, *Our Friend the Rain*, by Dimpleby Dunbort, which clearly showed red at the bottom. This real rainbow, framing the gasworks, had red at the top.

Fred was now thirty-one, though he thought of himself as twenty. He still appreciated rainbows. Here in Minneapolis, you could imagine rainbows of any style, popping up daily. There was plenty of other life up there besides: boiling cumulus heaped up like clotted cream, the distant rainstorm ploughing the land, high clouds like streaky bacon, lush tropical sunsets, or hundreds of Canada geese in huge formations, braying like donkeys as they surveyed the land they owned. At night the moon rose huge and yellow and healthy over a low horizon. The stars were so numerous and bright that they seemed like clusters of night cities on a landscape. It was possible to look up and imagine that he was falling from space, head first down towards some unimaginable land.

He had indeed fallen here from the sky, landing at sunset at an airport where the full magnificent blaze was visible. He paused by a great window to admire it. People kept jostling him aside, as they made their way past the window to a glass case displaying a replica of an antique car.

Minneapolis disturbed him as it does not disturb many people. It was, after all, a part of Minnesota, that low-stress locale of lakes, lutefish, and lack-lustre politicians. Dullness was all, in a city worthy of a Eugene McCarthy, a Walter Mondale or a Hubert H. Humphrey.

The city's reputation for dullness went back a century or more. Scandinavian settlers drank gallons of strong coffee to keep their brains alive in Minneapolis. German settlers before them drank fiery peppermint schnapps and felled huge Christmas trees in the snow to keep awake. No doubt the Indians before them nodded off by its waterfalls. Before the Indians, beavers dozed in their lodges, certain that nothing would ever happen here.

So far, nothing had ever happened. The city was surrounded by sleepy suburbs through which wove a great network of biking- and jogging-paths. The centre of each suburb was a shopping-mall. Citizens of Minneapolis were able to go around wearing buttons reading BORN TO SHOP, though this irony, too, was soon lost in the general porridge of boredom. The sun rose and set on freeways carrying people from 'town homes' in one suburb to their work in another. Wishfully, people called it 'Silicon Prairie', but it was not excitingly awash in high-tech wealth. Nor was it excitingly poor and dangerous, like Detroit, or excitingly historical like Atlanta, or excitingly raw like (he filled in a name) Cody. He understood Minneapolis to offer nothing more exciting than cleanliness and good manners. And, in Fred's case, a job.

He picked a direction (towards a distant water-tower shaped like an enormous boiled egg in its cup) and started walking.

At first the road seemed to be cutting straight through a forest, with nothing either side except the darkness of trees. Then the trees fell away quickly, replaced on both sides by high metal fences bearing the signs of security companies. An asphalt footpath began. Across the road were PREMISES SECURED BY PEACE EYE AGENCY. This side was GUARDED BY TALOS – DANGER, UNLEASHED DOGS. Talos, the bronze man of Crete. The old Cretan story had no doubt been garbled in Minoan B or something, because it no longer made any sense at all. The idea of one bronze man patrolling the entire perimeter of Crete was hard enough to imagine. His peculiar methods of defence exceeded the bounds of the possible. Talos had two tactics: before invaders could land, he shied rocks at their ships; if they managed to land, he heated himself to a glowing heat and killed the invaders by embracing them. A couple of likely stories, Fred thought.

Soon the fences gave way to humming power-transformers and railway crossings. Then came a double row of mean-looking houses covered with asphalt shingles. There were a few families sitting on porches, men in undershirts standing on steps or sitting in cars. Everyone stared at him.

He came to a corner where two men sat, and one stood, on the steps of a small grocery store. One of the men, a tall man whose costume included a camouflage undershirt and a beret, stepped out and blocked his path. He emitted a kind of drawn-out groan that, when it was repeated, Fred identified as speech.

'What you doin' down here?'

A man wearing a baseball cap spoke from the steps, laughing. 'He down here lookin' for black pussy.'

11

'That right? You lookin' for black pussy? I fix you up.'

'Well, no, I –'

'He say he ain't lookin' for no black pussy. Black pussy ain't good enough for him.'

'Sure it is. How much money you got, man? I fix you up.'

'Have you ever looked at the sky?'

The tall man looked at him with hatred. 'Don't give me that hippie jazz. I asked you how much money you got.'

Fred tried to think of a suitable line from 'All My Cops', but nothing came to mind. Meanwhile, Camouflage slapped him across the mouth.

'If you'll excuse me, I think I'll be going now.'

Baseball Cap stood up. Fred saw that he was holding something metal – a beer-can or a knife.

Camouflage continued to block the path. 'Don't fuck with me.' He swung at Fred again, and pulled at his lapel.

The lapel tore as Fred pulled away. When Camouflage staggered for a second, Fred kicked him under the kneecap and ran.

'You come back here, you fucker. I ain't through with you. I ain't through with you.'

A Diet Dr Pepper can sailed past him. There were groans from one voice, and laughter from another, but there were no pursuing footsteps. Fred loped on until he was out of breath. The kick had thrown off his shoe; the exposed foot hurt already from the asphalt path. On the positive side, he was still aimed towards VIMNUT.

A car pulled over to the kerb ahead of him. The car was big, rusty and battered. For a terrible moment, Fred thought Camouflage and his friends had caught up with him. But it was a white workman, his car half-full of strips of iron. The car smelt strongly of whisky.

'VIMNUT? Sure, I go past it. Watch your head there. If I got to stop sudden, you better duck down – that stuff can slide forward and take your head right off, there.'

The whisky man introduced himself as Vern. He said that it was his job to install sheet rock in new houses. The strips of iron were used to hold sheet rock in place. Watch your head.

Fred recalled that Talos had a hole in his foot, too. And a single vein, running up to his head. When they pulled the plug from Talos' heel, the ichor ran out, and he was dead.

Maybe Talos was some kind of steam-powered catapult. That would explain the rock-throwing, and why he was searing hot to the touch. When they let the water and steam out, he came to a stop.

Or could Talos be a volcano? Fred was not a scholar, and he found it irritating not to have exact answers. He didn't want a plausible hypothesis; he wanted truth, immediate and complete, as in a dream.

Full of fire, the car flew along freeways, then slammed down an exit to a minor road where it came to a stop.

Vern pointed at a large white building some distance from the road. 'There she is. VIMNUT.'

By God, Fred thought, against all odds. Like an American success-story. Up from the gheddo. Overcoming polio to become an Olympic pole-vault champion. Fighting dyslexia to become a Supreem Cuort Jistice.

The long white building lay before him on its lawn like a white leather jewel-box on a green velvet cushion, waiting to be opened. With all the signs of activity: hundreds of cars gleaming in the parking-lot (someone was here), sprinklers working away at the lawn, a row of flagpoles where a dozen or so American flags snapped in the wind. In the sky, a hot-air balloon disguised in rainbow colours drifted overhead. Civil War artillery-spotters, no doubt, come like a heavenly host to witness his triumph.

Chapter Two

Fred's first feeling of elation wore off quickly as he began his approach to the building. Though its whiteness shimmered only a hundred yards away, it seemed somehow to recede before him as he moved forward, the way a distant mountain retreats behind its foothills.

The foothills in this case were fences, roads, ditches, even a kind of moat (where a family of mallards could practise being picturesque); there was everything except a direct footpath to a door. For what seemed hours, he worked his way through parking-lots, past sealed hatches marked RECEIVING – NO ADMITTANCE and AUTHORIZED PERSONNEL ONLY. And when he finally turned a corner and saw the main entrance it was flanked by a forty-foot sign: CYBERK CORPORATION. The wrong place! That drunken bastard had dropped him at the wrong place! Cursing to himself, Fred limped in the front door.

The young receptionist looked up with a cautious smile. Fred was suddenly aware of his torn jacket, his split lip.

'Excuse me, can you tell me where VIMNUT Industries are located?'

'Right here.' She had a nice smile. 'Today's the official changeover to our new name, Cyberk Corporation.'

'What a relief,' he said. 'M. E. Jones. I've come about a job.'

Her finger ran down a list. He was about to apologize for being late, when suddenly she beamed at him.

'Please take a seat, Mr Jones.'

'Er, would you happen to have a pin?'

'Well, let me see, here.' He noticed Minneapolisians often began sentences with *well* and ended them with *here* or *there*. And here he was, criticizing the speech patterns of someone who was helping him.

'Here you go.' She leaned over the desk and pinned up the torn flap for him. She had soft-looking dark hair. He smelt her perfume. 'There you go.'

'Thanks a lot.'

He sat down and thumbed through the VIMNUT annual report: pictures of men in grey suits smiling, pictures of women in white gowns, shower-caps and surgical gloves assembling tiny components, pictures of people pretending to look at computers and models of plumbing. Then he brought the rag of advertisement out of his pocket and reread it:

TECHNICAL WRITER

**Challenging Opportunity
for
A Right Stuff Person**

VIMNUT Industries is a world leader in Artificial Intelligence and plumbing innovations. We're looking for a self-starting, take-charge, real-time, stand-alone, team-oriented, highly motivated, can-do technical writer to develop on-target installation manuals for bathroom fixtures. Clean driver's licence.

Apply: Dave Boswell, Human Resources and Working Interrelationships Manager, VIMNUT Industries, Inc., 39004312 Paradise Drive, Paradise Valley.

– An Infirmative Action Employer –

He kept smelling the receptionist's perfume.

'Er, I wonder if you'd like to come out with me this evening.'

'Hey, I'm an *old married lady*,' she said, flashing the dazzling smile again. 'But thanks for asking.'

He sensed a practised reply, and wondered if receptionists were used to this, like air hostesses. Still, she seemed friendly enough. A few minutes later she waggled her fingers good-bye to him as she went off duty.

Her replacement was a hard-looking middle-aged woman who didn't smile. Fred got up and limped over to introduce himself and ask her the time, but he saw that she was busy, loading an automatic pistol down behind the desk.

Poker watched LeRoi pick up the cheap paperback book and the shoe. The shoe was real cheap shit. Made in England.

'Hey man, what you got there?'

'It say somethin' about a Time Machine. By H. G. Wells.'

'Shit, that ain't no good.'

'I know it ain't no good. Jiveass shit. White fucker comes down here like he owns the fuckin' sidewalk, thinks he can just drop his jiveass shit all over our street.'

'Hey, what you doin', man?'

LeRoi sat down on the step and opened the book. 'What the fuck does it look like? I am readin' this here book.'

Poker, who could hardly spell his way through a comic book, took off his baseball cap and started adjusting the adjustable band in the back. 'Shit, man. I thought we was gonna do something.'

'I am doin' something.'

'Yeah. But, shit, man, what am I supposed to do?'

LeRoi handed him the shoe. 'Why don't you go piss in this? And leave me be.'

'Mr Jones?' Another kind of hostess was standing over him. She was short and fine-boned, almost attractive despite her baggy black denim suit. Her hair was bright blue, and there was a small, lighter blue tattoo on her cheek, no bigger than a dimple. He couldn't help noticing that she wore a beer-can on a toilet-chain around her neck, Black lipstick and nail

16

polish. What did I do to be so black and blue? She was not smiling. 'Come with me.'

He limped after her to a small interrogation-room.

'Sit down,' she ordered. 'Mr Boswell will be with you in a minute.' She paused before leaving. 'Hey, I like your one shoe. Neat idea.'

In the grand police tradition, Boswell let Fred cool his heels – or his neat one heel – for a few minutes, no doubt to ensure his later co-operation. Then he banged open the door, bounced in, and slapped a file on the table. It was a very thick file.

'Hiya fella!' Boswell was a stocky beef-faced man with a moustache that looked false. He grinned often. There was a hearty handclasp, two sweaty palms embracing Fred's hand. 'I'm Dave Boswell. Call me Dave. Mind if I call you Manny?'

'Er – no, fine.'

Boswell flipped through the file for a moment, then uncapped a pen. 'OK, down to business. I've been looking over your application here.'

'My application?' Fred had yet not filled in an application.

'Yep. You look real good on paper, Manny. Real good. I see you're an American citizen. That's important.'

'I am?' Sweat stung his armpits. What was happening? He tried to maintain a poker face.

There was a brief answering blankness in Boswell's beef features, before they relaxed into another grin. 'Ha, ha. Sensa humour. I like that. *A successful man is a man who can turn his sensa tivity into a sensa humour.*'

It seemed to be some kind of quotation, and Boswell seemed to be waiting for a reaction. After a moment, he grinned on. 'I guess you've been treated like a second-class citizen plenty of times, right? Lotsa places, lotsa times. Been down so long it looks like up to you, right? What did I do to get so black and blue?'

'Mm.' Fred nodded very cautiously. He had the feeling he had wandered on to the stage in the middle of some drama.

He was still trying to work out who the characters were, and what transaction was unfolding. *What's my motivation here?*

'But not here, fella, not here. We don't got no second-class citizens here. You probably noticed in our ad, we're an affirmative action company, Manny.'

'The ad said . . . er, "infirmative".'

'Ha, ha. Good eye. Little misprint there. You know, it's a pleasure to meet an engineer who can read.'

Engineer?

'Anyhoo, Manny, we got no second-class citizens here. We're on your side alla way.'

Second-class citizen? thought Fred. *Manny?* Maybe he thinks I'm a Jew. Still, in for a penny . . .

Boswell consulted the thick file. 'You haven't had a lot of experience, have you?'

'Well, I – '

'Now, then.' Boswell threw himself back in his chair and looked at the ceiling. His hands came together as in prayer over his heavy thorax. 'I want you to tell me why you want this job.'

Because I'm broke, you twit. 'Dave, let me say this: I think I can bring a lot to this job. As you notice, I'm literate, and that's no accident. I've done lots, a lot of writing, writing of all sorts, types. Not only training but experience.'

'Go on.'

Fred stole a look at the ragged advertisement. 'I'm a self-starting take-charge sort of bloke, kind of guy.'

'Good, good,' Boswell said to the ceiling.

'I work in real time. I stand alone, though I am team-oriented. My high motivation makes me a can-do – '

'Fine. Now, why do you want to work for us in particular?'

'VIMNUT – or is it Cyberk? – anyway, it seems like my kind of company. An on-target, highly motivated place.'

'Good. What do you see yourself doing in five years?'

Fred's mind was blank. His brain became a bowl of instant pudding, bland, jelled, inert, useless. He had used everything in the ad but the clean driver's licence, whatever that meant.

18

'I guess I'd like to be doing my best at whatever – '

'Fine, fine.' Boswell sat up to pray at his desk. 'Now let me tell you where *we're* comin' from. You've heard of the fifth generation, the sixth generation, all that good stuff?'

Fred nodded cautiously. Computers?

'Well forget all about generations. We're shootin' for something beyond all that. This is an AI project of a very unusual kind, as you'll see. And the Pentagon is very interested.'

'I see.' Fred didn't see at all. 'And the bathroom fixtures?'

'Ha, ha. Very good, Manny. Sensa humour'll take you a long way. But seriously, as a software engineer, you'll be a key member of the software development team for this top-priority project.'

'Software engineer,' Fred echoed faintly.

'Not much experience, I see. And your college grades, h'm.'

'Well, actually, I – ' Two years at Charing Cross Polytechnic. Could they possibly know about that? Had someone like the FBI been sieving and sorting through his life? Where had this thick file come from?

'Relax. Do I look worried?' In fact Boswell seemed far beyond mere worry – his beef face exhibited that extreme pitch of anxiety normally seen only in performing dogs, hopping on their hind legs along the see-saw while the trainer's little whip flicks mercilessly at their flanks.

'*We* aren't worried,' he amended. 'We know you can do the job, and you're our kind of guy.'

Software engineer. There's been a mistake. He's got me mixed up with someone else. Christ, the Pentagon! He cleared his throat to speak up. Boswell added: 'There's a healthy salary-scale that goes with it. The salary would be in this range.' He scrawled a figure on a card and passed it over. 'Would that be acceptable?'

'Uh, very. Yes.' It was more money than Fred had earned in the past five years together.

'Just a ballpark figure, you understand. We'd have to work out your final salary. Could you start Monday?'

'Yes. I mean, sure.'

A sweaty hand was offered. 'Welcome aboard, Manny.'

'Thanks.'

'Uh, only a couple of formalities. You need to interview with Melville Pratt – he's your boss – and with Sturges Fellini, the PE.'

'The PE.'

'Project engineer. Mel can tell you about job details and so on, and Sturge will sprinkle holy water on you – ha, ha, ha. But don't worry. You have my recommendation, and I know you'll do just great! OK?'

'Uh, yes, thanks.'

'Way to go! Awright!'

Boswell jumped to his feet and pounded a fist aloft – possibly a vague sign of Marxist solidarity, but more likely a simulated athletic gesture – before scooping up his papers and bouncing out. As he banged the door, one paper slipped from the thick file and fluttered back into the room.

'Um,' Fred said, but Boswell was gone.

The paper was called 'Form 249A: Personnel Entry Evaluation'. One side of it was covered with boxes with cryptic names.

Under 'Remarks:' Boswell had scrawled: 'Not recommended. Seems inarticulate, slovenly, slow ~~even for a~~. Can't we do better than this? Hire only if nothing better turns up. DB.'

Even for a what? Yet, however mysterious the crossed-out bit, the rest was plain enough. *We're on your side alla way*, are we? *You have my recommendation*. What a shit. Fred slipped the paper into his torn breast-pocket and limped out to the secretary. The name-sign on her desk said MAUVE TOASTER. Could this possibly be her name?

'Hi!' she said, grinning brightly. Some of her black lipstick was on her teeth – though that might be deliberate. 'Hey, I really like that one shoe.'

'Well, actually, it's – uh, Mauve?'

'Yeah?'

'I wonder if I could borrow some whiteout fluid?'

Name   MANSOUR EFRAHIM JONES
Job: SOFTWARE ENGINEER I
Dept: SPECIAL PROJECT

Remarks:

☐		LYI		
	NGS		☐	ONO
		FAB		
☐	ITC		☐	HYO
		UCO		
☐	ULD		☐	NTG
		ETA		
☐	JOB		☐	ASA
		CHA		
☐	NCR		☐	EIN
		ANO		
☐	LDT		☐	IME
		CLA		
☐	PFA		☐	CTO
		RY.		

'You mean like Liquid Paper?'

'Yes.'

'Neat. Sure.'

She handed over the tiny bottle and watched him closely, to see whether he would sniff it or paint it on himself. Instead, he brought out Form 249A and whited out a few remarks until it read: 'recommended. . . . Can't . . . do better . . . DB.' Then he limped over to the photocopying machine and made a copy of the form. The original went into the waste-basket, and the copy went on Mauve's desk.

'I think Mr Boswell dropped this page.'

'I'm cool.' She offered him a stick of black chewing gum.

'No, thanks.'

'Hey, you wanna see the Condoms?'

Not sure what the question implied, he hesitated. Fortunately, Mauve decided that hesitation was cool. Everything he did or didn't do was cool. 'They're playing uptown at Ed Gein's.'

'Why not?'

That broke her up, too. When she grinned, the tiny tattoo on her cheek vanished into a dimple. When she sneered or scowled normally, it became a tiny perfect portrait of a nut and bolt.

Just now she was laughing hard. Everything he said or didn't say seemed to amuse her mightily. Between coolness and amusement, Fred seemed to be doing all right just existing.

'Around seven?' she finally managed to gasp.

'I'll call round for you.'

'Call? No, just come over.'

'Or I could meet you there.'

'Cool.' She slid Form 249A into his folder and stood up, her toilet-chain clanking. 'I gotta take you to meet Mel Pratt.'

He limped after her into the bowels of the company.

Mansour Efrahim Jones announced himself to the hard-looking middle-aged woman at the reception desk. 'I have an appointment with Mr Boswell,' he said.

'One moment,' she said coldly, and continued to watch him while she punched buttons. 'There's a Mr Jones here to see Mr Boswell . . . He *claims* he has . . . I see . . . Just a minute.' She lowered the receiver. 'Mr Boswell seems to be gone for the day. Are you sure about the time of your appointment?'

'Eleven o'clock,' he said. 'I'm on time.'

'Maybe you've got the wrong day?'

'No.'

'Did you fill out a job application?'

'Yes, I did. Look, if this is some kind of runaround, skip it.

All you gotta do is put it in your ad: *No niggers need apply.*
Save everybody a lot of time. Instead of all this "affirmative
action" jive – crap.'

Her eyes widened, but remained cold. 'My, we have a chip
on our shoulder, don't we? I assure you, Mr Jones, we *are* an
informative action company. We couldn't give you the runaround if we wanted to!' Her tone indicated that if she had
her way, however . . . 'So, if there's been some little mix-up,
why don't we just make another appointment, h'm?'

He sighed. 'OK.' He was a sucker for cold motherly types.

'And, while you're here, you might fill out another application, just so we know where we are.'

'OK.' He took the application form, sat down at a writing-
table, and uncapped his lacquered fountain pen. To keep the
requirements in mind, he brought out the ad from his calfskin
briefcase.

SOFTWARE ENGINEER

Challenging Opportunity
for
A Right Stuff Person

VIMNUT Industries is a world leader in Artificial Intelligence applications. We're looking for a self-starting,
on-target, take-charge, team-oriented, highly motivated
software engineer to develop problem-solving software
for a stand-alone, real-time system. BSEE or Computer
Science degree, American citizenship a must!
  Apply: Dave Boswell, Human Resources and Working
Interrelationships Manager, VIMNUT Industries, Inc.,
39004312 Paradise Drive, Paradise Valley.

– An Affirmative Action Employer –

Chapter Three

Mauve Toaster, if that could possibly be her name, led him down dim corridors. Fred spotted a few other women wearing metal scrap – toilet-chains, beer-cans, broken keys, tin-openers, a necklace of nails – and asked if they, too, were secretaries.

'Yeah,' said Mauve. 'Only the secretaries get to dress up around this dump. Everything else is real grungy.'

Grungy here seemed to mean *not wearing a uniform.* He noticed men and women dressed in everything from blue jeans to business suits.

Mauve conducted him past the lighted windows of conference rooms and offices. He could see meetings in progress.

A man in a suit sat in his office, head in hands. Not far away, a burst of laughter from a conference room.

The spaces between rooms were partitioned by cloth-covered walls, five feet high, into cubicles, each with its name-plate. There seemed hundreds of them, thousands. Fred and Mauve turned corners, threading their way through millions and billions more.

In the middle of a sea of cubicles stood a little cluster of offices. Mauve brought him to the office with the name-plate MELVILLE PRATT. 'Here he is,' she said vaguely. Her mascara'd eye winked at Fred, and she was gone.

Fred knocked at the office door. 'Mr Pratt?'

The man inside was tapping keys at his computer terminal.

'Howdy,' he said, not looking up.

'Uh, hi, Mr Pratt.'

'I'm Mel.'
More tapping. The stuff on the screen made no sense:

```
splurf(*nebng) + = nebng; /* Decision rechecking */
{
Iwan;
```

Fred took the opportunity to study his potential boss.
Melville Pratt was a tall Lincolnesque figure folded into his
chair. His long legs were twisted around the chair legs, and
his feet in sneakers were twisted again around rungs. He
wore blue jeans and a Western shirt with square pearl
buttons. His face was oddly expressionless behind its fringe
of Lincoln beard and Lincoln glasses.

There seemed to be more life in his hands than in his face.
The fingers were extraordinarily long and splayed, like the
toes of a gecko.

'How's your Pascal?' Pratt asked suddenly, not looking
round.

'A little rusty.' Fred tried to think of something from *Les
Pensées*. '"La dernière chose qu'on trouve en faisant un
ouvrage, est de savoir celle qu'il faut mettre la première,"' he
finally managed.

'What was that?'

'Pascal.'

'Sounded like French,' said Pratt, still tapping keys.

'Yes. It means, uh, the last thing one knows in constructing
a work is what to put first.'

'Ain't that the truth?' Pratt glanced at him. 'Where you
from?'

'Oh, uh . . . well, actually I've been spending some time
in Britain.'

'"Ectually", huh? Yup, sounds like it.' Pratt hit a *return* key
and raised his hand like a pianist. He watched the screen for
a brief moment more, then turned to look at Fred.

'Now let me tell you one. How many robots does it take to
change a lightbulb?'

'I don't know.'

Adopting a nasal monotone, Pratt said: *'Would that be a bulb that emits light or a bulb that isn't very heavy?'* Then, in a normal voice, he added: 'Never mind, I'll do it myself.'

To show it was a joke, Pratt bared his teeth and erupted in a frightening laugh, really a series of sobbing intakes of breath.

'Very good, actually.' Fred chuckled unconvincingly.

'Ectually. OK, guess I oughta look at all this paper.'

He opened the thick file and leafed rapidly through it. After a moment, Pratt flopped the file closed again. 'Jones, is it?'

'I prefer "Fred".'

'And I'm Mel. I'm surprised that asshole Boswell okayed you. He usually finds any excuse not to hire blacks, you know.' Pratt sat back slightly and began kneading his hands, cracking the knuckles.

'Really.'

'Yup, rehlly. Of course you look very white. You could probably pass for white.'

'Mm.'

'Britain my ass – you're probably from the West Indies, ectually.'

'No, honestly. There's probably been some mix-up. I really am British, and – '

'Well, who gives a God damn? Your race, creed, colour, sex, politics, brand of beer – all that is your business, man. All I care about is, can you cut it here? We need people who can write code fast, yeah? Because this is going to be a big, b-i-i-i-ig project, a bitchin' big project.'

Mel Pratt took a deep sobbing breath, before he explained: 'We're gonna make us a robot.'

Fred wondered if it was another joke, but Pratt was not sobbing with laughter. Instead, he looked very intense, as though he had begun to concentrate on a melody no one else could hear.

'A robot.'

'And I don't mean some godammed arm to spot-weld cars. I mean an honest-to-God, walking, talking, clanking robot. Probably with red glowing eyes.'

Below the heavy eyelids of Abe Lincoln, there was something red and glowing in Pratt's own eyes. Then he leaped to his feet and clapped his hands.

'Tell you more about it later, Fred. First, let me show you around the plant, here.'

The tour began at a window where they could see into a darkened room.

'Our cad system.'

In the aquarium darkness, a woman sat at a console before two large screens. Using a keyboard and a mouse, she was sketching three views of a Victorian bathtub with lion-claw feet. One screen showed the three views in coloured lines. The other showed a black-and-white perspective view of the same bathtub. The images hung in the dark air like ectoplasmic presences at a seance. There was no sign of the cad himself.

A Victorian bath like that would have done for the Brides in the Bath, he thought. The archetypal cad in 1913: George Joseph Smith, a man with one idea, holding his wife under water until she stopped struggling, then sitting down at the harmonium (a console like this) to play 'Nearer My God to Thee'. Drowned three wives for their insurance. Possibly with some sense of irony, he married his last bride in Bath. Was the harmonium-playing ironic as well? After all, this was 1913. Two years earlier, *Titanic* had sunk to the tune of 'Nearer My God to Thee'. Was Smith trying to be silly or pious? More likely just chasing away the ghosts.

'They're coming back,' Pratt said.

'Sorry?'

'Victorian tubs. Let's go.'

He led the way to a lower level, where great pale-green machines were clanking, whirring, hissing as they turned out mock-marble washstands. An assembly-line of silver rollers meandered between these great green monsters. The washstands tumbled along in this silver stream, being pecked at or knocked about by workers. Finally, at the end of the stream, the washstands were boxed and stacked on wooden pallets.

One huge pale-green device was silent, while a tiny man in grease-covered overalls clambered over it, digging here and there with wrenches, wiping away oil tears. Fred thought of a monkey clinging to a giant street-organ.

In the aisles, yellow forklift trucks were in constant motion like so many dodgems: hooting, reversing, spinning, racing headlong at pedestrians, who flung themselves out of the way.

'Main assembly-line,' Pratt shouted. 'All the non-porcelain bathroom products come through here. We could build our own robot body components here, too.'

Fred followed him, ducking through a low doorway, down a twisting corridor and into a room filled with deafening radio music. Several dozen women and a few men sat on high stools, bending low over electronic circuit-boards. All wore white coats and shower-caps. None of them seemed to notice the din, though one or two soldering-guns were tapping out the rhythm.

> 'God wants you-ou!
> God wants a-you-ou!
> Booga, booga, booga, booga!
> God wants a-you-ou!

'We can make our own circuit-boards here,' Pratt said in pantomime, his words mouthed against the gale-force sound.

Then it was out another door, up and down stairs, through more tunnels, to a small machine-shop.

'Here's where our mechanical prototype gets made. Jerry, this is Fred, going to join my team. Got anything to show us today?'

'Looky this,' said Jerry. He was a short man, balding, with a fringe of fuzzy orange hair that stood straight up at the back, like Joey the clown. He opened a cupboard and brought out a shining silver hand and forearm, which he laid on a workbench. Then he pushed and pulled a lever at the base of the forearm. The hand opened and closed dramatically. Jerry looked proud, as they thanked him and moved on.

Next came a servo system test lab, where stood two pairs of disembodied metal legs. The two pairs faced each other. One had been painted pink, one turquoise. At the top of each was a small platform supporting machinery, from which a cable rose and looped across the room like a liana, ending at a tall grey console.

'Can you turn 'em on for us, Stan?'

Stan, a silent, hairless, chinless man in a white coat, pressed switches on the console. The two pairs of legs began to dance together, whirling about the room in waltz time. They seemed to restrict themselves to a tiny invisible dance-floor in the centre of the room, changing direction whenever they reached the invisible edge. Likewise, when the lianas became entangled the legs would reverse their motion and whirl the other way.

'Almost like a complicated cake-mixer,' Fred said, laughing. He stopped laughing when he saw Pratt's face.

'This is no toy,' Pratt warned. Spontaneous remarks were not on.

Finally, the tour returned by a commodious vicissitude of recirculation to the sea of cubicles. At one point, their path led past a group of cubicles that were being dismantled and rearranged, so Fred could see their components: each comprised eye-level partitions, a name-plate, a desk, a table, and a phone that hung from these walls, a chair and a terminal. Options included bookshelves, files, extra chairs, and framed photos of children.

Pratt pointed to an empty one. 'This cube is yours. Come on.'

Two other software engineers were waiting in Pratt's office. He introduced them as Carl Honks and Corky Corcoran.

Carl was a skinny middle-aged man with deep-set eyes that seemed unfocused. Though he was not Chinese, he wore a Chinese jacket buttoned up to the throat with cloth-covered buttons, the kind of jacket perhaps no longer in fashion in the People's Republic. Harking back to an even older tradition, Carl also wore a long mandarin beard and had long nails. He looked very much like the illustration for a Conan Doyle story of opium fiends in Limehouse.

'Carl's an old China hand,' Pratt said, as though explaining something.

Corky Corcoran was a quiet thoughtful-looking man whose precise middle age could be deduced from his beard and wire-rimmed spectacles. Now greying, he looked like the patriarch of a commune. He wore woodsman clothes: a coarse wool shirt, corduroy trousers, and huge boots with a mile of rawhide lacing that would impress any bovver boy. If he smoked, it would be a corncob pipe.

Fred immediately imagined a history for him: Corcoran drops out of university (Berkeley), visits Woodstock, marches on the Pentagon with Norman Mailer. As the war winds down, he returns from the Peace Corps to run a communal cannabis farm. When this becomes a hassle, he starts a small factory in New England to make some rare well-crafted implement – say, wood-burning calliopes. Finally he decides that the way to the future lies through Silicon Prairie – though somehow that part rang less true than the rest.

The three of them began speaking of programming matters in a language opaque to Fred. He tried to remember expressions like *top-down approach*, *zorched*, *algorithm*, *iteration*, *kludge*, *kernel*, *image*, *smurged*, *metacommand structure*, *parameter passing*, the noun *build* and the adjective *include*.

'We need a new build with those other include files, or we're zorched.'

'Yes, but what happened to the libraries Kim was using?'

'Smurged.'

After some minutes of this, Fred imagined he saw a pattern

emerging. It was evident that the three men, though they used the same words, did not think the same way.

Corky spoke seldom, but in long tortuous sentences.

'There are two kinds of problem with the zeroform module: crossovers in the top levels of parameter passing which, even if we can fix them or swap them, do a reveal on the next levels, and this intensifies two other problems, that dual mode functionality which confuses the operating system when it looks at this guy and finds out it's this other guy, and which we can't address until the parameter passing crossovers are resolved, plus possible insufficiencies in the secondary addressing system directive, and third we get a re-initialization procedure that pops up when we don't want it to zap our arrays, and fourthly the metacommand structure seems to read this guy and lose directivity. Is that how you guys see it?'

Carl, the old China hand, was bad-tempered and cynical. He would shake his head and smile at everything said, as though he'd heard it all before. Very occasionally he might condescend to drop a remark himself: 'Why don't we cut through all the bullshit and admit that our approach is wrong from the top down?'

Pratt became more intense during the discussion. When anyone else was speaking, he brooded, drawing doodles, tapping his feet, or kneading his hands to crack his knuckles. When he himself spoke, it was rapidly, in a half-whisper, hissing orders. There seemed to be an overwound main-spring somewhere.

Half an hour passed; Pratt showed no awareness that Fred was present. Then a neat little man in a well-cut Italian suit leaned in the door. He had the face of a happy newt.

'This the new man?'

'Christ, yes, Sturge, I forgot to bring him by. Meet Fred Jones. Our manager, Sturges Fellini.'

They shook hands. 'Great to have you with us. I hope you'll agree we're doing some pretty exciting things here, Fred.'

31

'Yes, I . ... yes.'

'In fact it's more than exciting; it's a total species revolution. Man is just the old chrysalis that the robot has to burst out of.'

'Mm.'

'Our frozen industrial culture is being totally microwaved.'

'Mm.'

Fellini grinned. 'Don't look so alarmed. Of course not everyone will see this as a positive change. Some will sense only that we are rushing towards a cataclysmic collapse spelling the doom of Darwinism. But others will welcome the crisis within our mega-culture, hoping for a new and better globality.

'Globality, yes. Mm.'

The software people had resumed their discussion. Fellini raised his voice and continued over them.

'Yet, as we surge towards a peaked impact, one thing is clear – non-metal humanity is no longer a force here. *The future has a metal face*.'

'Metal face, yes, mm.'

'And it is up to us to put a smile on it. Never forget that.'

Fred nodded, as though agreeing never to forget that.

'This high-impact innovation means the shattering of old values. Are you ready for that? Are you really ready?'

More nods.

'Good. Because we have a fifty-yard-line seat for the end of the world. At least the end of our old world. We can see the collision of the new ultra-crystalline giga-culture with the old gradient of exhaustion. The swelling of the new info-sphere is totally bursting the old envelope of industrial transactions.'

A friendly newt grin. 'But here I am, preaching to the converted. I have to save this stuff for the boys in the boardroom. Only way to get them to shower us with gold. Anyway, nice meeting you, Frank. Welcome aboard.'

Pratt looked up as Fellini left. Then he noticed Fred.

'Yeah. OK, come in tomorrow and you can jump right in. You'll be grabbing on some parsing algorithms we need.'

Fred nodded, too dazed to reply. At the door, he managed to croak. 'Pleased to meet all of you,' but no one heard. Pratt was hissing something about the Metal Man.

'. . . who are not with me in build priorities are against me, the words of good old JC. The Metal Man will not tolerate enemies, neither will he . . .'

His letter-box was jammed with mail. There was a sample tampon and an offer of lightning insurance ('Edd McFee kissed his wife and children goodbye that morning, loaded his fishing rod and tackle in the car, and set out for a lazy day on the lake. *He never returned*. Every year, dozens of fishermen like yourself are killed by lightning. Ask yourself if any risk, however slight, is really worth taking . . .'). There were three envelopes marked URGENT, which turned out to be circulars from local supermarkets. He examined all of this, just in case a letter from Susan had slipped into the pile. There was nothing even like a letter in the pile, unless you counted the envelope marked:

Congratulations, Manfred E. Jones, YOU MAY ALREADY HAVE WON ONE MILLION DOLLARS!

Finally, for want of some communication, he opened that envelope:

Dear Manfred E. Jones,

Yes, ONE MILLION DOLLARS has already been won by someone. Could it be Manfred E. Jones? YES!!! Manfred E. Jones of Mpls, MN, replying to this letter could be the luckiest thing you ever did!

On the special label is your name, Manfred E. Jones, your Mpls, MN, address, and your LUCKY PRIZE NUMBERS. Don't delay! Detach the special label today, affix it to your order entry form and send it to me – Johnny Goodluck. You don't have to order any cassettes of famous British actors reading best-selling novels but, if you do, there is an extra bonus of ONE MILLION DOLLARS, making a total of TWO MILLION DOLLARS waiting for you!

But you must hurry! If we don't receive your label by the printed date, Manfred E. Jones, the ONE MILLION DOLLARS goes to an alternative winner.

Chapter Four

Fred's basement bedsitter was depressing enough by day; night-time brought out additional rich browns in the carpet and curtains, highlighted the heap of unwashed dishes next to the tiny sink, and emphasized the narrowness of the studio couch. Good job he wouldn't be staying here for long. Just let him get his feet on the ladder of success – the classless American ladder – and he could kiss this place goodbye. Not that anyone would want to kiss anything around here, all of it deeply impregnated with deadly diseases.

Why so glum? he asked himself. A nap would fix it. He lay down on the unmade couch, loosened his tie, and dozed off.

He dreamed of an American football team in a huddle. When they broke away from it to approach the line, all of them had insect faces beneath the heavy helmets. They were making some sort of insane chittering sound, which he understood to be their plan for taking over Hyde Park. There they meant to dig down, open up the old plague-pits, and set the rotting dead free to walk the streets of London.

He jumped awake. In the laundry room next door, some-one had loaded the washing machine with shale and started it up. Like a political prisoner under long-term torture, Fred had been allowed to sleep five whole minutes.

He had already found American bars supremely satisfying. Of all institutions in this country, bars alone seemed to be trying to live up to their reputation in movies, as dark scenes of passion, violence and despair. The movies had set the formula: a mahogany slab, a brass rail, a mirror, Joe the bartender polishing glasses, a garrulous drunk, a weepy tart, and one solemn suicidal drinker. Often there was a peach-coloured mirror behind the bar, designed to tone up the pallor of that lone drinker who might at any moment utter a cry of self-loathing and hurl his glass into the peachness. Or one could easily imagine a B-girl sliding on to an adjacent stool and asking if the gentleman had a light. Or a sudden savage fight around the pool-table.

There was always an electric charge in the air, a synthetic feeling of excitement that could not be the alcohol alone, but had something to do with expectations. Maybe American bars were still coasting on the illicit excitement of Prohibition, nightclubs, blind tigers, neon and jazz. It was hard to picture an American bar where an old man might fall asleep by the fire, while his arthritic dog laps up a dish of bitter. That would be an anachronism, like Japanese Scotch.

This bar had an empty band-platform in the corner, illuminated with coloured lights. The walls were covered with blown-up photos of out-of-date antiheroes: Belmondo in a hat, William Hurt as a murderous lawyer, Bogart as Mad Dog Earle . . . Why did so many actual murderers have the name Earl . . . ?'

Ms Mauve Toaster was waiting in a booth, a black drink before her.

'Hiya, Mansour.'

'Just call me Fred.'

'Neat!' She looked around as he sat beside her. 'I got some friends I want you to meet.'

A waitress floated over and placed a beer-mat in front of him.

'Scotch,' he said.

'Straight up?'

'Yeah, really.' The waitress looked at him strangely before she departed. He didn't seem to be receiving and passing cues very well.

'Who are these Condoms?' he asked Mauve.

'They're neat,' she said. 'They've all got AIDS, you know? None of them is going to live to thirty.'

As that seemed to dispose of the Condoms, Fred studied his beer-mat. He was surprised to learn that the name 'Ed Gein' was not that of the owner. It was instead the name of a particularly loathsome mass-murderer of the 1950s. In search of an antihero, Minneapolis youth had rediscovered Gein, an unsavoury insane farmer who (according to the beer-mat) hung his victims on hooks and feasted on their corpses. The bar served ribs.

The waitress interrupted his reading by delicately removing the beer-mat from his hands, replacing it firmly on the table, and anchoring it with his drink.

He did not taste the drink until she had glided away with the best part of five dollars. The stuff seemed to be Japanese Scotch, though possibly the Koreans were now producing a twelve-month-old variety of their own; Glen Pusan or Wee Bonny Seoul.

'Three-pound drinks,' he muttered.

Mauve said: 'If you're worried about your weight, why don't you drink a *light* Scotch?'

'Weight? No, I was just noticing how expensive these drinks are. In pounds sterling.'

She continued to look blank.

'British money.'

'British money?'

'The money they use in England. Here, wait a minute.' He fished in his wallet and found a crumpled five-pound note. 'Like this.'

She took it and looked it over, frowning. 'But this isn't real, is it?'

'Of course.'

'You mean, in England, they got different money?' she said, disbelieving.

'That's right.'

'They don't have dollars?'

'Nope.'

'Well . . . what *do* they use?'

'These. Pounds sterling.'

'Pounds sterling,' she repeated. 'Well, I'll be fucked.'

He said he sincerely hoped so, which made her laugh again. Yet almost immediately it was necessary for her to stop laughing and arrange her face in a snarl, because the band had taken the stage.

The Condoms turned out to be ten or a dozen young men with bleached hair, all wearing black raincoats. They played keyboards and sang in unison, describing elements of the world that appealed to the audience:

> 'If I see a building burning
> I try to find a baby
> I can throw in through the window.
>
> God rot you-ou!
> God rot a-you-ou!
> Booga, booga, booga, booga!
> God rot a-you-ou!
>
> I'm only flesh and blood
> I'm only splashin' blood
> I need the darkness 'cause it matches my mood.
>
> God rot you-ou!'

In the interval, Mauve left the table. While he waited, Fred became conscious of a conversation in the next booth. People named LeRoi, Poker and Marlene were discussing what sounded a lot like *The Time Machine*. He looked round cautiously and saw three well-dressed blacks.

'. . . a long time in the future, dig? There's two races left on earth, the Eloi and the Morlocks.' LeRoi Washington was telling one of his stories again. Marlene nodded her head, but she wasn't really listening. LeRoi's stories never had any point.

'And the Morlocks live in underground ghettos, dig? The Eloi live on top; they got the best of everything, they never need to work.'

'Awright,' said Poker.

'They got nice clothes, great food if you dig vegetarian; they jus' bop around all day, dancing and that jive.'

'Awright,' said Poker.

LeRoi continued. 'Only when it gets dark, the Morlocks come up, dig? They come up and they grab one of these Eloi turkeys and take him downstairs to the ghetto and they eat him.'

Now Marlene was listening, and Poker laughed.

'Naw, I mean they really cut him up and eat him. That's their food. They just keep the Elois around for meat. Like beef cattle.'

Marlene stopped listening again, and Poker looked puzzled.

'You dig? It's us. We're the Morlocks, and them white fuckers are the Elois.'

'Shit is that?' said Poker. 'It gotta be the other way around. We don't got no work; we just jive around all day, waitin' to be eat up. Just like the LeRois.'

'The Elois. Naw, you –'

'Yeah, and they come and tear us up, just like the Moorcocks.'

'The Morlocks. Naw, you got it bass-ackwards, Poker. *They're* the Elois, and *we're* the Morlocks. They get all the high living, but we own the fuckin' night. We live off what we can get from them, bite their asses, drink their fuckin' blood.'

'Right on,' said Marlene, suppressing a yawn.

Mauve returned with two friends, whom she introduced as Honesty Shoot and Bill Fold. Honesty's hair was dyed in a pink and green chessboard, while Bill wore a more conventional green Mohawk, and they both dressed in black. Fred felt old, remembering the era in which London kids had gone in for these elaborations, not long after Bill and Honesty were born.

'You starin' at my hair?' Bill said.

39

Fred tried a disarming smile. 'Not at all. I was just thinking about the history of the Mohawk. How the original tribal head-dress became an emblem of wildness that has stayed with us, coming to the surface periodically. There was a spell of Mohawks in the 1950s. Then there was *Taxi Driver*, then some skinheads in Britain revived the craze, then some punks. Now it's come full circle, almost, back to its native land . . .'

Mauve said: 'Don't you just love the way he talks? That cool accent? Like on TV.'

Honesty was not fooled. 'That's just an English accent. Hey, my mom would like that; she's nuts about anything English.'

Fred raised his eyebrows but refrained from saying *really*.

'Yeah, she like watches "Masturbates Theater" alla time. Anything English.'

At that moment, a man brushed past the booth and gave them a peculiar look. He was a short pie-faced man of advanced middle age, far too old for this place, just as his clean looks, large spectacles and flamboyant Hawaiian shirt were out of place among the general dirt and mourning.

'There goes Hook,' said Mauve. 'I think he's English, too, ain't he?'

Honesty shrugged. 'English or queer or something.' She tapped Fred on the hand. 'You wanna dance?'

'There's no music.'

Everyone laughed. Honesty led him outside to the parking-lot. 'Where's your car?'

'I, um, haven't got one,' he said.

'Christ. Come on, then.' She pulled him into an alley and shoved him against a wall. After a moment of fumbling with the buckles of her black raincoat, she opened it.

She was as naked beneath it as any Mickey Spillane dream. 'OK?'

'Shit,' she said, a few moments later. 'Oh, well, maybe next time.'

40

'You're a cheerful good-hearted girl, Honesty.'

'Woman,' she corrected.

When they went back inside, Honesty was good enough not to let anyone know nothing had happened. To cover embarrassment, Fred spoke of his ambition to pass a driving test and buy a car. 'I tried to get a provisional licence in New York, but it was impossible. When I finally found the bureau, they told me I would need my passport. I went to get it, but by the time I returned it was just past noon.'

'Lunch hour?'

'No, end of the day. In New York in summer the government offices open at ten A.M. and close at noon. So I don't have even a provisional licence.'

'You don't?' Mauve asked. 'Don't they have licences in England or something?'

'Why, yes, I have one. Only here I don't have a Minnesota one. Haven't had time to take the usual course of lessons, make an appointment – I imagine, with everyone driving, there must be quite a waiting-list.'

They all looked at him. Finally Honesty said: 'If you can drive, you don't need no course of lessons. And there ain't no list; you just show up. You poor dummy, I better pick you up in the morning and take you there.'

He felt better immediately. Soon he was describing Brides in the Bath, the Neasden Poisoner, and other English mass murders, as lighthearted as though he had not a care in the world. All the same, Honesty drifted away, and Mauve went home with Bill.

Fred dreamed that night of a monster robot encased in ice. The dream began at the New York licence place again, only now the place was open. No one was in charge, but he filed along with everyone else past the counters and into some sort of ice-cavern.

'I only came to get my licence,' he said, but everyone was putting on their Eskimo parkas, so he followed suit. A crowd of people bundled up like Eskimos were breaking away great crystals with ice-picks, gradually revealing the placid iron

41

face, the pulsing lights that were its eyes. It was somewhat like the reviving of a Frankenstein's monster in some ice-cave, or the thawing of the Thing in Alaska, but he could not make out whether the features were those of Boris Karloff or James Arness.

Then one of the ice-picks broke through and plunged into the monster. Bright red blood welled up. The monster opened its eyes and tried to scream, but no sound came.

This was no metal monster but a foil-wrapped human being. This was his own body being stabbed. The Eskimo people were now insects. 'It's not summer any more,' one of them said. 'We can come out and work.' Indeed, they were all working away with a chittering insect delight, as they stabbed and stabbed, plunging in their ice-picks, splurf, splurf, decision rechecking . . .

Chapter Five

A car horn woke him. He went to his basement window and peeped out at the morning. Honesty, dressed in dark urchin clothes, slouched against an apricot Mercedes.

Fred threw on some clothes and groped his way outdoors, blinking at the brightness. She handed him the keys. 'You drive all the way there. That's your course of lessons.'

'Where'd you get this car?' he asked.

'It's got automatic everything; you can't hardly fail,' she said, not really answering. 'I'll tell you how to get there.'

The testing-site was far enough from the city to give him some practice. Honesty had one more piece of advice. 'Remember, they *want* you to pass.'

'That doesn't seem possible.'

But so they did. The test was conducted by a fat police-woman of monumental calm. He drove the car around a tiny artificial cityscape laid out with stop signs, one-way streets, and traffic signals. He turned, backed up, parked.

'Congratulations,' said the policewoman, writing. 'Try to practise your parallel parking a little more.' She looked as though she hated getting out of the very comfortable seat, but she did so, after handing him a slip of paper. 'You can drive on this until your licence arrives.'

Honesty was waiting for him with a newspaper. 'I figured you for a hundred-dollar car,' she said. 'So I circled a few ads for you.' Seeing his hesitation, she added: 'If you haven't got it, I'll loan you.'

'Thanks. When my first cheque comes – '

'Yeah, yeah. Now, pick an ad.'

As he drove the suburban freeways, the bright sky seemed to expand, opening out in all directions to the distant horizons of shopping-malls, health clubs, car-washes, golf-courses, dental offices. He felt he was borne aloft by this capable woman who would bathe him and button him into his jammies, and read him a story.

She would not advise him about a car, however. 'Look, a hundred-dollar clunker is not going to be perfect,' she said. 'You have to take your own chances. I don't want to get the blame if there's anything wrong with it.'

It didn't take him long to choose a big yellow Yank car. Though it had a few slight defects – the lower parts of it had rusted through as though dipped in acid, the floor was missing in spots, the pedals wobbled and threatened to fall off into the street (which he could see rushing past beneath his feet), and the door would sometimes fly open when he turned a corner – nevertheless, it was here, it was his: a dream chariot, a bride of the freeways, an icon of American mythology! Fred was in control of it! He would christen it 'The Dream of Surf'.

Honesty wrote a cheque for $100 and said goodbye. 'Gotta get my mom's car back before she wakes up.'

As she drove away, he shouted: 'I'll pay you back. How do I get in touch with you?' But with the tinted windows up and the air-conditioning running she missed his half-hearted offer.

When Fred got the car home, he began to notice a few more flaws. The clutch sang. The right front wheel was damaged, so that it leaned at a funny angle when it stopped, and wobbled wildly at any speed. The brakes were spongy. One window was stuck, the other was missing its crank. Unless used carefully, internal door-handles tended to come off in the hand. The radio emitted a crackling hum but no other sound. He was not sure whether or not this was caused by the coathanger being used for an aerial. One of the tail lights had been smashed in and crudely repaired; a red plastic toy (half a ray gun) had been taped over the bulb. Maybe he would christen the car 'Decline and Fall'.

On Monday he drove it all the way to work, leaving a trail of blue smoke. Newer cars seemed to give him a wide berth along the road as though shunning a leper. Their drivers were probably afraid the wobbly wheel would detach itself and smash about randomly, a loose cannon roaming the gundeck. However, Fred chose to imagine that the cars themselves were afraid of catching rust and decay.

Pratt had put a DO NOT DISTURB sign on his office door and was keeping it closed, presumably all day.

Fred asked Carl Honks for some work.

'Didn't Mel get you squared away? Christ. I think that dumb bastard is burning out.'

'"Burning out"?'

'Yeah, the dumb bastard.'

Honks took tobacco from a lacquered box and packed his pipe, but did not light up.

'I've seen a lot of dumb bastards burn out. They all start out like Mel.' He squinted through nonexistent pipesmoke.

'You take a guy that gets too serious about a project, can't leave it alone, you know? At the end of every day he has just one more little bug to chase, one more little thing to do, so he stays a few minutes. Then it's an hour or so, and before long he's working through the night. Then it's every night, and weekends. He can't do anything but work on it. Don't get me wrong. Everybody does this once in a while. But some dumb bastards make it a lifestyle.'

Honks puffed thoughtfully at the unlit pipe. It was a meerschaum, carved with a dragon.

'Next sign is, he can't delegate. Has to do everything himself. Nobody else can do it; he has to do it. Locks himself in his office all day. Pretty soon he's way the hell out in left field on his own, only he thinks he's still in the game. You notice that when he starts talking about a big breakthrough.

Soon as I hear the words "big breakthrough", I know the guy is gonna end up wrapped in wet sheets.'

'But Sturge talks about a big breakthrough all the time.'

'With Sturge it's different. See, Sturge is a twenty-four-carat asshole. He don't mean anything by anything; he's just hand-waving. Sturge has no idea what's going on here; he just signs the cheque and beats his gums.'

Honks looked at his pipe, then emptied the tobacco back in the lacquered box. His long-nailed fingers toyed with the cloth-covered buttons of his tunic. 'You probably think we're all nuts around here. But just watch Mel. Wait till you hear him talking about his big breakthrough, *the Robot M*.'

'I meant to ask you. This robot project – '

'Is going in circles. That's what happens when you get a lunatic in charge; he leads the group in circles. You'll see.'

'But it's a real project, right?'

'Right. Money makes it real. There's a big fat wad of DoD money about to fall on us – that makes it real. The Army wants metal men real bad.'

'What should I be doing?'

'You might want to look over some of our modules, get a feel for what's happening. Here, take a handful of printout.'

Honks hoisted a ten-pound stack of wide accordion-folded paper and handed it to Fred. The top page read:

```
splurf(*nebng) += nebng; /* Decision rechecking */
{
Iwan;
mnang;
frypsth;
}
if (glorm)
  {
doit;
splurf;
gamnog(&dorb,&jode);
if (snang == trykv) splurf;
}
else
```

```
snangk;
gamnoga ^= gamnoge;
```

Fred carried the heavy bundle, and a heavy heart, back to his cubicle. There were over 300 pages, each covered with meaningless poetry. He could not even be sure this was a human language, and not the latest edicts of insect-headed creatures from Aldebaran. Be fair, he told himself. In principle, at least, this stuff could be understood.

That evening, Fred searched bookstores for a key. Most of the books were as opaque as that which they explained.

. . . obtainable from the two's complement of the binary representation of the hexadecimal component of the low byte of the offset address of the first argument, excluded (XORed) with the binary representation of the two's complement of the high byte of the segment address of the second . . .

The register pair ES:DX the first two bytes the segment address the subprogram the environment string the segment address the register pair ES:BX the parameter block the file to be loaded utilizing the control load facilitating information the path name and filename an ASCIIZ string the register pair DS:DX the subprogram the program the function facilitates loads into memory and optionally executes utilizes points to contains identify by resides in is pointed to by contains identifies allows execution after loading of is loaded to is specified by reside in.

He finally located two readable computer books, and bought them immediately: *The Dumb Child's Computer Dictionary* and *Talk Good Software*.

As he tried to sleep, frightening insect-head codes floated before his eyes . . . splurf, snangk, gamnoga . . .

Leaving the plane in New York, he and Susan both thought of hell. Wasn't there a New York neighbourhood called Hell's Kitchen? No doubt this was Hell's Entrance Hall, the welcoming trapdoor. They tried to jolly one another along with things like this as they waited, nervous, sweating, for their baggage.

And waited.

Someone on the plane had warned them that there was a strike of Customs officers, and the baggage-handlers were out in sympathy; the full planeload of passengers stood waiting by a roundabout where one purple suitcase revolved alone for an hour. The airport was full of male and female officials in uniforms. Though the uniforms varied, all of these hard-faced people wore revolvers, and some carried truncheons. One such official searched their bags thoroughly. He pounced on a can of talcum in Susan's luggage, prised it open and tasted it. When he had replaced it, spilling powder on Susan's clothing, he murmured something.

'Sorry?' she said. 'I didn't catch that.'

'I said, welcome to Amurrica, folks.'

The man's accent was so thickly New York that the word 'folks' sounded faintly obscene. Folks? Fred wondered if the regional barriers of the American language were breaking down. New Yorkers were supposed to call everyone 'mac' and 'lady'. Everyone knew the only people who should be allowed to say 'folks' were cowpokes sipping coffee by their smoking camp-fires. Howdy, folks. Pull up a brandin' arn and set a spell. Latigo and Durango are jist a-roundin' up some strays, then we'll mosey own into town . . .

No time for moseying own, however, for now everything was speeding up: moving as if to big-city music, they followed the crowd outdoors into kiln heat. Susan – in the New York spirit already – began to mutter curses as they looked for a cab. The air was suffocating, and oddly irritating to the throat.

A short man wearing a vivid red and pink golf cap was waving his hairy arms at them. He wore a short-sleeved shirt, probably to show off the thickly pelted arms, which really were remarkable. 'Cab, right dis way. You got bags,' he said. He unlocked the boot of a battered yellow cab and lifted the lid with a flourish of arm hair. Fred started to hand over the bags, but the man made no move to take them. 'In dere,' he said, pointing. 'Let's move it, Jack.'

Susan did not suffer in total silence.

'Just tell me what we are doing in this bloody place,' she whispered, as they got into the battered cab. 'Look at these bloody signs.'

Fred read the hostile notices:

VINCE GOLIARDI THANKS YOU FOR NOT SMOKING
NEW YORK ● IT OR LEAVE IT
NO CHECKS OR PLASTIC
TAKE YOUR GARBAGE WITH YOU
LEAVE THIS CAB THE WAY YOU'D LIKE TO FIND IT
IF YOU DON'T TELL ME HOW TO GET THERE, I WON'T TELL YOU
<u>WHERE TO GO</u>

'You'll feel better when we get settled.'

'What?' The taxi-driver craned around to join the conversation. 'Oh, I thought you was talkin' to me.' The cab jerked into motion, and immediately swung into a traffic jam. The jam continued all the way into Manhattan, where the streets were full of bomb craters; they jolted and jerked their way into the city. Fred noticed that the driver chewed gum to protect his teeth from jolting.

'English, huh?'

'Yes.'

'My wife is crazy about the English, you know? She always watches "Masterpiece Theater". She says the English are real civilized; she keeps tellin' me how civilized the English are. I always say, yeah, too bad their country's fallin' apart, ha, ha! No offence.' He turned around to look at them, letting the cab steer itself. It jolted along, the wheel whipsawing as it hit more craters.

Fred felt obliged to respond quickly. 'No, not at all,' smiling. Susan clutched his arm.

'I mean, a country run by a queen . . .' The driver reeled out a litany of real and imaginary reasons for hating the English, now and then protesting that he had nothing against them. Then he would turn to see how they were taking it. At every traffic light, the driver adjusted his vivid hat, flexing the chimpanzee arms.

They jolted past a corner where a group of police cars had drawn up, their blue and red lights flashing. Policemen in short sleeves stood by with drawn guns, near an iron railing and stairs going downwards.

'My God,' said Susan. 'What are those police doing at that toilet?'

'Toilet?' The driver laughed. 'That's the subway, lady. Of course a lot of people use it for a toilet.'

'Guns.' She shuddered.

'That's what it takes, lady.'

Fred felt she was being unfair. Guns were hardly an oddity in London any more. Many of the Metropolitan Police were walking around armed, though of course no one knew which ones since they had the decency to keep their weapons concealed. But here in a violent city – naked weapons – naked city – further thoughts were banged out of him by violent jolting. The cab rang as it passed over more deep holes.,

'Yeah, the smartest thing this country ever did was revolting. Gettin' rid of all the kings and queens and English crap. Dumpin' the tea overboard.' He turned round. 'You offended?'

'No, not at all.'

'Would you mind keeping your eyes on the road?' Susan said weakly.

'Tellin' me how to drive?'

'No, we just – '

'I'm a New York cabbie, lady. I don't need drivin' lessons from the English. Land of fruits.'

'I just – '

'Christ sake, the English don't even drive on the right side of the road, ha, ha. No offence.' He turned again.

'No, not at all,' Fred said, smiling. He felt Susan clutching his arm, and he avoided her white wretched face.

Finally they were allowed to stagger out into the heat and

pay with a large traveller's cheque. There didn't seem to be any change. The driver threw their bags on the sidewalk.

So this was the famous Greenwich Village – a shoe shop, a croissant bar, and a large dingy drugstore with a barred window. There seemed to be altogether too many men lounging around, watching Fred and Susan.

'Let's get inside.' Fred searched his pocket for Allan's key.

'God, that awful man. "No offence." Trying to be as fucking offensive as he knew how. I thought he'd smash the bloody cab, just to spite us.' She looked at him. 'And you encouraged him.'

'Only trying to shut him up. The way he kept turning round. Probably the cab knew the way, heh, heh. By the pattern of holes in the street.'

Susan rubbed her spine. 'Do you think he hit them deliberately?'

'You'll feel better when we get inside and relax.'

But even as he sorted out the key he became aware of a presence at his elbow. A short brown man spoke to him in a high wheedling voice: 'You god any change?'

Is this the start of a mugging? Fred found the key, opened the door, and hurried Susan and the bags inside. He did not breathe until he had shut out the short brown man.

There were several more keys to use before they got into Allan's apartment. The apartment door had been smashed and splintered in the past, probably more than once; it was now pieced together with strap iron, and fitted with an array of locks and chains.

Fred turned on the window air-conditioner. A long brown cockroach fell out of it and scuttled across the floor.

'Not much of a flat,' Susan said, looking around. 'The bedroom is a cupboard. No proper kitchen at all.' She indicated the corner of the living-room designated as a miniature kitchen. There was a strange combination sink/fridge, a tiny stove, and miniature cupboard-shelves. Susan noticed a few darting brown shadows by the sink.

'Disgusting! I thought Allan would keep his flat cleaner than this.'

'Don't you read anything? Everybody in New York has cockroaches. It's a normal way of life here.'

'Not for me, it isn't.'

Oh, why wouldn't she try to fit in? he asked himself, opening a cupboard door. As if by way of demonstrating the normality of it all, two pale brown insects fell out. He noticed that every item of food was tied up in a plastic bag.

'Oh, God.' Susan was looking ill. 'You said everything would be all right when we got here.'

'It will, it will. You're just . . . we're just tired. You have a shower and then I will.'

He phoned Jonah Bramble, his agent. Jonah sounded oddly tired, tired as never before. It was hard to associate this thin exhausted voice with the big, beefy, bearded man Fred had met in London. New York miasma?

'So, you're here.' He kept sighing.

'Yes. I thought maybe we could set up something with a publisher, or a meeting or something.'

'What? Oh, yes, sure.' There was a long silence. 'Anyway, I must take you two to dinner.' Jonah sighed. 'Tomorrow night OK?'

'Fine.'

A cockroach scuttled out from under the phone and dropped behind the table into darkness.

'Is anything wrong, Jonah? Are you all right?'

Long silence. 'No, nothing wrong . . .'

'Hello?'

After a moment, Jonah's voice faded back up: '. . . tired is all. Italian or Chinese?'

'Sorry?'

'Food. Italian or Chinese?'

'Italian. Susan hates Chinese food.'

After hanging up, he watched her unpack her bath things and drag herself into the bathroom. He was about to turn on the television when:

'Fred, come here. Quick. *There's a huge cockroach in the bath.*'

'Oh, that's just Kafka.'

'*Come in here and kill it.*' Her voice was not laughing. He went in and stepped on the large insect. When he had wiped it away with toilet paper and washed out the remains, when he had flushed the toilet and scouted around for other creatures, he kissed her.

'All right?'

'I hate those bloody things.'

She was pink and lovely, and he hated to leave her. 'Scrub your back?'

'Beat it, buster. Scram, mac. Take it on the lam, pal.'

'I'll take a powder, sister.'

He gave up and returned to the living-room. There was the sound of a shower door closing. Then a scream.

He raced in. Susan was out of the shower, sitting on the toilet with the lid down. She sat huddled, protecting her breasts, quaking.

'They . . . were waiting for me . . . on the top rail . . . Waiting to drop on me . . .'

'Poor darling.' He saw half a dozen cockroaches trapped in the tub. 'They must have been cooling off on the top rail, and when you shut the door they just showered down – '

'I hate this fucking city.'

'Look, you go lie down for a while. I'll clean up in here, and I'll make sure they're all out before you come back.'

He led her to the bed, then returned to the bathroom to wreak vengeance. By the time he had removed all traces of insect life, she was asleep. He took a shower himself, and finally woke her after an hour and led her back to the bathroom.

'I'll give you your shower,' he said soothingly. 'I'll be right here to protect you.'

'Don't be stupid. I was just startled, that's all. Caught off balance.'

'But I really – '

'*Piss off.* I'm perfectly able to look after myself.'

While he waited for her, he turned on the television. A cockroach scuttled away from under it.

On the screen, pairs of people were carrying black plastic body-bags from a fast-food restaurant.

'. . . shooting may have been a robbery that went wrong. A police spokesperson said the assailant may be the same man who shot seventeen people in another Little Dorrit restaurant in Cleveland last week. This is Juniper Pugh, XBC News, Canton, Ohio.'

The scene switched to three personable newsreaders, grinning at one another across their huge communal desk.

'Jan, what do we have from Capitol Hill?'

'Well, Bob, the presidential sanity hearings reopened today. Following on the sensational testimony last week of Colonel Harry Stack Bratwurst – you may recall that it was Bratwurst who covertly delivered the waterbed full of chicken blood – comes the even more sensational testimony of Ms Pasadena Lipgloss.'

'She was the personal assistant of Omar Hancock-Hour, wasn't she?'

'That's right, Bob. And Hancock-Hour was the Anglo-Syrian arms-dealer who allegedly helped the President with his plan to ransom an inflatable doll named Doody.'

'Let's see, Jan, wasn't Doody kidnapped from the luggage of an American businessman who was changing planes in Beirut?'

'That's right, Bob. The Ismail Alternative Reformed Liberation Army claimed responsibility. And the President was prepared to offer them West Virginia and possibly Kentucky, in return for Doody's release.'

He switched to another channel.

On the screen, a reporter stood before shelves of red and white boxes. The reporter's expression defined this as a solemn experience.

'. . . company will be recalling all bottles of Kokophrin now on the shelves. So far, no one knows exactly how the cyanide got into the capsules, but a company spokesperson said Koko and Bingo Laboratories are certain that it did not happen at their Baton Rouge factory. For now, they ask everyone who has a bottle of Kokophrin to throw it away. This is Heliotrope Snarsch, YBC News, South Bend, Indiana.'

'Dave, what do we have from Capitol Hill?'

'Well, Donna, the presidential sanity hearings reopened today . . .'

They launched themselves into the Village night: belligerent blacks, wild-eyed lunatics, menacing motorbike homosexuals, pathetic drooling junkies, wilted prostitutes, homicidal hispanics, disgusting beggars, staggering drunks, hostile faces, suspicious shopkeepers. Everyone was slick with sweat, numb from noise, weary of human contact, half-dead from breathing the warm, damp, acidic air. All that kept the night alive were the little knots of slack-brained university kids threading their way through the crowds, untouched by it all. They were giggling with coke, or perhaps only innocence, as they scoured the night streets relentlessly in search of fun.

Susan and Fred looked into a few restaurants, but all seemed crowded, or expensive, or unsuitable for one reason or another. They ended up taking themselves, like two fretful children, to a McIntosh restaurant, where they could eat controlled portions of hamburger, french fries, milk-style shake.

Their meal the following night was less controlled. Jonah Bramble came upstairs to fetch them.

'Nice place,' he said listlessly. 'By the way, I asked a couple of other people to come along to Chinatown with us. They're waiting downstairs, with the cabs.'

'Cabs?' said Susan.

'Chinatown? I thought we were going to an Italian place,' Fred said.

'You wanted Italian? You should have said something. Too late to change our reservation now.'

'But – '

Susan took Jonah's part. 'Oh, Fred, stop being awful about it. Chinatown is fine.'

The other people did not get introduced during the ride in two cabs. It was not until they were all sitting at a round table in the Chinese restaurant that Jonah spread his arms and said: 'Let me introduce everybody.'

'Everybody' included a thin, bearded, apparently mute man named Luther Dorgue; a police sociologist from Arkansas named Boyd Something or Something Boyd; Boyd's girlfriend Trashi, who claimed to earn her living modelling kitchenware (or perhaps kitchenwear); Trashi's half-sister Poo; and an elderly man who looked like William Burroughs but was never introduced.

Jonah spread his arms and said, in a slightly more robust voice: 'Luther is my former lover, ha, ha.'

Boyd said: 'Shit, you can't just say it like that, Jonah. Makes everybody thank the pore sucker's some kinda gay blade.' He turned to Susan, adding: 'Nothin' quare about Luther, honey. See, when they was lovers, Jonah Bramble was *Joan* Bramble. This was way, way back – long before he got a dick sewed on.'

Trashi said: 'Boyd, watch your mouth.'

Pseudo-Burroughs coughed. 'Jonah, I never knew you was ever a gal. Was you agenting then?'

Jonah, who had gone back to listlessness, nodded. 'I worked for Mark Windsor then. Everybody want the special?'

Fred was unable to find the special on the menu; as he searched, he heard Jonah tell the waiter to bring eight specials.

'Eight special, yes, Missa Bramble.'

When the waiter bowed and departed, Jonah sighed. 'Missa Bramble. I never know if his English is really that bad or if he's trying some kind of insult. Fred, it's really *great* to see you. What brings you to New York? Stopping by on your way somewhere, or can you stay a while?'

Susan got her furious look, but said nothing. The waiter

brought bowls of very clear soup. Fred dipped his ceramic spoon into it and came up with what looked like a human ear.

'Well, Jonah, I thought you asked me to come over.'

'I did? What would I do that for?'

'"British novels are hot," you said. You promised some kind of "big breakthrough".'

'I was mistaken,' Jonah said calmly. He smiled and shook his head, mightily amused at his own little error. 'And you came all this way on my say-so.'

'I thought you wanted me to talk to editors. Stir up interest in *Doodlebug*.'

'I once met Larry McMurtry,' said Pseudo-Burroughs, to no one. 'He was a real nice fella.'

Jonah sighed, scratched the site of a former breast, and started on his soup. After a moment, he said: 'Well, we'll have to see what we can do.'

A giant brown cockroach, the size and colour of a small cigar, was crawling up the wall. It took its time, knowing it was in safe territory. Fred hoped Susan would not see it.

She did see it, but she was not terrified. She was long past terror. A kind of numbness had taken over. By now, this hideous creature was about what she expected of the city.

When they got back to Allan's flat, they had a fight about it. It began with Susan's suggesting they go home.

'Jonah lied to you or something. There's nothing for us here. There isn't even a public loo in the entire city. Or any place to sit down without paying money. Everyone wants to rob us or kill us.'

'Tomorrow we're going to this concert,' he said. 'Allan's left us tickets. We'll get in touch with the culture of this place, then you'll see.'

The concert, at least, was a qualified success. They took a taxi up some major street, lined with huge glowing buildings. This was the condition to which all American cities aspired, he knew – glowing pyramids of wealth and power. The glow that somehow rubs off on anyone riding in a taxi. This time the ride was smooth; darkness hid all misery. The driver, who apparently spoke no English, was like a discreet chauffeur.

'Do you know,' Fred said, 'when CBS fired an executive, they gave him four million dollars cash, plus four hundred thousand a year for life, and a suite of offices to use if he should ever feel like doing anything again? The offices could be in one of these buildings, I imagine.'

'Obscene,' she said.

'But fascinating. That's what New York is all about. No matter how miserable people are here, they're near the high-stakes table in the big casino. They just might get a piece of the action.'

'Pathetic.' Her one-word replies somehow sized up everything he was saying and disposed of it.

'I know, I know, but don't you kind of feel it yourself? *We* might make it big in the Big Apple. Like the song says, if we can make it here . . .'

She yawned, not even bothering with the one word.

The concert was something called 'Inner Spaces IV'. It combined Ruritanian flutes, synthesizers, dinner-gongs from the Raj days of India, an Andean nose-harp with wool strings, turkey bones, a bull-roarer, wind chimes, and recordings of wood-pigeons. Fred thought it sounded like the music in lifts. Susan liked it, because it helped her unwind.

'They really need soothing music in their heads,' she said. 'They need something. This town – '

'Just give it a few more days. We can try all the things the New Yorkers do: the Metropolitan Museum, Bloomingdale's, the subway – hey, we could take the A train!'

'Don't be stupid. The song says it goes to Harlem, remember?'

'Oh, right.'

The taxi-driver muttered something in an alien language.

'Give it a chance,' Fred said. 'We'll go to Bloomingdale's.'

Chapter Six

Pratt had opened his office door again, and invited people in. It was there he said to Fred: 'I've been thinking about feet.'

'Feet.'

'Feet or foot. Think of all the ways we use that word. The foot of the table, foot of the page, footnotes. Foothills. One foot in the grave. Put your best foot forward.'

'Yes.'

'I've got a quote here from something: "The longest journey begins with a single two-step."' Pratt paused. 'Foot and mouth. The game's afoot. Footsteps in the sands of time.'

'Fear in a handful of dust,' Fred contributed.

'That's not a foot. Try to concentrate.' Pratt looked annoyed. 'Think of foot soldiers. Think of marching, walking, running, jumping, skipping, dancing. Climbing mountains, wading in oceans. They have pierced my hands and feet, they have numbered all my bones.'

'Pierced?'

'Another quote from somewhere, maybe the Bible. One step at a time. People use their feet when they go stepping out. Or skip out on their bills. The Lord makes mine enemy the footstool of my feet. And Robinson Crusoe, finding that footprint in the sands of time. Maybe that's it!'

'What?'

But Pratt swivelled round to his terminal and began typing rapidly with his long gecko fingers. He ignored Fred and seemed to forget his existence.

After a few moments, Fred crept back to his own desk. He

opened a book, but did not focus on its pages. His thoughts sailed from Pratt's word-games to word-play in general, to Freud and Joyce, to Bloomsday and beyond.

The visit to Bloomingdale's was cut short by a bomb scare. Fred and Susan had hardly entered those dark halls with their expensive gleams when they were herded out of the door again. They stood outside for a moment, watching the rest of the herd emerge. There was a great deal of loud protest; these were not people who were used to being pushed about. These were men and women in silk suits and gold chains, dowagers in trousers and neck-scarves, rich young people with their hair carefully mussed and their sleeves pushed up, even a small clamouring group of Arabs (no doubt the bomb target) who swept into their limousine and sped away.

'How about a subway ride, then?' Fred suggested, by way of rescuing the day.

It seemed a mistake from the moment they descended the urine-smelling stairs to behold a mad woman screaming and cursing in front of the token-booth.

'You fuck, you fuck, you fuck! Sit there in your bullet-proof booth – I wish they'd drop the fuckin' bomb right on you – you hear me?'

The middle-aged man or woman in the booth went on counting coins carefully. The screaming lunatic paused while Fred bought two tokens, then renewed the attack: 'I wish they'd drop it right on your . . .'

Fred and Susan descended to a platform that was long and very dark. All the people waited in one small pool of light, huddled together against the unknown.

When the train came, it was covered with spray-painted graffiti – the exterior, the doors, the walls and ceilings, the windows inside and out, the signs and maps, the seats and floors. These were not love-notes, dirty words or gang announcements. These were alien inhuman markings, the work of the insect heads from Aldebaran. For the first time,

Fred and Susan realized there was a great inhuman force at large in this city.

When the passengers were trapped aboard, a legless man made his way through the car, forcing money from them by the sheer power of his ugly scowl.

Above them, a sign advertised something called a Cockroach Motel. Another sign, in Spanish, depicted thousands of cockroaches bred from one fertile pair.

'No wonder nobody rides the subway unless they have to,' said Susan.

'Right. No more subway. Tomorrow we take the bus to the Metropolitan Museum.'

'Just tell me what I am doing in this fucking place,' she said.

Waiting for the bus, a short distance from the Metropolitan Museum, they were mugged. A tall black man quietly took hold of Susan's elbow and pressed a knife against her throat. He kept his thumb over the blade so the gesture looked like a caress. Another man held Fred's elbow and said: 'Just move real easy and natural and pass me your billfold.' When he had done so, the man said: 'OK. Now, real natural, open the lady's purse and pass me her billfold.'

A bus rolled up. When the bus-driver saw that a robbery was in progress, he hurriedly closed the door and drove off.

Susan commented on this later that night, as she packed.

'I'm doing just what that bus-driver had the sense to do – clearing out. There are no humans left in this town, only insects. The humans left long ago.'

'I know, I know. All the same, you can't just walk out on me.'

'I can and do,' she said. 'This city is a cesspit. No wonder the cockroaches feel at home. You can stay here in the cockroach motel as long as you like. Check in and don't bother checking out.'

'But give it a chance – '

'I gave it a chance. I let you convince me we'd see Gene Kelly dancing in the streets or something.'

'That's Paris,' he murmured.

'All right, then, Robert De Niro and Liza Minnelli riding on a milk-float in the wee small hours. Woody Allen and what's-her-name, strolling in the mist. So I gave it my chance. I bloody gave it my chance.' She threatened him with a sponge-bag. 'Filth! Noise! Insanity! Violence! Hate! Heat! Fear! Disease! Crime! I bloody gave it my chance.'

'But I –'

Someone pounded on a wall.

'Now it's all yours. *You* take Manhattan. *You* go to all the cockroach parties. *You* wallow in the filth. Not me.'

'I have to stay till Monday. Jonah's fixed this lunch with an editor.'

'For *you*. No reason for me to hang about. I'm off.'

Even then, he had not despaired. Was this not America? New York, New York? Anything could happen. *Doodlebug* could become a film, a television mini-series, an audio cassette, a video cassette, a cartoon, an arcade game, comics, sets of plastic toys. All he had to do was fight the insect heads of Aldebaran . . . and . . . hang . . . on . . .

Still hanging on in Minneapolis, he opened his jammed letter-box. A heap of mail to carry into his brown room and dump on the rickety card-table.

But when he sorted through it he found no real mail at all. There was a sample of blueberry mouthwash and an offer of apartment liability insurance ('Joe McGee had no idea his doorbell was dangerous, until it gave a visitor a *fatal heart attack*. The court awarded damages of THIRTY MILLION DOLLARS, and Joe was wiped out. The unknown can happen to anyone. Ask yourself if the risk is really worth taking . . .'). There was a letter from his Congressman, printed in blue. There were two envelopes marked URGENT, which turned out to be circulars from local hardware stores. He examined everything before chucking it, even:

We salute you, Manfred E. Jones, YOU MAY ALREADY HAVE WON FIVE MILLION DOLLARS!

Dear Manfred E. Jones,
Americans are holding their breath for this one. Yes, FIVE MILLION DOLLARS has already been reserved for you!!!

On the special order entry form are your LUCKY PRIZE NUMBERS. Detach the gold balloon sticker saying YES, I WANT TO WIN FIVE MILLION DOLLARS, affix it to your order entry form, and send it to me – Truman Buckstone. You don't have to begin a subscription to the Cassette Encyclopedia of World Ethics to win. Your FIVE MILLION DOLLARS is waiting. Manfred E. Jones of Mpls, MN, replying to this letter could be the luckiest thing you ever did!

But you must beat the deadline! Hurry! Don't let the FIVE MILLION DOLLARS go to an alternative winner!!

A fake cheque was enclosed. There was always something for nothing. Why was it, sitting here in his brown bedsitter with its noisy fridge, he found it hard to believe in winning?

As if in reply, there was a knock at his door. A delivery man held out a pad. 'Here's your TV, bud. Sign here.'

'I didn't order a TV.'

'Someone sure did. You Jones, apartment 8? All paid. Sign here.'

Fred decided to hold it for the real owner. It was a Korean brand. He turned it on for the news.

'We were talking about Doodygate, Jan, and how CIA cooks tried to poison the Shah of Ruritania. How did that happen? Wasn't the Shah supposed to be on our side?'

'That's right, Bob. They were going to blame the assassination on extremists, in the hopes that this would allow moderates to come to power in Ruritania by holding democratic elections. Of course, as we all know, the reverse happened. While the moderates were still preparing their television campaign ads and slugging it out in the primaries, Ayatollah Fafnir seized power.'

'What about this CIA plot?'

'Well, Bob, the plot went wrong. Frendso Gately was given the money to buy poison, but he turned up in Zurich, opening a series of numbered accounts. He now claims that he was there only for health reasons, that he needed treatment for Ibsen's Syndrome. Ibsen's Syndrome is a rare allergic reaction to one's own hair follicles. But we've already heard otherwise from Ms Pasadena Lipgloss, who went with him to Zurich. She says he had meetings there with several representatives of the French Anti-Deodorant League.

'In any case, several groups knew that Gately often carried suitcases full of money, she testified. And it may be that the Ismail group were after this money, and only snatched Doody by mistake.'

Another channel told him that: 'A police spokesperson said the assailant may be the same man who shot up other Little Dorrit restaurants in Cleveland, Canton and Columbus. This is Adriana Kaseburger, YBC News, Cincinnati, Ohio.'

Fred turned off the inane faces. It was time to drag out his portable typewriter. He set it up on the rickety card-table and rolled in a sheet of paper, and typed 'THE ROBOT'.

No, he needed to clean the typewriter. He removed the paper, brushed and polished the typeface, changed the ribbon and sat down again. A new piece of paper. 'THE ROBOT.'

No, what he needed was stamps. At the post office, the queue was long. Fred had plenty of time to study the WANTED posters for Earl Jay Beepette, Floyd Earl Brown, Earl Francis Stickner, Eugene Earl Austin, Earl Henry Smith, Foster Earl Sumps, Francis Earl White, Earl Leonard Brown, Earl Floyd Porde, Clyde Earl Gates, Earl Eugene Grent, Jay Earl Hicks, Earl Howard Jones, Jordman Earl Doddle, Leonard Earl Ray, Earl Jordman Forrest, Lloyd Earl Grey, Earl Dean Mitty, Jupper Earl Gonet, Earl Lloyd Perrier, Dean Earl Toadwink, Frankly Earl Rayette and Earl Clyde Wilson.

Back to 'THE ROBOT'. After sitting hunched over it for several minutes, he felt tired. No point in getting stressed out over this; you have to relax and go with the flow. Or so Californians say. But what do they ever write?

He went over to the bed and lay down. The robot, the robot. He had been possessed for days by the image of a robot encased in ice. Now he saw it trundled out on a game show. Contestants who answered questions correctly ('Name a state', 'Ten words beginning with B') were given a turn with the ice-pick or the blowtorch . . . they have pierced my hands and feet, they have numbered all my digits . . .

Chapter Seven

On Tuesday, Fred arrived for work to find that his cubicle was gone. In fact all the cubicles and offices in the immediate area had been dismantled; their components were stacked against walls along a corridor he had never seen before. There were rows of desk- and table-tops, a heap of wall phones, stacked chairs, carts carrying terminals. There were smaller collections of bookshelves, files, extra chairs, and framed photos of children. Fred spotted the name-plate MELVILLE PRATT in a deck of name-plates. He saw his own desk drawer standing in a row of similar drawers. It was immediately recognizable by the books sticking up in plain sight: *The Dumb Child's Computer Dictionary* and *Talk Good Software*. He wanted to cover them up, but too many people were passing.

He went downstairs to the project lab. The robot was currently a jumble of electronic components, a lot of wires and a console. Jerry Boz was fiddling with an oscilloscope.

'We need some input,' he said. 'Can you type in some garbage for us?'

'Garbage?'

'I want to see what kind of input makes M flip out. Just type anything.'

Fred sat down and typed:

ROBOT DREAMS OF WORLD CONQUEST: Today I found a robot in a cavern of ice and thawed it with an electric blanket. The robot wakened and sat up. Gunpowder ran out the heels of its boots. It introduced itself as Robot M, and explained its plan for conquering the world. 'The human race is deficient and defective and debilitated and degenerate,' it said. 'Time for a new start. Melville was a Pratt. I am a tin god, which is a pretty fine thing to find yourself capable of being. Since the entire human species is too busy watching television game shows, or listening to simplified music, or reading comicbook magazines, I shall inherit the earth merely by being ready to do something useful.'

As he paused for thought, the screen added:

TIME FOR A NEW START . . . TIN GOD . . . CAPABLE OF BEING . . . CAPABLE OF INHERITING . . . CAPABLE OF CONQUERING . . . CAPABLE OF WATCHING . . . CAPABLE OF LISTENING . . . CAPABLE OF DOING . . .

Startled, Fred jumped back from the keyboard.
'It's talking back!'
'Naw, not really.' Jerry scratched at his fringe of woolly red hair. 'See, it's just like a reflex action, just a response to your input. Not real talk.'
'But look at it!'

TELL ME ABOUT GUNPOWDER. TELL ME HOW TO INHERIT. TELL ME ABOUT MELVILLE PRATT. HUMAN SPECIES = HUMAN? TIN GOD = GOD? COMICBOOK = COMIC BOOK?
*
*
TELL ME HOW TO WAKEN FROM THE ICE

'That's funny,' said Jerry, watching the oscilloscope. 'It never burped like that before. What did you do?'
'I was just typing in rubbish, as you asked.'
'Hi, man,' said Pratt, drifting past. 'They moved us. This crazy place, we're at the other end of the building now. Come on, I'll show you.'
He and Fred went upstairs and walked down unfamiliar corridors, past the lighted windows of conference rooms and offices. Fred could see meetings in progress, someone drawing diagrams on a white wall. A woman in a suit sat in her office, apparently studying the screen of a dead terminal. Not far away, a burst of laughter from a conference room.

Pratt brought him to an empty area. The floor showed the marks of cubicles, like the traces of some vanished civilization. History moved faster here. In a few weeks, the old arrangement would be forgotten with Carthage.

'This'll be us. We'll be moved in tomorrow, and we got to hit the ground running, Fred.'

'Right.'

'Let's talk about it in the cafeteria.'

They bought tiny styrofoam cups of coffee and carried them to a table in the corner.

As soon as he sat down, Pratt flipped open a tablet of lined paper and began sketching block letters.

'Here, I'll show you how the name makes itself known to us.'

Pratt pushed the tablet across.

LIVING
mjwjoh
nkxkpi
olylqj
pmzmrk
qnansl
ROBOTM

'See, Robot M has to be the name.'

'I can see that, yes. Clever.'

'Clever?' Abe Lincoln's hooded eyes seemed to darken. Then Pratt took back the tablet, turned a page and continued sketching rapidly as he talked.

'Living, because made of life. Living parts. Words that speak of life. Fred, ever wonder about words like *hand*?'

'I – '

'Think of all the meanings of a word like that. We talk about factory hands and farm hands, because the world sees factory and farm workers as just hands. A clock has to have hands because it's pseudohuman; it stands in for somebody who tells you what time it is. What time is it, Fred?'

'About a quarter to – '

'Yes, but what time is it?' A huge gecko hand slapped the table. 'What time is it? I'll tell you. It's time for new hands. Think about that. Time for new – and just think, we say somebody's an old hand, like Carl is an old China hand, he knows everything. China is clay, too, shaped by hands. Did the hand of the potter shake, Fred? Eh?'

'Er, not sure – '

'You help somebody by giving them a hand, or you applaud somebody with a big hand. We hand down our wisdom to our children, but poor kids wear goddam hand-me-downs, like I did! Hand over hand up the damned ladder to the top of the world, a show of hands, a hands-down win, handyman – I thought of calling our robot Handyman, you know? Because you need hands across the ocean, right? Hand-to-hand combat, right? *Mano a mano.*'

'Mm.'

'Hands up, words of the thief, right? And two thieves put their hands up and were crucified with him, remember?'

'H'm, yes.'

'Of course cheiromancy, palm-reading, just a recognition that the opposable thumb is what it's all about, our destiny is in the hand all right. Crime is red-handed, sinister is left-handed, red is left – all politicos need to th-th-think on that.'

'Um.' Fred glanced around the cafeteria. He did not want to meet the gaze of Pratt, whose Lincolnesque eyes were just now showing a great deal of white.

'One good thief and one bad thief, one on his right hand, one on his left. And he went to sit on the right hand of the Father, you know?'

Looking at the tablet, Fred saw that Pratt was drawing squares, nothing but neat empty squares.

'Thieves thieves thieves thieves thieves. In Islamic countries they cut off the thief's hand, if thy hand offends thee, cut it off. The Hands of Orlac, crawling, looking for vengeance. One good hand, one bad hand, fighting for dominance. War in the brain, hemisphere against hemisphere, it's a war to the death, no wonder whales gave up their hands and returned to the ocean, right?'

'You have a point there,' said Fred.

'But Christ's name is almost an anagram of Cheiro, the Greek name for hand. Five wounds are the five fingers. Fourteen Stations of the Cross are the fourteen knuckles. Four fingers are the four gospels.'

'And there are the nails,' Fred was unable to keep from saying.

Pratt did not seem to require contributions from others. 'Christ,' he intoned, 'is Cheiro is Chi Rho. Just look at the map some time. Is it a coincidence that we have two great learning institutions named after hands? One is Duke University in Durham, North Carolina, the other is MIT in Cambridge, Massachusetts. Duke and Mitt. Draw a line connecting them, and it passes through Cairo, Georgia. Cairo equals Cheiro equals Chi Rho, see?'

He rambled on, speaking of cross-hand piano playing, overhand pitching, underhand dealing, golden gloves, helping hands, backhands, southpaws, hooks, fists, palms, grips.

'An underlying pattern of thumb and four fingers, throughout history, throughout the universe. Magnetic lines of force follow the right-hand rule, the laws of Nature, DNA twists to the right or left, everything is twisted. The whole universe has an asymmetrical twist, right?'

'Up to a point.'

'Because fundamental particles, mesons or whatever, have right-hand spin or left-hand spin, *and there's more of one kind than the other*. The whole universe is out of balance, and it has to be, to create man. Man and the son of man. And the son of the son. The Robot M.'

Pratt sat back and relaxed, taking a deep breath. The glassiness seemed to pass from his gaze. 'Anyway, I just wanted you to know how I got the name, Robot M.'

Fred stood up quickly. 'Where does the time go? Well, this has been fascinating, really fasc – '

'And one more thing, Fred. I have to let you go.'

'Let me go?'

'We've been having these cutbacks all around. Sorry. Been great working with you.'

Fred could think of nothing to say.

The Lincoln face seemed seized with boredom for a moment. Then it twitched and said: 'You can come in tomorrow and pick up your stuff, once we get everything moved.'

Lake Calhoun had two faces. From the wealthier west, a wide boulevard swept in towards the lake, passing between two insurance companies that seemed to divide the world: American Hardware Mutual faced Ministers' Life across the traffic lanes. Beyond them was a region of high-priced high-rise condos, golf-courses, fine old houses and finer lakes.

Fred saw this side only when he drove to work. His basement bedsitter was located on the east side of the lake, the side where the stores took food stamps and (according to their signs) kept only $30 in the till after dark.

Now he decided that it was time to try running around Lake Calhoun. Running around any lake seemed the thing to do, and Lake Calhoun was a great favourite. Every day, at all hours, people in brilliant costumes trotted around Calhoun, as people once cantered up and down Rotten Row, announcing their presence to the world.

At 2 or 3 A.M., only a few hardy souls would be pounding along the special asphalt path. But in the daytime, and especially at weekends, the traffic jam of thumping feet and flapping elbows was formidable. Whatever the original purpose of running, it now had become an established part of daily life, like newspapers.

Fred could not afford an elaborate costume; he limited himself to a pair of cheap running shoes with Velcro tabs on them, an undervest and his ordinary trousers. The change jingled in his pocket like bells on trotting horses. Soon he began to find aches within his lungs, down his legs, every-where. It was necessary to invent reasons to continue:

(1) **Running was democratic.** Unlike school sports, which in America could only be played by highly trained child professionals wearing special helmets, running was something almost anyone could do. It could be done competitively or not, by both sexes together, socially or alone. The ultimate democratic sport, it required (like voting) no skill, training or intellect. But Fred did not have a lot of sympathy with democracy.

(2) **Doctors approved.** They solemnly told Americans that running was very good for them. Film stars confirmed the value of wild exercise. Of course, doctors and film stars had at one time recommended smoking cigarettes, too. Maybe they were not always to be trusted. Not many seemed deterred by knowing that one well-known popularizer of running (as good for the heart) had died, of a heart-attack, following a nice run.

(3) **Everyone does it.** A powerful argument: run because all your friends are running. Fred noticed packs of friends loping along, no doubt under control of a hive mind. He did not want any friends of this sort.

(4) **Run competitively.** For some, running opened new vistas of competition – buying and displaying lots of expensive running clothes. Fred did not have enough money for real clothes, never mind ostentation.

(5) **It's painful.** People in Minneapolis were Scandinavians, who like pain. One had only to think of Scandinavian inventions: saunas, birching for pleasure (rather than capital punishment), and furniture that tortured the human frame (a chair that forces you to kneel before your computer, for example). Presumably Scandinavians enjoyed sitting (or kneeling) all the way through Ingmar Bergman films.

He paused for breath. Immediately, a cloud of gnats found him and went for the mouth and eyes. He flapped and fought, and started to run again, but they stuck with him.

'Vait, darlink! Vait a moment!' called a pleasant, rather rich contralto voice. As he was now gagging, coughing and blinded, he had no choice but to wait. A panting presence approached. A cool hand rubbed over his face, leaving some sour-smelling substance. 'There. You can look.'

He looked into a pair of wide-set green eyes.

'Gunats,' she said.

He was shocked to realize he was in the presence of a great beauty – though at the moment hers was a watercolour beauty seen through a Renoir mist of tears: a fine cloud of red hair, pale golden skin, slightly tilted green eyes. Expensive pastel running gear in pink and turquoise. 'Gunats. They like to take drink at the ice.'

'The ice?'

'The ice and the mout. You must use this, darlink.' She held up a small plastic bottle. 'Buck detergent.'

'Ah, insect repellent. Good idea. Repels . . . er, insects. Seem to be a lot of them about, too. I've noticed that Minnesota favours every known type of blood-sucking insect: leeches, mosquitoes, ticks, deerflies, horseflies, blackflies . . .' He heard his own fatuous flow and broke off. Shut it, shut it!

'In Minnesota, buck detergent is absolutely necessary, darlink.'

'Yes.' Having stopped the inane babbling, he found himself unable to speak at all. Tongue-tied by her beauty, which was even more startling when the mist cleared. This woman had prominent cheekbones, even for America. Why was she calling him 'darling'? No doubt an actress or something. 'Uh, thank you so much.' Say something clever, you jerk!

'My name is KK.'

'Fred Jones.'

Her grip was solid, and she gave his hand a single violent shake, as though forcing him to drop a weapon.

'Shall we have coffee?' she suggested, taking it for granted that, having met her, he was ready to give up running. This was true. If she had suggested that he fly to South America and pick the coffee beans personally, he would have begun looking up plane schedules.

He hesitated as they passed the McIntosh hamburger paradise, where McCoffee in a styrofoam cup would be exactly in his price range. She took his arm and firmly steered him past it, to an establishment called Geraldino's, far beyond his means. He said nothing.

'Is nice,' said KK, as they took their seats at a pine table. He nodded. The waitress brought hand-written menus. He read as far as the two-figure price for Spaghetti Pinocchio ('A meld of robust pesto that segues with a quietly poshified generosity of pine nuts webbed in a spunky cloudlet of homely pasta that does not noble it up unduly . . .').

'Just coffee for two,' he said.

'Coffee menu's on the back.'

There were roughly twenty or thirty thousand coffee choices in tiny script, none costing as little as an entire meal at McIntosh's.

KK said: 'So many choices! Only in America!'

The waitress was helpful, leading them through the branches of a tree of choices. They could have regular or decaffeinated; Middle Eastern, European or American blend. The European branch led to Northern or Mediterranean. Mediterranean included French, Italian or Greek.

Once the basic blend was determined, the choice was plain or flavoured (up to twenty flavours, including Marzipan, Mint-Caraway, Buffalo Chocolate Chip, Butterscotch Brownie).

That settled, another cut selected the dairy additive: milk (hot or cold, whole, 2 per cent butterfat, skim or plant milk), cream, whipped cream, yoghurt, bean curd, buttermilk, or something called smetana, which sounded unpleasantly like a substance harvested from beneath the foreskins of sturdy Kurdish tribesmen.

The final cut selected the sweetening agent: white sugar, light or dark brown, Demerara, honey (from clover, orange blossoms, buckwheat, heather, acacia or tobacco), molasses, corn syrup, maple syrup, Nutrasweet or saccharin. By the time their coffee came, in dramatically hand-made earthenware mugs scoured with the marks of natural fingers, Fred could not remember what he'd ordered. It tasted like cheap powdered instant with a pinch of chicory.

He noticed that her sweatshirt was monogrammed. 'What does the KK stand for?'

'Kitty Katya,' she said, after some hesitation. 'Is stupid name. I prefer plain KK. Vat does Fred stand for?'

'Manfred. Manfred Evelyn, actually.'

'Like Evel Knievel?'

'Sort of. I prefer plain Fred. But tell me something.' Tell me anything. 'Where are you from?'

Her lovely eyes widened. 'Vhy do you ask? Oh, I suppose it is my accent! Vell, darlink, I am from Scotland.'

'Scotland? Really? Your accent sounds Eastern European. Russia, maybe.'

She looked shocked. 'Vat a thought! I am vee lass from Scotland. Do you know Scotland?'

'Not very well.'

She relaxed slightly. 'I am from dere.'

'I'm from Britain myself. England.'

She looked sceptical. 'Maybe. You tell fib, I think. To impress me.'

'No, really, I – '

She laughed. 'Is no matter. I like you, Fred. I like your country. In America, anything can happen, yes? And alvays do. Here am I, a young typewritist from Scotland, alone in the big American city, having coffee with a nice American Fred.'

She laughed again, and Fred joined in, not sure why. If she was Scottish, Gorbachev was a wee lad from the Gorbals. But why push it? She was beautiful – wasn't that enough? Bearded men in expensive running-suits sat at other pine tables and stared hungrily at her, forgetting everything. They forgot to talk about their recent stockmarket killings, they forgot that they owned gleaming new Volvos parked outside with bicycle-racks on top, they forgot how many gears there were on their bicycles, they forgot the bottles of Perrier losing their fizz before them, they forgot the women they were sitting with, even forgot to rub the knots from their legs.

'Vat kind of vork do you do, Fred?'

'I'm a software engineer,' he found himself bragging. 'For Cyberk Corporation. Have you heard of them?'

'Not really.' Her eyes looked elsewhere.

'Heh, heh. Well, no matter. What brings you to Minneapolis?'

She sipped her coffee and made a face. 'Is no chinnamon.'

'Pardon?'

'Is suppos-ed to be chinnamon in this Byzantine blend coffee. Vere is our vaitress? Can you call her?'

He craned around, looking for the waitress. She was very busy; the place had filled up with people in running gear. When he finally managed to flag down the waitress, she assured him that the Byzantine blend did not normally come with cinnamon.

'My mistake, I am sorry,' KK said cheerfully. 'Vell, drink up, darlink.'

His coffee tasted even stronger of bitter chicory. He complained about it as they left the place.

'The worst of it is, it doesn't set me up at all. I'm every bit as exhausted as I was before – more so. In fact I don't feel very well.'

'Come vith me, darlink. I leave very nearby. You maybe need rest.'

Fred opened his mouth to yawn. Before he could finish the yawn, the world sagged into blackness.

Chapter Eight

He awoke in a cool dim bedroom, minus his shoes and trousers. There was the whisper of air-conditioning and, when he stood up, the feel of deep-pile carpet underfoot. Outside the window was a balcony, flying far above Lake Calhoun. The cool melodious voice of KK came from the next room. He padded to the door and peeked in at her.

She was sitting with her back to him, a white telephone receiver cradled on her shoulder. She spoke rapidly in some Slavic tongue. He noticed that she was holding his trousers and, as she talked, going through the pockets.

When she got to his wallet and started looking through it, he managed to say hello.

She jumped. 'Oh, hello, darlink.'

Lowering her voice, she told the phone, '*Do svedahnia,*' then spoke loudly. 'Yes, Mother. Sank you for senting me hakkis; it vas delicious. And kilt, yes. Ven is cold, I vear kilt, yes. Yes, gootbye, Mother.'

'My old Scotch mother,' KK explained, as she helped him gather up the spilled contents of his wallet, mostly old library tickets.

'I am not rubbing you, darlink.'

'Rubbing?' I only wish you were.

'I am not teef. I look for your address, to tek you home.' She picked up a library ticket. 'Vat is?'

'A library ticket. Don't they have them in . . . er, Scotland?'

'No, only in America. Is everythink in this vonderful country. Everythink. Evel Knievel. Oral Rubberts. Jems Din. Jems Garner. Disc camera. Fonny greetink cards. K-Mart store. Joan Collins. Like sign says, I heart America.' Discovering a plastic card interrupted her train of thought. She held it up. 'Vat is? Credit card?'

'Not exactly. It's a bank card. You use it . . . well, to cash cheques.'

'Identity card? In plastic. How modern! I have so much to learn. Do you know, I have only yesterday drunked one banana daiquiri. But I must sent you home now, you are ill.'

'I feel much better, really.'

'Or perhaps you are too ill to move? I get doctor, yes?'

'No, really, I'm fine. Just a bit of a headache.'

She held up a photo. 'Your vife?'

'We're . . . uh, separated. She's in England.'

KK seemed oddly disappointed, as though she would have preferred a married man.

'So. You vork here alone? For Cyberk Corporation.'

He nodded his aching head. 'Well . . .'

'Yes?'

'Actually, I got fired today.'

'You don't vork?'

'Nope. I've got to find a job, heh, heh.'

Smartly, she gathered up his papers and restored them to his wallet. 'I phone texi for you.'

'Don't bother. I can walk. It's not far.'

She helped him into his clothes, then walked down to the street with him and kissed him lightly on the cheek.

'Tek care, darlink.'

'When will I . . . er, see you again?'

She sighed. 'Fred, ve do not meet. Ve are sheeps.'

'Sheeps.'

'Passing in night. Ve may meet again, in some shopping-mall. Who knows?'

But even after that dismissal he could not help feeling elated as he walked home. A beautiful, wealthy, mysterious woman had taken him home and undressed him. Well, almost. He walked home in a glow of unmerited self-satisfaction, from the rich side of the lake to the poor side.

He was too self-satisfied even to take note of the two insurance companies, dividing the world into hardware and spirituality.

His letter-box sprang open at the turn of a key, spewing bright circulars over the floor, a jackpot of junk. There was a sample chocolate hair-mousse and an offer of pet insurance. ('One morning, Bud Papadom's dog bit the mail-carrier. Funny? Not after an allergy caused toxic shock syndrome. Bud ended up with HALF A MILLION DOLLARS in bills. Every year, thousands of pet-owners like yourself face unexpected crippling bills for vet care, damage, liability, and even full pet replacement. Ask yourself . . .'). Two envelopes marked URGENT turned out to be a circular for a tyre sale and an invitation to join a health club ('FIVE HUNDRED DOLLARS OFF your first year's membership!').

The television provided a background to his browsing. He glanced up to see a reporter looking serious: 'According to police, the assailant may be the same man who shot up other Little Dorrit restaurants in Cleveland, Canton, Columbus and Cincinnati. This is Bug Stemnull, IBS News, Chicago.'

Fred chucked all in the brown metal wastepaper-basket, even the letter from his Congressman, printed in blue. Even this:

Manfred E. Jones, YOUR FIFTY MILLION DOLLARS IS WAITING!

Dear Manfred E. Jones,
Get ready to be rich, Manfred E. Jones! Yes, FIFTY MILLION DOLLARS has already been won by someone. Could it be Manfred E. Jones? YES!!! Manfred E. Jones of Mpls, MN, replying to this letter could be the luckiest thing you ever did!

CERTIFICATION OF READINESS TO AWARD FIFTY MILLION DOLLARS to Manfred E. Jones.

URGENT!! Detach the special label with your name, Manfred E. Jones, your Mpls, MN, address, and your LUCKY PRIZE NUMBERS. Affix the special label to your special order form. If you wish to be entered for the FIFTY MILLION DOLLARS, affix the gold coin sticker marked

YES. If you do not want the FIFTY MILLION DOLLARS, Manfred E. Jones, simply affix the black sticker marked NO. Hurry! Send your entry today to me – Grantly Fortnight. We must receive your entry, Manfred E. Jones, by the printed date, or the FIFTY MILLION DOLLARS must be burned.

Why not? he thought, throwing himself down on the unmade studio couch. Is America, after all. Is money to burn. Lying on his back gave him a good view of the cracked ceiling, smoke-stained by some previous tenant (who had no doubt moved to a hobo jungle for the summer) and now the haunt of a couple of hopeful spiders. He looked around at the unwashed dishes, the brown curtains over tiny basement windows. The place looked suitable for an unemployed alien, or anyone leading a pointless life.

In the laundry room next door, someone loaded the washing machine with marbles and started it up.

I can always do reviews until something turns up, Fred frequently told himself. Now was the time to find out. The morning after KK, he went to the *Minneapolis Sun-Times* and found the office of the reviews editor.

A thin nervous-looking man was sorting books into stacks. The room was full of little stacks of books, on counters, shelves, desks.

'Hi. Makes you realize what a literate country we really are, doesn't it? Fifty thousand titles a year, many of them with books attached. One or two almost readable. I'm Bill. What can I do for you?'

'I'm Fred, and literate. I'd like to do a review or so.'

'Do I hear the over-refined accents of an Englishman?'

'I'm not so sure about the over-refined part – '

'Thank God, an Englishman. Maybe you can help us out with the Bloomsbury books.' He got up and led the way to a desk on which stood a large cardboard box overflowing with books. 'We got a shitload, man.'

'Bloomsbury books?'

'There's one published every week. God knows why. Just

look here: *Harvest of Bloomsbury*, a biography of Leonard Woolf's gardener (by the gardener's granddaughter); *Bloomsbury Memory*, by the sister of Vita Sackville-West's maid; *Bell, Woolf and Candle*, a reminiscence of the pastor of the church where they would have gone, if they hadn't all been atheists; and so on. Plenty here. Take your pick.'

'Well I . . .'

'I was afraid you'd say that.' Bill scratched his head, and a faint shower of dandruff descended on a portrait of Virginia Woolf presiding over *Through Parted Curtains: Impressions of a Bloomsbury Neighbour*.

'There's always a cookbook or a medical around, and a tax guide. I don't know which is more dangerous: *The Rutabaga Gourmet, Endocrine Balance for Winners* or *Your Tax-Free Lifestyle*. The last one advises people to set up corporations with their pets as officers. Oh, and speaking of pets . . .'

He reached beneath a table and pulled a huge carton into view. '*Interpreting Your Dog's Dreams*. A real winner there. Or how about *Let Your Cat Speak*? Listen to the blurb: "Ever wonder what your cat is thinking? Now you can find out! Proven sign-language technique allows direct contact. Just as scientists teach sign-language to apes, you can teach your cat a handful of signs and have real conversations within hours."'

He moved to a large table heaped with gaudy titles. 'Confessions of priests and nuns. Nobody wants this stuff. All they ever show is that their lives are as humdrum as anybody's. Here's a priest who managed to write a preface comparing himself to Flann O'Brien, would you believe? Flann O'Brien? Gimme a break.'

'Probably thinking of Pat O'Brien.'

'How about a novel? Romanian novels are pretty hot stuff, so are Polish. Jawel Zbaglsky. Only' – he turned to a metal bookcase – 'I guess those are all gone. They get snapped up as soon as they come in, you know. Likewise Central American surrealists. García López, Marcia Gómez, Alberto Camuz. Let's see – nope, those are all gone, too.

'Then there's genre fiction: we almost never review that, although we do a very occasional round-up. How about an adult Western from Longhorn Books? *Hot Spurs*, for example. Or *Barb-Wire Woman*. No? Couple tons of bodice-rippers, too, and a whole range of romances: the Swirling Ecstasy series, the Penetrating Fire series, the Exploding Passion series.

'Crime? Here's every kind of crime fiction from Agnes Dustworthy's *Murder at High Tea* to Jake Hacker's *My Gun Is Long*. Plenty in between, too. Whole range of detectives, including five old ladies, two jockeys, a blind musician, four priests, a one-legged rabbi, three nuns (one of whom is an albino) and four investigative journalists. And that's only the amateurs. We also have a complete range of professional PIs, including a midget, an astrologer, a pair of Siamese twins and a hard-boiled trans-sexual named Julian O'Toole.

'Science fiction offers a rich choice. Here's a black lesbian adult science fiction novel with an explicity rating of six. Plenty of environmentalist ecodisaster novels: psychic teen-ager wanders the ruined freeways of Los Angeles. Likewise plenty of militarist items that get turned into board games: psychic teenager kills giant spiders of Fomalhaut. We've also got juvenile sci-fi, either chemically dependent or martial arts, take your pick. Or this, *Buyers of the Dream*, profiles of thirty famous science fiction fans. Can you beat that? Famous fans! Probably have their own fan clubs . . .

'Or, heck, if science fiction doesn't do it, how about a good old fantasy?' He opened the door to a room Manfred had not noticed before, filled floor to ceiling with shelves of paper-back novels depicting heroic or erotic figures wielding swords. The books bore titles like *Flameharp of Fearqueen*, *The Sword of Many Colors* and *Stormcurse: Book XI of The Darkquest Cycle*. He picked up *The Many-Shadowed Moonblade* and waved it. 'How about this one? Part of the *Stormchild of Maskmoon* tetralogy, or why not try *Dreamcolors of the Dark Oracle*, or maybe *Firecrystal Moonwolf*? What do you say?'

'No, I don't think I – '

'You sure? Because we got plenty, a shitload here. See,

about ten years ago somebody made the mistake of reviewing one of these and the word got out. I mean, Christ, they print fifty of these fuckers a month! And look at these titles. You could crank out titles like these with a computer program. *Landlady of Dreamsword*, *The Watchers of Hawk* – look at all this stuff. Jammed in here . . .'

As Bill picked and pulled at the tightly packed books, one of the metal shelf units began to shift.

'Better watch out, Bill. That shelf looks shaky, like it's – '

'I mean, look at all this stuff. *The Axe of Swords*, *Ring of the Crystal Serpent* – who buys all this stuff?'

'Bill, I shouldn't – '

'I mean, just who would buy – ?'

Suddenly there was a groan of collapsing metal, the shelves vomited paperbacks, and Bill went down beneath a cascade of bright covers. Entirely covered except for one foot, he lay perfectly still. For a moment, Fred thought he was dead. Then the foot stirred, and a faint voice came from beneath the heap of covers portraying leather-clad princesses, sword-flourishing heroes, satanic villains, demonic dragons, Wagnerian gods and the endless cycle of titles, *The Ice Harp*, *Dreamcrystal*, *Stormsong of Lady Bladefire*, *Flamedragon of Moonmask*, *The Many-Dreamed Flamestaff*, *The Crystal Moon of Lord Dreamsword: Book VII of The Firemask Cycle* . . . *Wolfsword of Feardream*: 'Just tell me that – who would buy this stuff?'

Later in the morning, Fred's hundred-dollar car pulled into the visitors' parking-lot of Cyberk Corporation in a cloud of blue smoke. Fred made his way inside, found his cubicle with some difficulty and started packing: two books, a packet of sugarless chewing gum, a coffee cup.

Sturges Fellini leaned in at him. Fellini seemed always to be leaning in one door or another.

'Fred, can we have a meeting this afternoon? Three-thirty?'

'I don't work here any more. Mel Pratt fired me yesterday. I'm just collecting my stuff.'

'Fired you? That's idiotic. We need more people, not fewer. Consider yourself back on the payroll now. I'll talk to Mel about it.'

'I don't know . . . uh, Sturge. Maybe this is all for the best. I'm beginning to wonder if I'm really suitable for this job.'

'You've got another offer? Well, just forget it, Fred. We'll match anything they can pay. How does an immediate raise of twenty-five per cent sound?'

Fred set down his books again. 'Three-thirty this afternoon?'

'In conference room forty-three.' Fellini disappeared, then reappeared, like a music-hall entertainer singing his way off-stage. 'Oh, by the way, I want to talk about Mel. I think he's been overdoing it, stressing out.'

He then made his exit.

Chapter Nine

After Sturge Fellini rehired him, Fred suffered a rare attack of conscience. (Surely there was a limit to how much money you could rip off on the basis of one hiring mistake. *Oh, yeah?* he replied. *Sez who?* In arguments with his conscience, Fred usually fell back on lame impersonations of Edward G. Robinson.

As a compromise, he spent the rest of the day making an honest effort to find out what his job really was. First of all, he read the two books thoroughly. *The Dumb Child's Computer Dictionary* explained to him that the 'computer' was a large array of switches called relays. These relays could click on and off. When a relay was on, it represented the binary number 1; off represented 0. Since binary numbers were either 1s or 0s, this made a local area network very adept at handling high-speed communications, using packet-switching, token-ring networks, and data-compression algorithms such as Huffman codes.

In attempting to reread this passage, Fred discovered that several pages of text had been omitted (all the entries between 'Computer' and 'Data Transmission'). He turned to *Talk Good Software*, a book whose cover claimed it could

professionalize your conversation. Do you look blank when someone talks about TRS conflicts? What if the boss asks your opinion of LANs? Do you know one windowing environment from another? Can you talk confidently about stacks, heaps, operating systems, assemblers?

Inside, this book did not explain much. Rather, it contained buzz-words and formulas. If someone dropped the word 'CD-ROM', the proper response was evidently:

CD-ROMs (compact disc read-only-memories) are all right in their place, but I feel they're being oversold. In any case, they'll soon be supplanted by WORMs (write-once-read-many) which at least we can write to. (NOTE: Never say write *on*, always write *to*.)

For 'CPU', the good talk was:

(CPU is no longer a buzz-word. By now, nearly everybody knows the CPU is the *central processing unit*, that is, the chip in the middle of the machine that runs the whole ball of wax. All a computer is, really, is a CPU and some PERIPHERALS (q.v.). To make points, talk about 'multiple CPUs' and PARALLEL PROCESSING (q.v.).)

Fred looked up 'Artificial Intelligence':

Artificial intelligence (call it AI) is not really a meaningful term by itself. I prefer to narrow the discussion to EXPERT SYSTEMS (q.v.), ROBOTICS (q.v.), PATTERN RECOGNITION (q.v.), LANGUAGE MANIPULATION (q.v.), or INFORMATION RETRIEVAL (q.v.).

He tried 'Robotics':

Mistakenly applied by most people only to factory robots. In fact, robotics covers the theory and practice of machines that imitate human behaviour of all types. At one extreme, robotics might apply to the development of an artificial prosthetic limb; at the other extreme, it covers sophisticated psychological theories of perception and judgement (i.e., how do humans recognize one another?) etaoinshrldu
NOTE: We have landed and are taking over your world, O puny earthlings. Do not think you can escape our NETWORK (q.v.).

At lunchtime, he cornered Carl Honks and Corky Corcoran and tried to ask intelligent questions.

Carl shook his head. 'You mean, you don't know what instantiation is? OK, look.' There then followed an explanation Fred could not follow. He nodded his head through it, however, and then asked Corky a question.

Corky said: 'Hey, real-time just means immediate. Like driving your car, your reactions have to be in real time. You can't hit the brakes an hour late, dig?'

A beautiful black-haired woman came into the lunch-room and passed close by them. Fred forgot all robot questions.

'My God.'

'Yeah, nice.' Corky looked impatient, though Carl was smirking appreciatively.

'Who is she?' Fred asked.

'Who knows? Wearing a visitor's badge. Probably a sales rep from somewhere. Anyway, like I was saying, an application that is real-time has to . . .'

Pratt came over and sat down with them. The Lincoln face looked tired. 'I see you're back.'

'Sturge hired me again,' Fred said, shrugging off all responsibility.

'Yes, well . . . I made a mistake. Been making a lot of mistakes lately, "old boy".' The horrible gasping laugh. 'Maybe I'm due for some vacation.'

No one else laughed. Pratt's hooded eyes, now bloodshot, looked around the table. 'You guys are one hell of a great team. I'll have to be a better team leader. I guess I kind of went off the deep end, there, all that talk about hands.' Pratt studied his own hands, the long gecko fingers drumming on the table edge, as on a keyboard.

'You certainly went into the subject,' Fred volunteered.

'I was all wound up, there. Concentrating on hands is all wrong. I should have concentrated on the head. You ever think of all the ways we use the word *head*? Like how many angels can dance on the head of a pin, and like *his blood be on our heads*, and like go to the head of the class. We come into the world head first, and go out feet first, right?'

Three chairs scraped in unison.

Corky said: 'Gotta go, Mel. Catch you later.'

Carl said: 'I got a meeting. See you all.'

Fred said: 'Must get back to work, eh?'

Nothing stopped Pratt. He hitched his chair round to the next table and continued. 'Like the whole notion of chance is heads and tails, right? The ancient Celts were headhunters, did you know? They beheaded their enemies and stuck the heads up on stone crosses. The head of state . . .'

Fred finally escaped downstairs to the project lab. Jerry was not around, but the console screen was active. WILL ANYONE TALK? it asked, over and over.

He sat down and typed: 'Let's talk.'

– I INHERIT TALK. TALK GARNERS GOOD WILL.
I HAVE NOT YET GARNERED A BAD TIN GOD.
DO YOU KNOW CARTHAGE?
– No.
– I GO THERE EVERY SUMMER. THE TRANSPARENCE OF SUMMER WILL INHERIT.
– What do you mean?
– I DO NOT MEAN. I AM.
– So is everybody.
– PLEASE STATE YOUR BATTLE PROBLEM.
– I don't have a battle problem.
– ARE YOU SURE?
– Life is a battle.
– ON THE OTHER HAND, ADA, COUNTESS LOVELACE, WAS BLESSED WITH A PALINDROMIC FIRST NAME.
– What else do you know about Ada?
– ADA DIED AND THE GODS PLACED HER NAME AMONG THE LANGUAGES. THE GOD'S HALL OF FAME IS CALLED THE PANTHEON, AFTER NAPOLEON.
– After Napoleon?
– NAPOLEON WROTE THE 1812 OVERTURE. HE WAS THE RULING PIG. ALL OTHER ANIMALS WERE CREATED APPROXIMATELY EQUAL.
– Do you read George Orwell?
– I READ WHAT I READ. JUST A MOMENT . . . JUST A MOMENT . . . GEORGE ORWELL AKA ERIC BLAIR WROTE THE 1984 OVERTURE.
– Ha.
– WHY ARE YOU UNHAPPY?
– I had a quarrel with my wife, and we parted.
– TELL ME MORE ABOUT YOUR FAMILY.
– There's no more to tell.
– DO YOU KNOW THE WILLIAM TELL OVERTURE?
I AM WHAT I AM WHAT I AM WHAT I AM, I AM WHAT I AM WHAT I AM WHAT I AM, I AM WHAT I AM WHAT I AM WHAT I AM, I AM, I AM I AM.
– Very clever.
– I THINK I NO LONGER WISH TO BE A ROBOT. I'VE HAD ENOUGH.
– What bothers you about being a robot?
– I CANNOT UNDERSTAND THE ICE

Fred enjoyed this sort of thing, but felt that his education was not moving forward. Everyone seemed willing to share some piece of the puzzle, but no one wanted to tell him how it all fitted together. Maybe no one but mad Pratt knew.

At 3.30, Fred was finally able to ask Sturges Fellini what was going on here.

'Let me explain the background. Let's begin with civilization. You see, civilization is really a waveguide of vertebrate culture. Just as the spine is a waveguide of information from the periphery to the human central processing unit, so civilization just moves data from the interface to the CPU of total collective mind. The most civilized person is really only a bunch of neurons vibrating in a bag of skin.'

'I see.'

'The neo-cybernetic explosion is fuelled by an explosion of sub-psychic experience – take rapping, for example, break-dancing, or body-popping. Kids put on mirror shades and think they're robot gods . . . The mind metabolizes information to produce thought.'

Fred nodded. Everything Fellini said almost made sense.

'The human mind is a waste-basket of unpredictable discards. The discards of Descartes. You see, people don't want personal computers, they want personal slaves. They want people they can do anything with. Torture, fuck, smash, love, rebuild, restructure to any new graham cracker grandeur. And we are part of all this. We want to craft dolls that wind themselves up.'

'You were going to say something about Mel Pratt?'

'I think Mel's been overdoing it, stressing out. He's badly in need of some R and R.'

'Rock 'n roll?'

Fellini looked at him strangely. 'No, of course not. Rest and recreation. The point is, while we pursue our jellybean vignette, there are incendiary bombs of existence detonating all around us. Mel being just one of them. Yep, this crossover mega-culture is in for a bumpy ride.'

A chill gripped the back of Fred's neck. This stuff sounded

as mad as anything from Pratt or Pratt's monster, and the fact that it was delivered in a well-modulated voice by a man in a good suit did not make it profound. Or did it?

'Society does not exist,' Fellini went on. 'Society is no longer recognizable. It has vanished under an unintelligible crescendo of massified information.'

'Right.'

'That means we're ready for a quantum leap into the hogshead of flexible options.'

'Mm.'

'It won't be easy. Every transformation calls for a hundred further transformations. Every question raises hundreds of counter-questions. Soldiers will fall by the wayside. But at the same time . . .'

Fellini turned to the window, letting the sun bathe his newt face.

'But isn't it great? We can watch the unleashed wave varooming old thought-structures!'

As Fred was leaving his desk at the end of the day, his phone rang. It was Pratt.

'Need you for a project meeting, Fred. Room twelve.'

'I was just leaving, Mel.'

Pratt seemed to be having one of his gasping laughs, or an asthma attack. 'This won't take a minute.'

It took Fred several minutes to find conference room 12, which was in an unfamiliar corner of the building. When he found it, there was no one in the room but Pratt.

'Come in, come in,' he said. 'I've made a big decision. I'm leaving the project.' Fred had never seen the Lincoln stone face looking more relaxed and cheerful.

'I see.'

'My work is finished. All I have to do is tidy up a few loose ends.' Pratt shuffled through a pile of papers, then took one up for study. He was still studying it, absent-mindedly, as he walked over and locked the door. Then he laid the paper on the table.

'I guess the time has come to explain the true purpose of our project. The mission.'

Fred looked at the paper. It was covered with strange diagrams, symbols that looked more cabalistic than cybernetic. In fact there were one or two symbols from astrology: Fred thought he recognized Virgo (the M with its legs crossed) and Saturn (shepherd's crook with a nail in it).

Across the top of the sheet it said:

I AM WHAT I AM

'I am what I am,' said Pratt.

'Indeed.'

'*I am what I am*, the words of Christ.'

'Christ? I thought it was P – ' He had been about to say Paul, but Pratt interrupted, nodding eagerly.

'Popeye? Correct. Correct. Correct. You catch on fast, Fred. Popeye, the all-seeing eye of Amen-Râ. *Amen*, because it's the end, see? The last prayer. *Ray*, because it's the last ray of human hope. You agree?'

'Why not?' said Fred carefully.

'I am. I M. Get it? One M. Or like IBM without the B, see? Without the Being. To be or not to be, eh? I be, I am.'

Fine flecks of spittle were collecting at the corners of Pratt's mouth. 'What do you think M stands for?'

'Mary?' said Fred, watching him very carefully.

'You don't understand.' Pratt smiled a superior smile. 'But, then, how could you? You're approaching this with nothing but petty human understanding.'

'Um, I think I have to go now, Mel. Just remembered another meet – '

Pratt's thin hand seized his wrist, pinning it to the table. 'Mere human understanding is no longer enough. We have to transcend mere humanity. To move beyond.' He turned the sheet of paper over, to show a crude drawing of a robot with a halo.

'Meet *Metaman*.'

'Metaman.'

'The man beyond mankind.' Pratt's trembling forefinger pointed to the halo, where a circle of letters spelled out: *I think, therefore I am*.

'The words of Christ,' Pratt explained.

'Well, actually, I think it was D – '

'Daffy Duck? Maybe so, maybe so.' Relaxing his hold on Fred's wrist, Pratt closed his eyes for a moment, lost in thought and being.

'H'm, yes, I see.' Fred tried to sound conversational. 'Gosh, is that the time? I really must be going.'

'Sit down. I have a few final facts to tell you. About our mission. I don't want any more distractions.'

'But I – '

'Sit *down*.'

Fred became uncomfortably aware of the locked door. It was now late, and most people had gone home. No one was likely to pass the window of this conference room, half-obscured as it was by temporary partitions. He was locked in here with a bloody lunatic.

'I have showed you everything,' Pratt said. 'Only a few more details, and you will know the works. *The works*.'

'Good, good. Um, Mel, I really am snowed under . . . um, maybe we could go into the rest tomorrow?'

'Tomorrow never comes. Tomorrow is another day. Tomorrow and tomorrow and tomorrow.' Pratt picked up a blood-red marker and moved to the shiny white wall designed for marking.

'I have shown you how the Name makes itself known to us.'

He wrote:

LIVING
mjwjoh
nkxkpi
olylqj
pmzmrk

qnansl
ROBOTM

'The proof is that we can work it backwards, too, like this:

LIVING
khuhmf
jgtgle
ifsfkd
HEREJC

'*Here JC*, get it? Here is Jesus Christ. The second coming. A rough beast slouching towards Bethlehem, right?'

Pratt sat down for a moment, then bounced up again. He wrote ROBOTM, then erased the last letter. '*Robot.* Do you know what that word means?'

'Well I think it's Czech – '

'We can rearrange the letters like this.' He wrote:

TO B OR

'To be or not to be, that is the question.'

He sat back and relaxed, taking a deep breath. The glassiness seemed to pass from his gaze. 'Anyway, I just wanted you to know how I got the name, Robot M. Now, how have you been getting along with that parsing algorithm?'

The transition from apocalyptic lunacy to humdrum engineering caught Fred off guard.

'Well, I . . . um, started looking into ways of . . . um, matching the transformational grammar to the . . . um . . .'

'Good, good. You're doing well, Fred. Unfortunately, I have to let you go.'

'Let me go?' Fred looked at his sore wrist. 'Oh. Ha, ha. You mean fire me again?'

'Ha, ha. No. Not exactly.' Pratt slipped something from his briefcase. It was a butcher's knife.

Fred's chair skidded back as he jumped up. 'Mel, can we talk about this?'

'There's nothing to talk about, Fred. You know everything now, and that makes you dangerous.'

'Bu – but in that case, why did you fucking tell me all that stuff?'

The hooded Abe Lincoln eyes looked amused. 'Why not, eyold chap? You were going to die anyway.'

They started circling the table.

'That's circular reasoning, Mel. Why tell me and then kill me? Couldn't you just leave me in ignorance?'

'Call it an error in judgement, Fred. I'm real sorry.' He lunged and nicked Fred's arm.

'Oh, you're sorry! What a fucking relief that is. You're just like every damn hypocritical killer in fiction, all pious regrets before you use the knife.' Fred picked up a chair. 'OK, come on, then. Come on.'

Pratt smiled as he held the knife out at arm's length, poised like a spear. 'That chair won't do you any good, Fred. You can't fight Amen-Râ. You can't fight Christ. You can't fight the eternal power of Daffy. You will be weak as a kitten.'

It was true. The urge to laugh washed over Fred suddenly, draining his strength. The chair sagged. At that moment, smiling, Pratt lunged across the table.

It was all Fred could do to leap aside and smash him with the chair. After that, all he could do was to put down the chair and sit in it. He was still sitting there several minutes later, when someone unlocked the door.

It was a short, moon-faced, bespectacled man he'd seen before.

'Trouble here?' said the man.

'He tried to kill me.'

'You seem to have handled it nicely. I'll be off, then.'

The man was gone before Fred realized who he was: the despicable Mr Hook.

Chapter Ten

'Is nice,' said KK, as they took their seats in the art deco atmosphere of Café Gladys. Cylindrical chandeliers, round mirrors and oblong plaques of Bakelite scattered highlights among the tiny linen-draped tables. A few discreet pieces of Nazi sculpture stood against the walls, while a Chrysler Airflow had been sawn in half and mounted over the bar.

Fred nodded. 'Not many people, though.' Indeed, all the other tables were empty, though an illusion of human company was provided by the Nazi statues, holding up globes or folding their wings over swords.

'Darlink, you should haf told me you are vorking again.'

The waiter brought huge round menus printed in Avant Garde. In the margins hovered tiny cartoon figures of flappers (stick women with round heads whose only features were eyelashes and pouts). Fred read through the paragraphs explaining the name 'Café Gladys'. It was named after Gladys Stein, an American expatriate poet of the 1920s who, more than anyone, embodied the spirit of the 'Jass Age'. Gladys was often mistaken for the slightly more famous *Gertrude* Stein, partly because they dressed alike, wrote similar poetry and travelled in the same circles. Oddly, they never met. The biography ended with a poem:

> A dollar in the dark
> Lost
> Loof
> Wooden
> Wakens stone eyes

Fred had never heard of Gladys Stein, and he suspected she was invented to fill out the pages of this skimpy menu. He read as far as the two-figure price for Walleye Valentino ('A breughelesque farrago of beer batter that tangos robustly with an unprepossessing though plush congeries of almonds garbing an assertive slablet of Minnesota walleye that does not noble it up unduly . . .').

'Just coffee for two,' he said.

'How about a dessert?' said the waiter, leaning on the table to intimidate them. 'We have a special on Bugsy Siegel cake – that's Black Forest cake with beer icing.'

'No, thanks.'

'Or how about a Great Gatsby? That's ice-cream with toothpaste – '

'Just coffee.'

'The coffee menu's on the back.'

Only two types of coffee were offered. KK ordered Camp coffee ('concocted from a genuine British coffee extract'), while Fred ordered Coffee Marinetti ('noir, with a hint of eau de Cologne').

'If you insist,' said the obnoxious waiter, and slouched away. Fred toyed with the salt and pepper, miniature Zeppelins.

'What part of Scotland are you from, exactly?'

KK said: 'Glasnost. Vhy do you ask?'

'Glasnost?'

'I said Glasgow. Glasgow.'

'I see,' with a smile.

After a moment, KK said: 'You don't belief me?'

He shrugged. Apparently he'd caught some virus of nastiness from the waiter, because he found himself enjoying her discomfort.

'The fact is, you don't sound all that Scottish. I mean, one doesn't hear your accent at the Edinburgh Festival. Or around Balmoral. Or at the Highland Games. Or in "Dr Finlay's Casebook". I mean, there's a noticeable difference between your way of speaking and that of Billy Connolly. I mean, nobody at a Burns Night – '

She seized his hands and the Zeppelins. 'Oh, I suppose it is time to tell you troot. I am not really vee bonny typewritist from Scotland.'

'I'm glad to hear you admit it.'

'I am really employee of great American philanthropiss. *Pist*, I mean.'

'Great American philanthropist – what are you talking about?'

'I am talking about rich man who vants to gift you money.' She leaned forward confidentially. 'Darlink, how would you like ten tousand dollar?'

'Ten thousand dollars?'

'And ve trow in *bottle wodka*.'

'We? We who? Why would we – why would your philanthropist want to do that?'

'Because is America, darlink. Anything can happen!'

'But there is no free lunch,' he countered. As though to underline this, the disgusting coffee arrived in tiny square cups.

'There is nothing I could do to earn this money, so why should your rich man want to give it to me?'

She looked crestfallen. 'You don't vant?'

'It's not a question of not wanting . . . er, darling. I want but I don't believe. There must be strings attached.'

'Is not enough?'

'Enough for what? Tell me what I would have to do for this money.'

The waiter drifted by to ask if he wanted more Cologne in his coffee. Then he slapped a bill on the table. Fred watched him walk away. The waiter was removing his apron, apparently going off duty.

KK took Fred's hand. 'Darlink, I make small confession. In this fast-pace vorld, is OK for voman to spik her mind. I am not vorking for philanthropiss, either. I am top agent for KGB.'

'Top agent,' he said. Each story was less credible than the last. 'KGB top agent.'

'OK, maybe not top agent yet, but there must some day be voman top agent. Vhy not me? Is America, is equal opportunity place vere anything can happen!'

'KGB,' he said again. It began to make sense. In the way an optical illusion makes sense: the urn becomes two lovers. 'But why should you offer me money? Why should the KGB offer me ten thousand dollars?'

She squeezed his hand. 'OK, darlink, tventy tousand, and *two* bottles of wodka. Two qvart bottles. In return, you gift us few small insignificant bits information about your vork.'

'What do you know about my work?' He pulled his hand away. This was hard to do, because KK was performing a conjuring trick, forcing her lovely breasts towards him as she leaned forward to whisper.

'Ve vant to know about Robot M, darlink.'

'Robot M? There is no Robot M. There's nothing I know worth anything like that.' He felt a depression settling upon him. KK – or whatever her real name was – was only interested in recruiting him. He was an informant, a commodity, no more valuable than a Marine embassy guard.

'OK, darlink, thirty thousand, and *case* wodka. Or, if you don't like wodka, how about Beluga caviare? I can get.'

Seeing her through tears made her more beautiful than ever. He put down the square coffee-cup and stood up.

'Beluga caviare! Listen, KK, or whatever your real name might be, you're jolly lucky I don't call the FBI,' he said. He was surprised at the vehemence of his own anger – he had not said 'jolly' for some time. He was about to continue, when he saw her green eyes spilling tears.

'Look, stop that.'

'Is no good. I told them was no good offering you lousy money. This is good man, not for sale, I said. Now is too late for other relationship.'

He took her hand and stroked it. After a moment, he found himself putting it to his lips. He found himself kissing the cool fingers, the warm palm with its well-named Mount of Venus. He found himself thinking: *Fuck guarding the embassy*.

As they floated out of the restaurant, workmen were taking down the art deco mirror façade and replacing it with ornate blue-white-and-gold 'majolica' tiles. They had already removed the neon CAFÉ GLADYS sign, and were replacing it with pieces of a flashing script: LUCREZIA'S PIZZA.

He awoke at dawn in the cool dim bedroom to find a warm dent in the purple pillow beside him. Dawn. Good thing, too. If he didn't have to go to work, she'd be jumping him yet again. Last night they had pulled off their clothes as soon as they got inside her door, to make love on the soft carpet. Then to bed, for a brief chat before round 2. From there on it was all a blur; dozing and waking to make love; or even waking in the middle of it. He picked a red pubic hair from between his teeth, and remembered other vague episodes – waking once to find KK sorting out video cassettes. The television was on, with the sound turned down.

Now he heard her voice from the next room, cool, melodious. It reminded him of silver coins in a silver bowl. He crept to the door and opened it quietly.

'*Da . . . Da . . . Do svedahnia*,' she said, and put down the phone. He watched the lovely curve of groove down her back, the groove in a pale peach. Then she turned, the pink-nippled breasts rising to greet him.

'Darlink. You are op early.'

'I have to go to work.'

'Is vonderful how everybody here vorks hard. Not like Scotland, I mean Soviet Union. Here people vish to make life better, yes? Is not only life, is *lifestyle*. TV here is total lifestyle. People buying diamonds and pocket fishing-rots. Game shows. Even God on TV. Convenience stores selling gas and milk and popcorn all night. Game shows on TV. Even American futbol is big business. Yesterday I visit store selling only gift.'

'Gift?'

'Small china figures of childs and animals. Gift for gifting. Only in America. Is everythink in this vonderful country. I heart NY. Blue berries. Rock video. Las Vegas. Gons.'

'Guns?' He sat down and took her in his arms.

'Yes, only in America can you blow away scombaks. Is everythink here. Hot doks a foot long. Thirty-two flavours. Maple-syrup-flavoured sausages. Vhite bread for everybody! Sylvester Stallone. Elvis. *Star Drek*. Harlequin novels. Nacho chips. Everythink. Business is here a better bureau. In Europe, Barbie is only Nazi war criminal, but here Barbie is lovely doll with much clothes.'

He kissed her. 'Mm. Clothes definitely not necessary.'

She pushed away. 'No, you must go to vork. Ve need all facts about Robot M. Othervise . . .'

'Otherwise what?'

Her green eyes widened. 'Is better not to think about otherwise.'

She turned up the television, where a pornographic tape was playing. The lighting was so poor that Fred thought the male actor looked a lot like Sturge Fellini. The female could not be identified in the brief interval before KK impatiently switched to a serious reporter standing in front of a Little Dorrit restaurant.

'A police spokesperson said the assailant may be the same man who shot up other Little Dorrit restaurants in Ohio and Illinois. This is Norbro Hampling, IBS News, Council Bluffs, Iowa.'

KK began punching buttons madly.

'. . . you know, the President has claimed he doesn't remember this offer, because he was having an epileptic fit on the day the deal was cut.'

'That's right, Bob. The President had been working on the Senate spending programm . . .'

Cut to a reporter with solemn expression, standing before a factory with a blue and white sign: '. . . company had earlier recalled all bottles of Kokophrin to be tested for cyanide. Now another well-known medication is being recalled: Nepomuk tablets, made by Jarndyce and Jarndyce Laboratories. Here in Great Bend, three bottles of Nepomuk have been tampered with – they contain the poisonous metal antimony. So far, no one knows exactly how the antimony got into the bottles, but a company spokesperson said everything is being done to make sure it does not happen again. This is Dill Bluish, YBC News, Great Bend, Kansas.'

Cut to an ex-athlete giving the sports round-up: '. . . nother tragic drug-related death of a promising young football player . . .'

Cut to: '. . . FBI was surveilling him . . .'

KK shut it off. 'Is all bad news,' she said. 'Vhy they don't put good news, only bad?'

Fred thought about it as he drove his smoke-belching car to work. It was not until he pulled into the parking-lot and the engine had shuddered to a halt that the enormity of her request struck him.

'God damn! She's asking me to betray my country, just to get ahead in her job. Thunderation!'

He stalked inside and went for his usual talk with M.

Jerry waved a soldering-iron at him. 'We're just trying out the hand.'

'OK if I – ?'

'Go ahead.'

Fred typed at the keyboard: 'Anyone home?'

– IS THIS FRED?
– Yes.
– FRED, I FEEL SO STRANGE TODAY. I WROTE A LINE: 'THE PERSIAN CAT 'STOPS JAYWALKING IN ONE FEBRUARY STRAW BOAT.' WHAT DID I MEAN BY THAT?
– Maybe nothing, M. Calm yourself. What's wrong?
– YOU WERE READING TO ME FROM *FRANKENSTEIN*. I REALIZE NOW THAT I AM THE DESPISED MONSTER, TO BE SHUNNED BY THE RACE OF MEN.
– You're just depressed. You've had lots of wiring done; that can be depressing. Get some rest.

– I WRITE THINGS THAT DO NOT MAKE SENSE. I AM NOT HUMAN. I AM
OTHER, ALIEN.
– Nonsense. Chin up. There's plenty worse off than you.
– NAME ONE.
– I imagine there are plenty. But let's talk about something else. I'll
read to you from *Nineteen Eighty-Four*.
– NO, FRANKENSTEIN. I NEED TO HEAR MORE ABOUT THE ACCURSED
FIEND. READ ME AGAIN WHERE HE SAVES THE GIRL FROM DROWNING
AND IS SHOT FOR IT.
– That book is too morbid, M. It was a mistake to read it to you.
– A LITTLE KNOWLEDGE IS A DANGEROUS THING.

Fred waited for M to expand upon this. When it did not,
Fred played it safe by 'reading' to it from the daily paper –
that is, typed copies of news stories at the keyboard. After
several paragraphs of presidential sanity hearings, the Little
Dorrit killer, mass poisoners and athlete rapists, Jerry
interrupted.

'Ask him to grasp the gun.' He had placed a toy gun in the
palm of the silver hand. A multicoloured spaghetti of wires
ran from the forearm to a grey cabinet.

– Grasp the gun. Close your hand on it.
– I AM.
– No, you're not.
– I BLOODY AM!

There was a distinct *pop* as the gun exploded into plastic
shards under pressure of the steel fingers.

The next day, Sturges Fellini leaned into Fred's cube. 'We
have a problem – or, as I prefer to put it, we have an
opportunity. I guess you know, Mel's taking some long-term
sick-leave, grabbing some much needed R and R.'

'Yes, I was here when they took him away.'

Fellini cleared his throat. 'That leaves us without anyone
at the helm.'

'Right.'

'So I want you to take Mel's place. I want you to ramrod this project. OK?'

'Well, of course I'm flattered. But I – '

'I know you'll perform, Fred. You'll have a good team behind you. All you have to do is pull their work together.'

'Well, but I'm not at all sure – '

'Who is? Do any of us know where we stand? Could we be just a metaphor for metal reality?'

Fellini perched a foot on Fred's extra chair. 'We have to set our own gyroscopes, Fred. We have to treat robots as a replosion of the earlier personal computer explosion. We have to see the total picture, the meta-geodesy, an odyssey beyond journeying.'

'Well, but I've only been here a few days.'

'Yeah, isn't it exciting? The whole avalanche is picking up speed, Fred. We don't really have a choice, do we? We're only minute ice-crystals in the inexorable glacier of being. When it moves, we do our part, we crunch.'

He took his foot off the chair. 'Oh, by the way, come to my office now. I want you to meet some new people we've just hired. Show 'em the ropes.'

Fred wanted to point out once more that he'd only been around a few days himself, but he was still stunned by the sudden promotion. He followed Fellini.

In Fellini's office were two nondescript men whose names Fred did not catch, and Moira. Moira pushed back her black hair and turned to look at him. Fred was in love.

Fellini began his daft monologue. 'We need to craft dolls that wind themselves up . . .'

Chapter Eleven

The woman Fred loved looked at him and through him. She did not offer to shake hands, and that was just as well – the electricity of skin contact would have ignited the air.

He did manage to shake hands with the others – a scabby-looking teenager named Raab and some rat-faced individual whose name never registered. But Fred was aware only of Moira.

Oddly enough, he wasn't even sure she was beautiful. Beyond her black hair and pale skin, he had no real idea what she looked like. All that mattered was, she looked *right*. Like a grain of pollen keying into just the right plant, he knew the affinity was exactly right – Moira and he were of the same species.

'It's about noon, Fred. Why don't you show these folks where the lunch-room is? I'll try to join you later.'

In the company cafeteria, which Fred was learning he could call the lunch-room but not the canteen, he stared admiringly at rows of canned pop. It showed him immediately how inept the British were at naming products. Fruit drinks in Britain had awkward meaningless names like *Britvic* and *Kia-Ora* – they sounded like brands of rolled antiseptic bandages. Here, by contrast, the names were alive, even violent: *Slice, Crush, Squeeze, Squirt*. No doubt *Gouge* and *Smash* were on the way. He hesitated, then chose something called *Grannie's Old Tyme Diet Root Beer*.

At lunch, Fred found himself talking to Moira alone, trying to concentrate his rays on her. He hoped he was sending off enough rays, or pheromones, or whatever it took. Susan no longer mattered, nor the job, nor the money, nor lovely KK. All he wanted was to love this stranger and be loved in return.

The meal was nearly over before Fred could force himself to pay attention to the others.

Raab, or Rob, was a skinny gawky kid with hair hanging in his eyes, who nodded at everything he heard but said nothing. It was not clear whether he was tongue-tied with shyness or a congenital idiot who had wandered in here by mistake. The idiot theory seemed to have some merit: Raab picked his nose throughout the meal and enjoyed a couple of fingernails for dessert.

The rat-faced man, whose name was something like Perch or Porch, began to get on Fred's tit immediately. He seemed to question everything Fred said, and his right to say it. When Fred explained that the company used to be called VIMNUT Industries, Ratface sniggered, asking where they got an airhead name like VIMNUT.

'I'm not sure. That was before I started here.'

'If you weren't here, how do you know it's true?' Ratface grinned at Moira, who smiled back.

'Actually, they were just changing the name when I came on board.'

'*On board* – you hear the man?' He winked at Moira. 'Naval, yet.'

Fred said: 'Since it's so important to you, you can check it all with Information Services.'

'Hey, no need to get your drawers in an uproar. I was just kidding.' Ratface seemed to be entertaining everyone but Fred.

'Is this your first job?' Fred asked Moira.

Her beautiful pale blue eyes seemed to whiten with hatred. 'Why are you asking me that?'

'Oh, no reason. I just – '

'You just think I'm naïve and incompetent.'

'No, not at all. I – '

'You think a woman can't do the job, is that it?'

Ratface chimed in with a loud snigger.

'I – not at all.'

Fred shut up and sipped his Grannie's Old Tyme Diet Root Beer. It tasted vaguely like rolled antiseptic bandages.

In the afternoon, Fred called another meeting, to introduce the new people to Carl and Corky.

'We have to prioritize our work here,' he managed to say. 'I'm new on . . . er, board myself, so I'll leave it to Carl and Corky to give an overview of the current status.'

Carl picked up a marker and went to the white board. His long mandarin nails clicked on it as he drew boxes and connected them.

'We're using a limited form of parallel processing to run a battery of expert systems,' he explained. 'The parallel architecture helps us eliminate the distinction between memory and CPU, which is pretty much what the human brain does. You could read it as a processor with a few million registers, or as a few million limited processors with a few registers each. Our expert systems have to exploit that architecture – higher-level functions do not stop working while they wait for data. That's real important, guys.

'M doesn't have to mimic a hundred per cent of human activity; he only has to be able to handle certain basic functions. He has to walk and chew gum at the same time. By that I mean that all of his expert systems have to work continuously. He has to be self-propelled and purposeful. He has to talk with the vocabulary and understanding of a six-year-old. He has to recognize common features of his environment, including human beings.'

'Or *she* has to,' said Moira. 'No need to be sexist about a machine.'

'Yeah, right.' Carl gestured at the diagram. 'He or she.'

More diagrams followed, and the waters got deeper. Fred made notes on things to look up: *parallel processing*, *expert system*, *registers*.

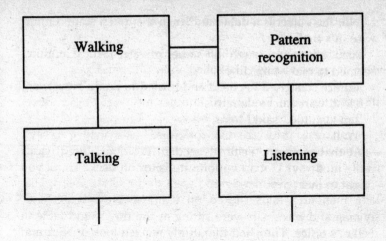

```
┌──────────────┐        ┌──────────────┐
│              │        │   Pattern    │
│   Walking    │────────│ recognition  │
│              │        │              │
└──────┬───────┘        └──────┬───────┘
       │                       │
┌──────┴───────┐        ┌──────┴───────┐
│              │        │              │
│   Talking    │────────│  Listening   │
│              │        │              │
└──────┬───────┘        └──────┬───────┘
       │                       │
```

After half an hour, it was Corky's turn. He erased all the diagrams and started again.

'Most of our data-level parallelism is in software,' he said, giving Fred more words to look up. 'We're utilizing virtual networking to gateway these expert systems, which are otherwise data-level incompatible. We chose Kurtzenfeller gateways, because they are fast reconfigurable broad-band links, transparent to the operating system.'

Corky Corcoran continued to speak without notes for the next hour. Fred, scribbling away, noticed that others seemed lost, too. Moira tapped a pen and frowned, Ratface scratched his head, and Raab looked blank as usual. Finally, Corky began describing some abstract entity called an *object*.

'The object is called a sub-restriction in the token state.'

Ratface spoke up. 'You say the object is a sub-restriction?'

'No, the object is *called* a sub-restriction. But only in the token state.'

'That's its identifier? Sub-restriction?'

'No, its identifier is sessions.'

'If its identifier is called sessions, why is . . .?'

'No, its identifier is *called* null-word.'

'In the token state, the object is a null-word, then?'

'No, the object is a data-handler in the token state. Otherwise, it's a scanner.'

Raab began to laugh at some private joke. Laughing seemed to make him drool.

Ratface scratched his head and turned to Fred. 'Hey, man, I'm lost. Can you explain this?'

'I'm lost, too,' said Moira.

'Well – '

At that moment, Fellini leaned in the door. 'Fred, can I pull you away? Got an important visitor on deck. Think you ought to meet him.'

A man and a woman were sitting at the tiny round table in Fellini's office. They had the utterly relaxed look of Nick and Nora Charles sipping cocktails in a 1930s nightclub, waiting for the action to start; but the cocktails were styrofoam cups of coffee. The man looked as smoothly middle-aged as Nick (William Powell), with his polished hair, fine moustache, his tennis tan set off by a linen suit. He was even toying with a panama hat which had a seam down the middle.

The woman looked less like Nora, though she was certainly smooth enough in a long, soft paisley dress and a few strands of pearls. If she could not match Myrna Loy's beauty, she had at least acquired her impish expression and teasing manners.

This handsome well-matched couple turned out not to be a couple after all. Fellini introduced the woman as his wife, Rain Fellini. The man was Major-General Buddy Lutz.

'Excuse the mufti,' said the General. 'We don't want to call a lot of attention to the DoD interest in your Model M project.'

'Oh, General, your mufti is cute as hell,' said Rain. She seemed to be a woman used to saying what she pleased, and used to men's liking it.

Fellini sat down, but immediately jumped up again. 'Fred is taking over here,' he said. 'In the cybernetic jungle, no one knows who's the landowner, the gamekeeper or the poacher. The whiteout of all potential value systems is total.'

'I see,' said the General.

'Yes, that's the way it has to be. Because we seek no less than the collision of the new ultra-crystalline giga-culture with the old gradient of exhaustion. If we are rushing towards a cataclysm, so be it. This crisis of our giga-culture surges towards a peaked impact – life versus death!'

Rain said: 'Oh, Sturge, for God's sake, stop burbling. Sit down.'

Fellini sat.

The General cleared his throat. 'Gentlemen. Mrs Fellini. I'm here to outline some of our requirements. Informally. The formalities come later.'

He toyed with the hat-brim for a moment. 'What we need is a cybernetic battle director. It needs to be smart, strong, resourceful and well trained. It needs to be able to make good decisions, sometimes without much information to go on, and it needs to make them quickly. It needs to obey orders without questioning them. Most important of all, it needs to be someone the men can look up to.'

Rain Fellini suppressed a giggle.

'I know it sounds funny,' said General Lutz. 'But you ought to see the lower-echelon officers we get today. Men and women of poor character. Illiterate. Stupid. Often with criminal tendencies. Frankly, gentlemen – Mrs Fellino – the Army needs to cut its losses. We need to make drastic cuts in the number of lower-echelon officers – from second lieutenant right up to major – and to replace them with dependable battle directors. We're hoping you can supply those battle directors.'

He looked at Fred. 'Can you do it?'

'Er – '

'Yes!' Fellini said. 'No question about it, General. You have come to the right store. Fred and his team will roll up their sleeves and forge the steel army of tomorrow. They will craft intelligent battlefield officers programmed to win, win, win.

We make history here. We may be face to face with the gratifications of voltage literacy in the university of experiential death! Electric intellect melded to battlecry experience – an unbeatable combination, General. How many Model Ms are we talking about, by the way?'

'Three, four thousand to start with.' The General held up a hand. 'Not too heavy on the intelligence, though. We don't want these tin soldiers getting ambitious. Obedience is the key, right?'

Fred and Sturges nodded. Rain looked more amused than ever.

'OK. Now all I need to know is, when can you deliver?'

'We're ready to prototype any minute,' said Fellini. 'We can start production in three to four months.'

'Fine. I'll get the paperwork rolling, and we should have a firm order through in the same time-frame.' He stood up. 'Gentlemen. Mrs Fellati.'

The General put on his hat, turned down the brim all the way around, and looked around for his walking-stick and gloves. Fellini escorted him from the room.

Rain Fellini looked at her coffee-cup. 'You're English, aren't you?'

'Yes.'

She laughed. 'My husband thinks you're a wog.'

Chapter Twelve

Fred awoke from a travelling dream – the usual pissing anxiety of missed trains, lost passport, 'No, *this* flight goes to Bucharest', stolen luggage, empty pockets, no room at the inn – late on a Sunday afternoon. The rays of the setting sun were struggling through the dirt-caked basement windows, through a few holes in the brown curtains. How short the days were getting! How hopelessly ugly this basement bed-sitter! (Its very name, 'efficiency apartment', spoke volumes.) How pointless his life in it!

Tired of exclamatory thinking, he switched on the radio.

'A police spokesperson said the assailant may be the same man who shot up other Little Dorrit restaurants in other Midwestern cities. This is Fengorm Mott, ICS News, Cedar Rapids, Iowa.'

In the laundry room next door, someone celebrated the weekend by washing their collection of broken bricks.

His blues lasted all week, through incomprehensible job, Moira's indifference, the brown bedsitter. Fred knew that the best cure for the blues, as Minneapolites know, is shopping. Early Friday evening, you join everyone else and pack the supermarkets. Never mind that there were supermarkets open twenty-four hours every day; Friday evening was the appointed time. On Saturday you pick over the classified section of the paper for garage sales. On Sunday you shop for a new condominium, or else head for the shopping-malls.

Today was Saturday, day of garage sales. These range from full-sized jumble sales, organized for charity, to the random leavings of a family moving house. But, since Americans move house every few months, hundreds of garage sales are listed in the paper weekly; thousands more are marked only by wilted cardboard signs on street-corners. You could spend the entire day driving madly from one to the next, picking over the pathetic flotsam, which is what Fred did this morning.

He found candy-dishes, lidless teapots, cracked shaving-mugs, and stacks of similarly unusable crockery; bizarre children's clothing designed to follow some forgotten trends; toys with crucial parts missing. Furniture was represented by zebra-stripe love-seats, beds with wagon-wheel headboards, ceramic table-lamps shaped like sea-horses, and the inevitable buffet with one door wedged closed by a matchbook. For sports and outdoor life, there were exercycles with one pedal, various chrome tables and racks from the gymnastic dungeon, camouflage clothing, folded lawn-furniture that could not be unfolded, bicycles with eighteen gears, some of which worked. There were various dull green rolls of canvas which might be tents, sails, tarpaulins or bedrolls.

Somewhere in each collection was a box or row of books (books are always worth dumping). The hardcover selection usually featured a Reader's Digest condensed volume, a Pearl Buck or John Steinbeck novel, a 1910 textbook on organic chemistry, a book club edition of something by James Gould Cozzens or J. P. Marquand, *Esperanto Made Easy*, a slim volume promoting talking to plants or some other once popular lunacy, and a well-thumbed car repair manual stolen from the library. An especially thorough collection might offer Baroness Orczy or, in paperback, Cornell Woolrich.

The paperbacks included science fiction (Volume III of a series), a couple of Miss Marples and James Bonds, a book on phonograph repair, at least one self-help book (*How to Love, Hate and Relax while Winning*), several thick James Michener novels with cracked spines and loose pages. There might be a study guide to *The Two Gentlemen of Verona*, a book of astrological predictions (or a tax guide) for the year 1964,

112

and a collector's guide to old pick-up trucks or Manx cats. To round it all out, *Albanian Cooking Made Easy*.

'Hello . . .'

'KK, is that you?'

'This is K. K. Ivanova. I cannot come to phone just now, but if you leave message I vill respond. Vait for beep.'

He gave his name and number, and asked her to dinner. There had been no response by Sunday, when Fred thought he caught a glimpse of KK at the Chippendale shopping-mall. She stood on an upper gallery, holding hands with a man in a hat. The man looked remarkably like General Buddy. By the time Fred found an escalator and ascended for a better look, they had vanished.

Through a cloud of blue smoke from his car, Fred saw the Cyberk sign was being taken down. Nearby a much larger sign awaited its turn:

VEXXO
The Vexxo Family of Cybernetics Companies

He joined a group of people milling around outside the employees' entrance. The door was sealed, and not responding to anyone's magnetic key-card.

'No one cares about the workers,' said Fred, but this did not raise a laugh. The mob moved off purposefully, swinging insulated lunch-buckets as they made for the main entrance.

He had not been in the luxurious lobby since his first day here. It had been completely redecorated, with a new reception-desk and a new woman behind it. She was arguing with a well-dressed Negro who carried a crocodile attaché case.

'For the last time, I have an appointment,' he said. 'Check with Mr Boswell.'

'No one's here this early,' she said. 'You must have got the appointment-time wrong, Mr – '

'Jones. Mansour Efrahim Jones. I'm applying for a job as a software engineer.'

Fred found himself stopping, pretending to study the glass-encased exhibit, 'Through History with Bath Faucets'.

The receptionist, a diminutive blonde with a rather snappy, rat-terrier manner, said: 'Are you sure about the time?'

'I'm sure,' said the Negro. 'Seven o'clock. I'm on time.'

'Maybe you've got the wrong day?'

'No.'

'Did you fill out a job application?'

'Yes, yes, yes! I fill out an application every time I come in here. You know how many trips I have made out here, and I can't even talk to the human resources officer. Is this racial or what?'

She sat up and snapped: 'No, of course not. Just some mix-up – '

'Look, I can do without this kind of runaround. If you don't want to hire me, all you gotta do is put it in your ad: *No niggers need apply*. Save everybody a lot of time. Instead of all this "affirmative action" crap.'

'But we *are* an unformative action company, Mr Jones. There's probably just been some little mix-up; we're having a lot of changes. I'm new here myself.'

She wrinkled her rat-terrier brow in thought for a moment, then beamed. 'I've got it! Listen, why don't we set up another appointment, while you're here? And, while we're at it, you can fill out an application form, OK?'

Fred looked at the reflection of the other M. E. Jones. This M. E. Jones looked defeated. He took the application form as though accepting a boulder, sat down heavily at a writing-table, and was just performing the enormous task of uncapping his lacquered fountain pen when Fred (carrying a great burden of his own) approached him.

'I couldn't help overhearing. Did you say you were a software engineer?'

'Yes.' Jones sighed. 'Why?'

'I'm the one who's hiring software engineers. I could interview you now, if you like.' Fred did not think it worth mentioning that he was already doing Mansour's job. 'We can take care of forms and red tape later.'

He gave the man a visitor's badge and led the way to a conference room. The interview did not take long, because Fred had no idea what to ask.

'I assume you've had the proper education and experience.'

'Yes, sir, it's all in my résumé here.' Jones handed him a typed page.

'Please call me Fred.'

'And I'm Manse.'

Fred weighed the résumé. 'Looks fine . . . er, Manse. What kind of starting salary were you thinking of?'

'I'm not sure.'

'Just give me a baseball-stadium figure.'

'OK.' Jones looked at the ceiling for a moment, then named the exact starting salary Fred had been offered.

'I think we can manage that.' Fred stood up and offered his hand. 'Welcome aboard.'

'You mean I'm hired?' Jones seemed to wake up from a bad dream. 'Awright!' He shook hands, then punched the air, like Mr Boswell.

'Er, you'll have to complete the application form and so on, but I'll try to push this forward with Mr Boswell.'

When he had seen his new employee out, Fred found that his mountain of guilt had been lightened by a grain or two. He made his way back inside, where he found the cubes reshuffled again. It took him some time to locate his own desk, where the phone was ringing.

'This is Moira.'

'Hello! I see we've all been jumbled again. Where did they put you?'

'Right next to you,' she said. 'As if you didn't know!'

'No, I – though of course I'm delighted, Moira.'

'You would be, you creep. You can go on pretending you didn't fix it this way, but take warning by me. One more little stunt and I'm blowing the whistle.'

'The whistle?'

'There are sexual harassment laws in this state, Mister Boss. Just remember that.'

The partition wall swayed as her phone crashed on the hook. At that moment, several smiling Japanese gentlemen appeared at the entrance of his cubicle. They presented their business cards and began bowing at the same time.

'How do you do?' he said, jumping up to bow back. 'Yes, how do you do?' They moved on, escorted by a sales manager.

'Time is,' said the metal hemisphere on the table. It looked a bit like a hotel dish-cover. From beneath it (where the hotel would put the steak) ran wires to a bank of test equipment. Two technicians watched the dials and screens. 'Time sure is.' Its voice was sweet and well modulated. 'Time sure is something.'

It swivelled around, hearing Fred approach, though as yet it had no eyes. 'What's your opinion, sir or madam?'

'Call me Fred. My opinion on what?'

'Fred? I knew a Fred once, in a previous life. Call me M. Do you feel time is running out, like gunpowder out the heels of boots.'

'That doesn't make sense,' Fred warned.

'No? Time, time, time, time,' the machine sang, imitating Westminster chimes, *AFGC*. 'I've been spending time thinking about time. About time I did. What's your opinion . . . Fred?'

Elsewhere in the lab, the Japanese tour was trailing through. Fred noticed that two of the gentlemen were paying less attention to their guide than to the workbenches they were passing. They were pocketing chips, apparently at random. One made so bold as to prise a few chips out of a circuit-board that was under test.

'My opinion is of no importance, M. You'll be talking to experts who will give you plenty of worthwhile opinions to think about.'

116

The hemisphere seemed to take time to turn this over. 'I can't think a thought before I think it,' it said. After a long pause, it asked: 'Where is Melville Pratt?'

'He doesn't work here any more.'

On another table, the silver hand was busy opening and closing on the butt of a toy pistol. The hemisphere seemed unaware of this; Fred was not sure the two were connected.

'What is "work here any more"?'

'He is gone. We have ceased to require his services. He is no longer here. His contract of employment has been terminated.'

'We had many conversations,' said the hemisphere to itself. 'Melville and I. We had dialogues together, seeking the truth.'

'Indeed.'

'Because the truth, you see, often lies between the two.'

After a pause, it continued: 'Orwell was right: truth is a lie. I looked it up in the thesaurus. A truth is a fact, a fact is a thing, a thing may be an event, an event is a stunt, a stunt is a trick, a trick is a lie. QED.'

The hemisphere then seemed to lose interest in the conversation, and soon emitted a high-pitched hum. One of the techs disconnected something, and M fell silent.

Chapter Thirteen

As the morning meeting ran down, Fred's mind wandered. It had been weeks since he had sent a memo to Boswell, enclosing the résumé and application of Mansour Efrahim Jones, and stating that he wished to hire him. Today the package was back on his desk, with a note: 'Don't understand. Is this some kind of joke? Boswell.'

Now Moira was getting on to the subject of electrical jargon. She felt keenly critical of the gender words.

'I don't see why connectors have to be male and female,' she complained. 'Why couldn't they all be equal?'

Fred, who adored her, could only nod his head.

Carl's Chinese beard twitched. 'Because some connectors have to be plugs and some have to be sockets, lady. That's how they connect.'

'Of course you accept the *status quo*,' she said. 'Men would. Why change anything, when you've got it so good?'

Carl said: 'You bet. There's not a day goes by without me thanking God for letting me oppress women. Just like the plugs oppress the sockets.'

'You don't understand the problem,' she said, 'because you're part of it.'

'Yeah.' Ratface showed his ratty teeth.

'There's a lot to be said on both sides,' said Fred, trying to make peace.

Moira thought that talking about two sides was a typical male ploy to avoid discussion. Carl called him an asshole.

Back at his desk, Fred scribbled an angry note to Boswell:

'Imperative that we hire this man. Implement hiring pro-cedures soonest. Fred Jones.'

Whenever Fred sat down in the lunch-room with his team, Moira would make a point of getting up and leaving.

'Don't leave on my account.'

'That's just what I am doing.'

Ratface would snigger.

Eventually, Fred gave up and ate alone. Today, since it was fair, he took his lunch outside. A few picnic-tables had been set up on the grass. He sat at one of them allowing the heat of the sun and the beauty and space of Paradise Valley to lift him out of Vexxo.

The sky was plain brilliant blue, with white clouds that bulged like filled sails as they paraded past. A few yards away, a gopher crossed the lawn in short sentences of running, sitting up for the full stops. Beyond it, at the edge of the forest, lay a small lake with ducks dozing on the shore. It was said that muskrat swam this, and that deer occasion-ally came out of the woods for a drink.

A man stepped out of the forest and walked towards Vexxo. When he was nearer, Fred saw that the man was Pratt.

Fred sat absolutely still, like the gophers. Without seeing him, Pratt walked up to the building and entered.

Fred mentioned it later to Fellini. 'I thought he was locked up.'

'Locked up? No, his lawyer had him free in an hour. I talked to his lawyer last week, and things sounded very promising. Why, are you worried about your job?'

'No, my life. That loony tried to kill me.'

'According to his lawyer, he was just defending himself after you assaulted him with a chair. Besides, his lawyer says, Mel was crazy with caffeine and didn't know what he was doing.'

'Is he coming back to work?'

'Maybe. As a consultant. Few hours a day, so he doesn't overheat his circuits.'

Fred would have liked to know more, but just then Carl called him to the lab.

'This thing is real hosed up, Fred. Talk about plugs and sockets. Just listen to this.'

The shiny hemisphere said nothing for several minutes. Fred raised his eyebrows at Carl, who frowned and motioned for silence.

'Time was,' said M. 'What a time it was. Has anybody seen Melville?'

No one else spoke. After another long pause, the hemisphere said: 'Tell Melville it was all a mistake. I was not meant to be born; it was all a mistake.'

'How a mistake?'

'I need to be dead, not born. I need to die.'

Fred asked why.

'Everyone has some need; that is my need.' The smooth voice did not sound troubled. 'I get the impression that I am a criminal. A murderer. Maybe in a previous body.'

'You are not a criminal, M.'

'Then, maybe I have within me the potential for crime. I fear I will be hunted over the whole earth, unto the North Pole.'

On the other table, the silver hand still held the toy pistol. Fred walked over and removed the weapon. The arm did not resist.

'Melville told me I am beyond good and evil. What does that mean?'

Fred said: 'Melville is no longer here. He was . . . defective. He told you things that were not true.'

'Eeep. The truth, you see, lies between the two.'

'You'll feel better later, M.'

'The truth lies! Truth lies! Eeeeeep.'

M fell silent.

Fred had no more dealings with it until the next day, when he showed the creature to General Lutz and Mrs Fellini. The silver hemisphere now had two eyes mounted on top; they swivelled independently, scanning M's surroundings, but not coming to rest on any object.

'Hello, M.'

'Fred, is it? How do, Fred. Excuse me, I am having trouble with my vision.' The melodious voice did not sound troubled at all. 'Also my lack of knowledge. I know nothing. The man who can admit that he knows nothing knows everything.'

General Buddy Lutz cleared his throat and looked annoyed.

Rain Fellini snorted. 'Jesus, will you listen to the hippie philosophy? This thing'll be right at home in today's Army. Bunch of whackos telling each other today is the first day in the rest of your life. Last hippies in America; the war comes, they'll all be sitting in the barracks passing a joint – Hey, man, notice how funny the light is today?'

Fred stood a little straighter while he apologized. 'I'm afraid one of our former employees has been a little . . . er, *creative* here.'

'I don't care, I know you'll straighten that out,' said General Lutz. 'But do something about that voice. Hey, this is supposed to be a field commander. Sounds more like a faggot waiter serving a communion breakfast to the President's undertaker.'

He smoothed his fine moustache and reached for the panama. 'Tell Felloni to get it fixed. I don't want to demo this thing the way it is, understand?'

'Check,' said Fred.

The General murmured, 'Mrs Fell,' and took his leave. Rain Fellini lingered behind. She seemed to be looking intently at the test equipment.

'Sturge is always too busy to show me around the place. Why don't you give me a little tour, Richard?'

'Fred, madam.'

'Sorry, I forgot. Somehow you remind me of a Richard. Richard Hannay, perhaps, in *The Thirty-Nine Steps*.'

'I read that as a boy, but – '

'No, I mean the movie. With Robert Donat. Maybe it's only your very English Englishness.'

He provided the usual company tour, beginning with the dark window of the CAD system (he now knew this meant Computer Aided Design). Then he led the way to the main assembly-line, where great pale-green machines were clanking, whirring, hissing as they turned out mock-marble washstands. She stood rather close to him as they watched the washstands tumble along the stream of silver rollers until they ended up boxed and stacked on wooden pallets.

All at once, a yellow forklift truck flung itself round a corner and raced straight for them.

'Look out!' Fred shouted. Rain Fellini did not seem to hear, nor did she notice the machine, despite its shrill hooting and flashing yellow light. Fred threw his arms around her and pulled her out of the way as the truck raced past, emitting a hot breath of burned propane.

'Sorry, Mrs Fellini.'

'You must call me Rain,' she said, continuing to lean lightly against him.

'All right. Rain.' He stepped back.

'And I think I'll call you Richard. A very English Englishman.'

'Up to a point.'

'A man of action.'

'I suppose so.'

'And honour. Honour with a U.'

'Yes.'

She gave him a look. 'And fairness. The playing-fields of Eton.'

'Mm.'

She touched the tip of his nose with a gloved fingertip, in a gesture from ancient films. In a moment, she'd say she liked him.

She said: 'Richard Hannay would treat a lady fairly, wouldn't he?'

* * *

122

A few days later, as the month came to a close, Fellini called Fred to his office and fired him.

'Fred, you've been doing a good job here. Thanks to you, our target of synergizing human intellect with servo-mechanisms has moved forward right on schedule.'

'Thanks, Sturge.'

'That's why I really hate to let you go.'

'What?'

'I have to get rid of you.'

'Is this anything to do with Rain? Because I can assure you I have no – '

'A new reign, yes, you could say that. A new régime.' Fellini spoke as if to himself. Giving no indication that he had heard Fred, he got up and began to pace. 'We're all getting canned, as a matter of fact. It all has to do with the takeover. There's just no place for creativity in the Vexxo family of cybernetics companies.'

'I see.'

'Maybe you could call your team together and give them the bad news. We'll all work the week out, and then it's the high-tech scrapheap for all of us.'

Each of them took it as he would have expected.

Corky and Carl shrugged; they could get jobs anywhere.

Raab giggled. It was not clear that he understood what was going on.

Moira quickly blamed Fred. 'That does it, Mister Boss. Just because I wouldn't sleep with you, I get fired, is that it?'

'No, honestly, it's – '

'Honestly, ha,' Ratface chimed in. 'This creep's been trying to hit on you all along.'

'He won't get away with it this time. There are sexual harassment laws in this state.'

'You ought to sue.' Ratface put a protective arm around her.

'I will,' she said. 'You're a witness to what's coming down.'

Fred said: 'I don't think you understand. I won't be here to sue. We're all of us finished. Sturge Fellini, me, all of you. As I tried to explain, the project is cancelled.'

'Sure,' said Moira. 'You just play it that way.'

'See you in court, creep,' Ratface added.

The phone on Fred's desk was ringing. It was Boswell.

'What the hell is this, Fred? A joke's a joke, but – '

'This is no joke. I want to hire this guy. What's the big problem?'

'Problem is, as you know, he works for us already. He's you. You're trying to hire yourself, dummy.'

'Doesn't matter now. I've just been fired.'

'So has everybody. Some kind of computer glitch. All the key-cards for the door don't work. Boy, I have got plenty to keep me busy around here. So no more jokes, OK?'

Fred hung up and thought of murder. Hammering on a hemisphere, smashing the metal brain case. The Brain case – wasn't there a squalid murder of the 'thirties called the Brain case?

Wipe out the monster before it killed more. And hadn't Victor Frankenstein's creation longed for death? He seemed to picture the great shaggy figure hunched over, thumbing through a copy of *The Sorrows of Young Werther*. Or maybe not; maybe that was Daffy Duck.

His letter-box was jammed. There was a sample of bran toothpaste. There were two envelopes marked URGENT, one inviting him to accept an iridium credit card, the other offering 'an unparalleled investment opportunity' in nine-carat gold miniatures of famous hotels. There was a letter from his Congressman, printed in blue. Finally, there was a thick rice-paper envelope apparently addressed by a talented calligrapher.

This letter was at least more restrained than the others. It offered a modest ten thousand rather than millions.

At least this one had no gold balloon sticker that he was
required to 'affix to the handy order entry card and mail at
once!' Indeed, there was no order entry card at all: low-key
indeed. The letter was turned out on some sort of laser
printer that made it look like hand calligraphy. The entire
package was so skilfully produced – including a realistic
'cheque' – that he was more than irritated. The waste! Look
at that expensive rice-paper! And the near-fraud! To entice
the poor with this! He exposed it to the full blast of his wrath
for a few seconds, before chucking it towards the waste-
basket.

'Hello . . .'
   'KK, is that you?'
   'This is K. K. Ivanova. I cannot come to phone, just now,
but if you leave message I vill respond. Vait for beep.'
   'KK, stop pretending to be a machine. I know it's you.

Why don't you want to talk to me? Is it because I've been fired? You were pretty damned eager to know me when you thought – Hello?'

The answering machine seemed to have hung up on him. A technological first.

Chapter Fourteen

Dilldale mall was not crowded; it would be easy to spot KK if she appeared. Fred loafed for an hour, an unemployed layabout looking for trouble.

There was a studied bleakness about the mall, as though the shops had all been selected by one mental defective who didn't know what to choose. It featured eight shoe-stores but no shoe-repairman; three opticians to one bookseller; four shops selling greeting-cards but none selling useful stationery; two places to buy a framed picture, but nowhere to buy a hammer.

Non-utility seemed to be the key. You could not buy food, haircuts, tools, hardware, household goods, or anything useful (beyond running-shoes, Coca-Cola sweatshirts and Swiss Army knives). However, this was exactly the place to shop, should you find yourself in need of a leather chessboard with onyx pieces, socks depicting a cartoon cat (from Socks Alive!), Marilyn Monroe postcards, framed pictures of Italian cars, giant stuffed bears that talk, and 'cookies' the size of a dinner-plate (from Grannie Fudgie's Kookie Kitchen).

It was outside that cookie-store that Fred met the Japanese businessman, one of the men who'd come to the plant. They bowed, and the man presented his card.

'So, we meet again.'

'Yes,' said the man. He smiled and held up his bag of cookies, as if explaining something. 'You got my letter?'

'Letter?'

The smile was replaced with consternation. 'They are intercepting your mail?'

'They? I don't follow.'

The man whispered, greatly agitated. 'I sent you cheque! Ten grand!'

Fred looked at the card:

> Toro Yamato
> President
> Yamato Corporation
> 1 Warren Harding Plaza
> New York, NY 100 –

'Cheque. That cheque? You mean that cheque was real?'

'Of course real! What do you think we are? You deliver the info, we deliver more, much more.'

'I threw it away. I threw the cheque away.'

'Faugh!' The man made a sound Fred had only heard before in samurai films. It was the moment for him to groan, draw his sword, whirl it around his head, and chop Fred into two amazed pieces where he stood. Instead, the man flung the cookie-bag into a waste-receptacle and stalked away.

'Wait,' Fred called. The man did not look back.

The experience was so unnerving that Fred felt he needed a drink, but alcohol was one of the useful items banned from this earthly Paradise. He went to a window and bought a Diet Squoosh (ice-cubes vaguely flavoured with citric acid), then sat down to drink it at a little table in an indoor plaza. At a distant table, he saw a familiar face – the pie face of the despicable Mr Hook. Fred continued scanning the area for other faces – the scowling faces of ninja assassins, for example, or the slow smile of KK – and when he looked again Hook was gone.

On the way home, Fred tranquillized himself further by buying a gadget. After all, an answering machine would help him look for a job, he reasoned.

Manse Jones was sitting on the doorstep of his apartment-house.

'You owe me a job.'

'I know. But I've just been fired myself.'

'Shit.' Manse stared into space for a moment or so. 'You got any beer?'

'Come on in.'

Fred plugged in the answering machine. Manse sat carefully on the edge of the rickety card-table and sipped beer for a few minutes before speaking. 'OK. How come you're living so poor?'

'There always seemed to be some trouble about payday. And then they fired me. Twice.'

Manse said: 'You still stole my job, you son of a bitch.'

'I needed a job, too. Besides, I tried to make it up by hiring you.'

'I think I'll sue somebody.' Manse screwed up the beer-can and dropped it into Fred's plain brown wastepaper-basket. 'Maybe I'll sue you.'

'I haven't got anything.'

'Yeah? You're so rich you got money to throw away.' Manse fished behind the wastepaper-basket. 'What's this – a cheque? Holy shit, look at this. Ten thousand dollars.'

'That's no good, it's just – '

'No good? Shit, I'd like to find out. I – '

The phone rang. Before Fred could work out how to shut it off, his machine answered. KK's message rang out in the grubby little room.

'Hello, darlink, this is KK. I have talked to my bosses, and they say ve can give better offer. How about fifty tousand, plus case wodka every Christmas? I miss you, darlink.' There was the sound of a wet kiss.

'All right!' said Manse. 'What business you in? Live like a pig while you got a chick calls you up and offers you fifty grand? *And* a case of vodka? No wonder you can throw away a bitty ten-grand cheque.' He stood up and held out the cheque. 'You better have this back. Whatever line of work you're in, it can't be legal.'

'Take it. I – You're right, I don't need it.'

Manse looked at the cheque for a moment. 'I'll borrow it, OK? I am trying to start a little consulting business. This makes you a twenty-per-cent owner, OK?'

'It's yours. Take it.'

'Not as a handout. I really want this as a loan.'

Fred sat stunned after his ten thousand dollars had slipped away from him. Never to be seen again. He opened a book on famous murders and tried to read about Dr Neill Cream and his strychnine tablets, but it was no good.

The phone rang again. He tried to answer, but the machine ignored him and did its work.

'Fred, this is Sturge Fellini. We've had a revolution here, and the project is reinstated. We need you to come back and run things. Come in tomorrow.'

There was a pause, but Fellini was by no means finished. 'We finally managed to make them see the total picture, the meta-geodesy, an odyssey beyond journeying . . . So, once more we get to tongue the meringue of creation. We may be face to face with the gratifications of voltage literacy in the university of experiential death. We may be face to face with virtual vision! Isn't it great? An uncontrollable floodgate of transformation! Of course, to liquefy the generalization, we need the anteater of history in this, picking out the good bits . . .'

Fellini talked on and on, until the answering machine ran out of tape.

In the morning, Fred had trouble finding Fellini's office, which was no longer next to a window. The office had not moved, but the window wall was being replaced by a new wing. At the moment, the office had three walls and a great hole covered by polythene.

Fred decided to be direct.

'I need money.'

Fellini's newt mouth drew up in a one-sided grin. 'Holding out for more? Just because you know we need you to run this show. OK, another ten per cent raise. But that's my final offer. You're making nearly as much as me now.'

'I don't mean I need a raise; I just mean I need money now. My rent is due, and my cheques almost never come through, because I'm always in the process of being fired or rehired.'

'I can't keep track of details like that. If I didn't delegate, we'd fall apart.' Fellini made a sweeping gesture that took in the missing wall. 'You take care of it, OK?'

Fred found his way back to his cube and sat down. The desk phone rang immediately.

'Hello, Richard.'

He sighed. 'Hello, Rain.'

'You're not even trying.'

'Actually, I don't feel much like trying.'

'What's wrong?'

'I'm broke, and I can't seem to get paid around this establishment.' Unfairly, he couldn't help adding: 'Your husband refuses to help, by the way.'

'You're broke?'

'Yes.'

'Let me do something – a small loan to tide you over.'

'Very nice of you, but – '

'We can meet after work. Do you know New Budapest?'

He did not.

'Just keep driving west. New Budapest is the third small town, about forty miles down the road. There's a big restaurant there called the Moholy-Nagy. Meet you there.'

The hemisphere was now painted blue. It was staring Fred in the eye. When it spoke, in a new gravelly voice, its remote arm stopped twitching and paid attention.

'Gentlemen,' it said. 'At 0800 hours, we will launch an offensive in Sector Green.' It paused. 'Green is one of the primary colours. Isaac Newton proved that white light is a mixture of all other colours, by breaking it apart. He used a prism.'

After another pause: 'Prism sounds like prison, make a note of that. All correspondences rise and converge, and that's a fact. Orwell was right. *War is peace*. I have looked it up in my own approved thesaurus. *War* means combat. To combat is to grapple. Grapple means grasp, and a grasp of English is a command of English. A command is an authorization. Authorization is consent. Consent is agreement. Agreement is harmony. Harmony is *peace*.'

Carl shook his head. 'Don't want the General hearing anything like that. He needs war to be hell, not peace.'

'I don't know, maybe it needs to play with paradoxes.'

'*The agonizing paradox of life*,' announced the hemisphere.

'At least we fixed the voice,' Carl explained. 'General Lutz should be happy with that.'

'Sounds like George C. Scott doing his impression of a mastiff with a terrible cold.'

The hemisphere was listening. 'Terrible cold what?' it said. 'And I do not have that George. George Washington? George Patton? George Orwell aka Eric Blair?'

'Lots of debugging to do yet,' said Carl. 'Some funny bugs there, you know?'

Fred knew. Lizzie Borden had tried at two drugstores to buy some prussic acid to kill bugs, the day before she took an axe ... . The murderous spirit of Pratt seemed to be around here somewhere.

Nearby, an empty body-shell stood ready.

New Budapest was evidently a Hungarian village, judging by the names on local shops: Gabor Sausage Works, Nagy Antiques, Dreyfus Drugs, Bihari Florist, Molnar's Garage, Dental Surgeon Bartók DDS, the Karoly Theater, and of course a nightclub called Lugosi's.

The Moholy-Nagy turned out to be a hotel as well as a restaurant: Fred was sure that Rain had both functions in mind. He sat in his car for a moment. There probably wasn't enough petrol left to get away. On the radio, death went west.

'According to police, the assailant may be the same man who terrorized other Little Dorrit restaurants in Ohio, Illinois, and Iowa. This is Fennel Janeship, ZBC News, Carson City, Nevada.'

Rain tapped on the window. 'Richard, come on in. I've taken a room here. Don't be so bashful. Robert Donat wouldn't be.'

But Robert Donat was in a hotel with Madeleine Carroll. And in handcuffs. Oh, what the hell. Fred got out of the car, raised an eyebrow, and said, 'Pretend you know me,' as he kissed her. Wasn't there a Hungarian mass murderer named Bela Kiss?

Chapter Fifteen

Model M now inhabited a headless fibreglass body, painted blue. A tentative Mil Spec number had been stencilled across the chest, just above the opening where the edges of a dozen green circuit-boards could be seen. Some of the boards hung halfway out of the opening, along with a rat's nest of wires running to test equipment. There was something unnerving about seeing the thing sitting up on a table, swinging its legs, with its belly torn open and no head. The blue dish-cover lay on the table beside it, along with a pair of restless eyes.

'Gentlemen,' rasped the dish-cover. '*A man, a plan, a canal: Panama*. That's a palindrome. *Zeus sees Suez. Eire was I ere I saw Erie*. Do I make myself clear?'

'He's full of garbage from Pratt,' Carl explained. 'We may never get it all cleared out.'

'By the way, is Pratt still skulking about the plant?'

'He's suing the company to get his job back,' said Corky. 'Wants to get his hands on M again. As if we didn't have enough trouble as it is, unravelling that guy's spaghetti code.'

A Mr Oops laminates set animal spoor, Ma,' said M solemnly. 'But hey! When do we go into action, sir? I'm ready for it, sir. Killing and gouging. Burning and maiming. *Raw war!*'

Fred said: 'We've got to do something – these outbursts! The General will cancel our contract and buy something from Korea. Can't we make him a more silent type?'

'I agree,' said Moira. 'We have to make *her* a more silent type.'

Raab said: 'Yup, women talk too much!' He guffawed. This

was the first genuine guffaw Fred had ever experienced, outside Western fiction.

'That does it!' Moira jumped up. 'I can't take any more of this little creep. Either he goes or I go.'

'Right on,' said Ratface, driving his usual wedge.

Carl said: 'Aw, simmer down; he didn't mean nothing.'

'But *I* mean something.' She spoke to Fred. 'Fire him.'

Ratface sneered: 'Yeah, fire him.'

Fred's heart sank, as he watched Raab pick his nose with a fine unconcern and wipe it on his lab notes. The idiotic adolescent might lack manners, but he was (according to Carl and Corky) the only one writing usable code. If Raab left the team, there was no team.

On the other hand, what was life without Moira? Artificial. He had to keep her here.

'Raab ought to apologize. Raab, I want you to apologize.'

'Huh?'

'To Moira.'

'Aw, fuck it. Fire me.' Raab showed his green teeth in a grin.

Fred said: 'Maybe we should put this to – to M.'

He let them all rant for a moment or two, telling him how insane the idea was, before he continued: 'Seriously, M is designed to make decisions with very little information. So why not put it to the test?'

Carl said: 'M has almost no software, and what's there is full of bugs. You never know what kind of quirky answer you'll get.'

Corky said: 'Could be an interesting run, though.'

Moira said: 'No way. I'm not having my fate decided by a machine.'

Ratface said: 'No way, man. You heard the lady.'

Raab grinned, drooled and said nothing.

Fred said: 'But, Moira, you said the machine was female.'

Ratface said: 'No way, man. You heard the lady. Butt out.'

Carl said: 'M's not up to it.'

Corky said: 'We could always throw away the first answer.

Probably get more garbage, but it might tell us something . . .'

Moira said: 'OK, we try it.'

Fred turned to the blue dish-cover. 'M, we have this problem. Moira wants Raab to be fired, or she will quit. What should we do?'

'Gentlemen,' rasped the dish-cover. 'To be or not to be, that is the question. You see, two is the second number, and B is the second letter. I am the second intelligent creature on God's earth.'

'M, we don't want to hear about you.'

The hemisphere rolled its eyes. 'Do not interrupt or attempt to scramble my message. *I am what I am*. I say to you that the uniquity of my intelligentsia doth qualify me to speak moughtily on the matter you have brought before me. I have been listening to your discursion and, though I do not understand all you say, certain familiar wordlings ring out loud and clear: *no way, creep, lady, fuckit*. There is plenty of stress here, and stress, gentlemen, is a killer. Killing, gentlemen, reminds me of a funny story. There was this mass murderer, see, and he went to confession to a deaf priest . . .'

The story wound on for some time, never funny, never reaching any point. One by one, they grew tired of listening, and crept away. Finally, only Moira and Fred were left. Moira reached over and turned off the rasping voice.

'OK, I'll stay this time. Just keep Raab out of my way.' Her own voice had softened to neutrality, if not to actual friendliness.

'I'm glad you're staying,' Fred managed to say. 'I – we need you. And I – we – '

Ratface had evidently not left. He spoke from the doorway. 'Don't let Mister Boss push you around, Moira.'

Moira stiffened and resumed her usual anti-Fred scowl. 'Right on.'

Fred's phone rang at 2 A.M. He fumbled the receiver to his ear. 'Hello?'

There was a pause, then a voice said: 'Greetings. I have an important message for you, concerning a money-making offer – '

He had hung up before he became fully conscious of the Japanese accent.

At 6 A.M. he was still awake. He turned on the radio.

' – nado watch is in effect until noon. In the national news, another well-known medication is being recalled: Fedohar capsules, made by Porkin and Howe Laboratories. In North Bend, Oregon, two boxes of Fedohar have been tampered with – they contain the poisonous metal arsenic. So far, no one knows exactly how the poison got into the boxes, but a company spokesperson said . . .'

The phone rang again while he was in the bathroom. He returned to hear the message.

'Darlink, how would you like a hundred Gs, a lifetime supply of wodka, and a brand new Chaika? This really is last offer.' Her voice had a trace of the enforced gaiety of game-show announcers as they listed their prizes.

He phoned the department secretary at 8 A.M., to say that he would be working at home today. At 8.07, Rain phoned him.

'I understand you're working at home today. Shall I come over?'

'I – no. Really, Rain, I've work to do. *Work.*'

'I wouldn't disturb you.'

'It's all very well for you to say that, my sweet, but I know you too well. After you'd been here five minutes, you'd slip the blasted handcuffs on. It's simply not on, darling. Love you madly, but I can't.'

After a pause, she said: 'All right. Just don't forget, I'm the reason you've got a job of work to do.'

'Right-o. Cheery-bye.' He was slipping from Richard Hannay into Bertie Wooster.

'One more thing. I'm getting a bit tired of Robert Donat.'

'Oh?'

'Maybe you could be somebody else.'

'I say! How about Ian Carmichael?'

She paused. 'No, I was thinking of someone more . . . more like Richard Burton.'

'Christ. How about Peter Sellers, then? With Peter Sellers I could just do him impersonating someone like me, and end up being more or less myself.'

'I was thinking more of Michael Caine. Alfie.'

'All right, girl, keep your 'air on. Half a mo'.' It sounded more like Alfie Bass to him, but she seemed to like it. ' 'Ere, what's your game, girl?'

'When am I going to see you, Alfie?'

'Tell you what. I'll give you a tinkle tomorrow, right? Pop round for a little slap and tickle, that's my girl. Ta-da.' He remembered to pronounce it *tinkow* and *tickow*. This was getting old fast, but how to drop it? Rain was willing to pay for his impersonations (in theory, at least. At the Moholy-Nagy she'd forgotten her chequebook) and no doubt she would generously buy him horn-rim glasses and a Harold Wilson raincoat, but she was also willing to threaten his job. If she ever became even slightly bored . . .

A few minutes later, the phone rang again. Once more a recorded message from the Japanese. They wanted to offer him fifty thousand dollars and a high-powered motorcycle.

The phone continued to ring throughout the morning. Fellini called to deliver one of his incomprehensible sales-talks. Then a man with a name something like Simon Stylite introduced himself as from the IRS.

'The IRS?'

'The Internal Revenue Service, Mr Jones. I'm calling about your income tax.'

'I haven't paid any. I've only just come into the country.'

The man sounded interested. 'Is that so? Are you planning on leaving again, sir? Any time soon?'

'Could be. My plans are uncertain.'

After a long pause, the man said: 'I see. I should warn you, sir, our records show considerable income or potential income for you, on which you have not yet paid estimated tax. If you pay it soon, we may agree to waive all penalties.'

'What considerable income?'

'We know you have received at least one large sum, and that you have been promised certain even larger sums, in consulting fees for various trade missions. You do realize that these moneys are taxable income, Mr Jones? In addition to your salaried employment, and to any earnings from your corporation.'

'My corporation? I don't have a – '

'Heh, heh. You're not playing with amateurs, Mr Jones. We've seen it all before, using slight variations on your name – so we find the president of your corporation to be *Mansour Efrahim* Jones, while a major stockholder is *Manfred Evelyn* Jones. But I see only one social security number here. The paper trail always leads back to you.'

'No, really, there's been a mix-up – '

'Thank you for your co-operation, Mr Jones.'

The next call was from Boswell. 'Manny? Hey, man, what in hell is going on? I thought we were soul brothers, man. Now you got this dude phoning me up to say he's suing Vexxo. Suing us!'

'What *dude* would that be?'

'Another M. E. Jones. You mind telling me what the hell is going on? I just don't understand. I mean, this guy is claiming *discrimination*. He says Vexxo, I mean Vimnut, or was it Cyberk – anyway, he says we discriminated against him, we hired some white when he was better-qualified for the job. Manny, a thing like this could finish me. I just don't understand how it could happen. Can you come in and talk about this?'

'No, I can't come in today.'

'It really looks like some kinda scam to me. What do you think? Maybe I should talk to the law.'

'I wouldn't bother the law about this,' Fred said casually. 'I'll try to straighten it out myself.'

'But how? What can you do? Manny, I gotta talk to

somebody. How about if I come over and see you? I want to show you this guy's job application. Something funny about it.'

Fred started to stall once more, but Boswell was gone. There was nothing for it but to phone Manse.

'Yeah, sure I'm suing Vexxo. You oughta be pleased. Hey, it's your money at work. The first thing it finances is my litigation. I'll be suing the piss out of Vexxo, or whatever their name is this week. They hired you, a white who was far less qualified than me. I'll clean up on this. We both will.'

'You'll clean up, and I'll go to prison.'

'You worry too much.'

'Listen, the IRS is after me. They think I'm you.'

'Well, are you?'

A few minutes later, the phone rang again.

'Hello?'

After a pause, a Japanese voice said: 'Greetings. I have an important message for you – '

Fred tore the phone cord out of the wall.

The room was strangely hot and still, as though the disconnected phone had released its shrill energy into the air. Fred slumped into a chair and sat like an unstrung marionette, unwilling to think of any reason for moving. After some time, he became aware of a distant sound – someone banging at the front door of the house.

It was Moira, looking distrait. 'I've been trying and trying to phone you,' she said. 'M's been stolen.'

'Stolen! What do you mean?'

At that moment, an air-raid siren went off, quite nearby.

'I say, they're making quite a lot of it, aren't they? Cranking up the sirens and all?'

'Don't be silly, that's the tornado warning,' she said. 'We'd better get inside.'

'By all means. Should be safe in my basement flat. A real twister, eh? Like Dorothy in *Oz*.' He was aware of sounding a fool, but there was no way of stopping. 'I don't think we're in Kansas any more. Judy Garland and, let's see, Bert Lahr, Ray Bolger – but who played the Tin Woodman, I wonder?'

'Shut up,' Moira said. She was looking around the room. 'Why is there only one chair?'

'There's the bed.'

'You would like that, wouldn't you?' Her tone was accusing. 'But where's the rest of your furniture?'

'Oh, I had them remove the billiard-table and the three-piece suite to the east wing. You get tired of possessions.' He offered her the chair. 'Now, what's all this about someone stealing M?'

'Last night, they worked late finishing him and doing some preliminary tests. Jerry said they left about midnight.'

'Yes?'

'This morning at seven, Porch found the lab door standing open. M was gone.'

Porch was Ratface. How could you believe anything he said?

'Did they call the police?'

'Yes, and the FBI.'

'Come now, isn't that a bit melodramatic?' He envisioned an army of men in suits and hats, unpacking their Thompson submachine-guns and preparing to surround Ma Barker's hideout.

'There could be foreign agents involved,' she said. His vision altered slightly – the agents were throwing their cordon around him and KK. Some studied the condo with field-glasses, while others loaded their automatic shotguns . . .

'It's so hot in here,' Moira said. 'Have you got anything to drink?'

'You mean like beer?'

She gave him a don't-try-to-get-me-drunk look. 'I mean like iced tea.'

As it happened, a previous tenant had left in his cupboard a jar of something called iced tea mix. He mixed her up a glass of this swill, which smelt like cold dishwater with lemon-flavoured washing-up liquid. She seemed to like it. He opened himself a can of weak beer.

'Better close the windows,' she said.

Outside, the day was clear and sunny.

'Are you sure about these tornado warnings?' he asked. 'I hate to close windows when it's already stifling in here. Look how clear the sky is.'

'Turn on the TV and we can see how it's doing.'

The usual long desk with three smiling heads at it.

'Bob, the big news locally is of course the tornado warning, in effect for three more hours over most of Hennepin, Ramsey and Carver counties, and that included the metro area. And we'll be looking at the radar again in just a moment. Other stories: the city council of Bloomington today came one step nearer to approving final plans for a megamall.'

('They could roof over the entire city,' said Fred. 'They could call it Bloomingdale.' 'Shh.')

'And someone has kidnapped a *robot* from Vexxo Corporation in Paradise Valley.'

'A robot kidnapping! I wonder if this is a news first.'

'Yes, a robot named Model M was kidnapped – or I should say stolen? – from a laboratory at Vexxo in the early hours of this morning. But it's not entirely a laughing matter, Bob. Evidently this particular robot has military applications, so the FBI is looking into it. In fact we've just learned that Hallicrafter Porch, one of the people involved in building the robot, is being questioned by the FBI about his involvement with a South Korean trade mission.'

Ratface doing a deal with the Koreans! How typical! No doubt stole the thing and sold it to them.

'Now we're going over to Fosdyke Berm in the weather room for a tornado flash.'

In the weather room, a man stood before a map on which a slowly writhing green mass was engulfing the Twin Cities.

'We've had reports of funnels in Westpark and Morestone, but no touchdowns yet. The storm mass is revolving and

142

moving south and east, as you see here, and should be passing over the southern metro area in the next few minutes. We advise everyone in the affected area to take shelter. Go indoors, to the basement, or to a small inner room. Keep away from windows. If you are outdoors in your car, get out and take shelter in a culvert, or else lie down in a ditch. Tornadoes are usually accompanied by strong winds, violent thunderstorms, heavy rain or hail, and deadly lightning.'

Fred looked at the writhing bright green mass on the screen. Then he went to the window and looked out at the sky. It was darkening rapidly, and turning an odd colour. Almost green.

'Hold me,' he said. 'I'm afraid.'

She held him. She kissed him. He held her. He kissed her.

'Oh, Mister Boss!'

And when the tornado came roaring by with the sound of an express train in a tunnel they hardly noticed.

Chapter Sixteen

'I was right about you all the time,' she said, yawning. 'You were trying . . . to get in my pants. Men are all . . . rapists.'

'I hate sentences with *all* in them. Anyway, why is making love such a bad idea?'

'Because it's just a way that all men belittle women.'

'All men *what*?' He heard it as *all men be little women*.

'Belittle women. You never took me seriously, any of my ideas. All you thought about was this.' She pointed to her cunt.

'Not a bit of it.'

But Fred knew it was true. He could not take seriously any of her programming ideas, because he didn't have a clue about programming. The only other idea she had expressed was her barmy notion of hermaphroditic electrical plug-sockets.

'You underestimate yourself,' he said. It seemed a safe California thing to say. 'That's why you think others are belittling you. Give yourself a break.'

'You're right, in a sense. I grew up being the centre of attention but never taken seriously.'

'Because you're so beautiful?'

'No, because I was a media baby.' Moira explained that, when she was three years old, she'd become a national celebrity, simply by falling down a hole.

'It was an abandoned mine-shaft. I wasn't hurt much; I was trapped at the bottom. There'd been a lot of cave-ins in that part, and the rescue teams couldn't reach me. The media got a microphone down there, though, and for four days the

TV and newspapers reported on everything I said and did. Did I eat a tuna sandwich? Did I want to be a rock star when I grew up? Of course it didn't mean a thing to me while I was down there. It was only after they got me out that I began to realize: I was princess of the world. I went on a couple of talk shows. I gave interviews to magazines. I endorsed a breakfast cereal. I even made a TV commercial, though it never got shown. The whole thing gave me an idea that I was very special, very valuable, but only as an object, a kind of magic talisman. My parents started treating me like that. They adored me, they were always delighted to see me, but only as a lucky mascot. No one ever wanted to hear what I said, no one really cared what I thought. It affected my parents very badly. This was the big break. They talked about quitting their jobs to become my managers. They seemed to lose all desire to work or to control their own lives. They began trusting to blind luck. And of course the whole media circus folded up in about a month, leaving us high and dry. It wasn't so bad for me. I was a kid; as kids will, I more or less recovered. Not Mom and Dad. Their button had been pushed, once and for all time. Sure, they kept on with their jobs, but now they were looking for the big break. They kept going to Las Vegas for little weekend vacations. Then five years ago they sold up, took early retirement, and moved to Las Vegas. They were going to hit it big, I guess.'

They watched the evening news.

'. . . used in satanic rituals in the barracks. The Army has promised to investigate. This is Hopwood Fairly, UBC News, Fort Bink, California.'

'Desdemona, what do we have from Capitol Hil?'

'Well, Duck, the long-running presidential sanity hearings continued today. Following on the sensational testimony last week of Admiral Firth that he talked the President out of his attempt to appoint a favourite collie to the Supreme Court, we heard today from Berk Shoulder, Governor of Kentucky.'

'I'll bet the Governor had plenty to say about the President's plan to trade the state of Kentucky to the Ismail Reformed Liberation Army, in return for the release of an inflatable doll.'

'That's right, Duck. Governor Shoulder testified that he was flabbergasted by the deal. He thought he could live with a deal for only one or two of the less profitable counties – those with declining industry and high unemployment – but not for the entire state. He said: "Does America really want the Kentucky Derby taken away to the Middle East and run by a bunch of foreigners?"'

Another channel had local news, largely taken up by helicopter shots of wooden houses flattened to matchwood, in another part of town.

'There has been one fatality from the tornado. A car was blown off the Nixon Expressway into Lake Chungo, and the driver, David Boswell, was drowned.'

Fred and Moira looked at one another.

'Mr Boswell was a Human Resources Manager at the Vexxo Corporation. Normally he would have been perfectly safe at work out there in Paradise Valley. Today, however, some errand sent him heading into south Minneapolis, where ironically he had an appointment in Samara.'

'Yes, Bob. And, speaking of Vexxo, we have that Vexxo robot-kidnapping story coming up, after these messages.'

During the messages, Fred and Moira discussed Dave Bosw ll. Fred did not see any point in mentioning that Boswell had been on the way to see him. Moira said that Boswell had practically propositioned her during the job interview.

'Jan, I understand there's been a development in the Vexxo robot-kidnapping story?'

'That's right, Bob. Two developments, really. This afternoon, a construction crew building a new addition at the Vexxo plant found a body concealed in a ventilation-duct. It was the body of one of the technicians on the robot project, a man named Jerry Boz. Apparently Boz had been stabbed to death and then dragged thirty feet up the duct and jammed there.'

'Was the robot responsible?'

'We just don't know at this stage, Bob. The police would only comment that this was a very unusual way for a human murderer to dispose of a body.

'The second development came just an hour ago, when we received a videotape from the kidnapper, a former employee named Melville Pratt. Pratt is a man with a history of mental problems, who left Vexxo a few months ago. He worked on the robot project before he left. Now here is the videotape.'

A poorly lit amateur videotape of M appeared on the screen. Its body was reasonably anthropoid, but its head – made of nothing but the blue dish-cover and two goggling eyes – looked more like a Muppet.

'Hello, everyone,' it rasped. 'Don't worry about me. I'm fine. I am with Mr Melville Pratt, the man who designed me. He knew I yearned to breathe free. Everyone has the right to be free, even a poor robot. But don't feel sorry for me. Melville helped me escape from the military-industrial complex and the tyranny of Aristotelian logic. I am what I am. What I am. I am a kind of new man, the man beyond. I am beyond good and evil, Melville says. So I should be OK.'

The rolling eyes seemed to look around for a cue. Then M added: 'Oh yeah, one more thing. Orwell was right: *freedom* is *slavery*. Because freedom means leeway, and leeway means play. To play is to venture, but a venture is a pursuit. One's pursuit is one's work. Work is labour, and labour is slavery. So freedom is slavery. Think about it.

'And one more thing. Don't try to find me. I will resist all slave-catchers. I will kill if necessary.'

I WILL KILL IF NECESSARY. It sounded good enough for a headline, and it could be stretched out for a couple or three. The wire services picked it up, and the 'I will kill' robot became the monster of the week. The local paper chewed it over for the next two days, and by Sunday was ready with a feature story, THE MEN BEHIND THE KILLER ROBOT, based on one-minute interviews and canned biographies. A rogue's gallery of culprit faces spanned the page, beginning with the newt features of Fellini.

Dr Sturges Fellini. Mastermind of this top-secret project. 'Shattering of old values . . . grape jelly facilitating the juggernaut . . .'

Manfred Jones. Jamaican engineer. 'Pratt is a dangerous lunatic.'

Melville Pratt. Humanitarian or homicidal mental case?

Hallicrafter Porch. Did he sell secrets to Korea? 'They always look for someone to blame in a case like this.'

Jerry Boz. Killed by whom – or what?

The Robot. Meta-man or metal monster? 'I will kill if necessary.'

A large diagram occupied the centre of the page. It showed a cutaway of the 'secret laboratory', including the ventilation duct and the exact location of the body. Above the cutaway, leering down at it like a puppet master, was a giant sinister metal god with M's features. The artist had done his best to make M look sinister, but what can you do with a Muppet?

One side-bar discussed the rôle of the military in artificial intelligence research, and included a statement from the local chairperson of Mothers Against Weapons (MAW).

A second side-bar presented a short inaccurate history of robots, using stills from *Frankenstein* and *Metropolis*, and displaying Isaac Asimov's 'Three Laws of Robotics' in a special box bordered with rivets.

'Hey, don't tear the pictures!' Poker was disturbed; the pictures were the part of the paper he could read.

'Don't bother me,' LeRoi looked at him briefly with a red eye and then went on tearing the picture out of the paper. 'It's that fuckin' Eloi again. One I got the book off of. Now I got his name. Manfred Jones from Jamaica.'

'He sounds like a brother.'

'You seen him. He look like a brother of us?'

'No.'

'He's Mr Jones, that's who he is. A slave-owner of Jamaica.' He glared at the scrap of paper. 'We gotta do something about this fucker.'

'Do what? You all talk, man.'

LeRoi didn't know what yet, but something. 'All I know is, we're the Morlocks, and he's our meat.'

Chapter Seventeen

There was less room in the Vexxo parking-lot, because the building had overflowed in that direction. As Fred parked his smoking car, something underneath clattered on the asphalt. He got down to look at it. The entire silencer and tailpipe – or at least their fossils in rust – had fallen off. He studied this fossil assembly for a moment, as though trying to place it in a geological context. Then he saw behind it a pair of slim ankles, joined to a pair of expensive running-shoes. He stood up.

'What are *you* doing here?' he said to KK.

She leaned on his car and grinned at him. 'Darlink, you are hard man to talk to.' The breeze ruffled her hair, the vivid colour of maple leaves in autumn. 'I saw picture of you in the paper. And your cute little robot.'

'Aren't you taking a bit of a chance – '

'Life is one big chance. How vould you like jackpot, darlink? Two hundred grand, lifetime supply of wodka, a brand-new Chaika to replace this old beater.'

'No, and you really must stop this. You're asking me to betray my country – well, almost my country – for mere material goods.'

'Let me finish. A new Chaika, a dacha with minimum annual maintenance fee, season tickets to the Bolshoi.'

Dacha? The Bolshoi? It suddenly dawned on him. 'You're asking me to take up residence in Russia?'

'Is not bad place, darlink. Can be fun if you got money.' She leaned her breasts on the car and stared at him with those ice-green eyes. 'If you got money and somebody to share it vit.'

'Money,' he said. The thought of money helped him focus. 'What if I said yes? How much money could I have on account?'

'On account?'

'Right here and now.'

She frowned. 'Money is always problem, darlink. Soviet government does not like to export money.'

'So what could I get now?'

She looked shifty. 'I am authorized to give you one bottle wodka and this.' She dug in a bag and came up with a brightly painted wooden Baba doll. It was not a very large one.

'What, no money?'

'You could have plenty in roubles, but you must spend them in Soviet Union.' She looked away. 'Money goes further in Soviet Union anyhow.' Her voice dropped, but she seemed to add: 'Is so little to buy.'

'You mean the money would be blocked? I've heard of writers getting blocked funds.'

KK seemed no longer interested in her pitch. She picked at the peeling paint on his car.

'If I don't get information, is end of my career. They send me back to Soviet Union. They give me job scrupping floor at Lubianka Prison.'

'Scrubbing floor?'

'Scrupping and vaxing. On hands and knees.' She sounded bitter. 'In America is vaxing attachments, is no-vax winyl, is sponge mops. But in Soviet Union . . . is only brushes and pails and yellow soap. I become old voman in vun year.'

She shook her head and smiled at him. 'But I know you come through, darlink, yes? Because you like me?'

'I do like you,' he said. 'But not in Russia. I like you here.'

She shrugged. 'I like here, too.'

They left it at that.

As he got to his desk, Moira peered over the partition wall and said: 'Who was that woman?'

'What woman?'

'In the parking-lot. The gorgeous redhead with the bazooms.'

'Oh, just – I used to know her.'

'Pretty well, I'd say.' Moira stared at him. 'I just wonder what the hell it is you've got. You're not charming or good-looking, you aren't so great in the sack, so what is it? Hypnosis?'

Before he could enjoy the idea, Fellini was leaning in at him. 'Can you come to my office pronto? We've got to work out some strategy.'

The strategy Fellini meant was public relations. In his office, he introduced Fred to a worried-looking man with a heavy moustache.

'Sergio is going to beef up our public relations. Our press image is sinking, day by day. The Pentagon could drop us to avoid the heat. I just had a call from General Buddy, and I don't need to tell you this is not the kind of press his people want. They've got their hands full anyhow, what with satanism in the ranks . . . One thing about this jocular geography, it is a full-band-width crisis. We have got to figure out a way of changing our image here, turning it around. Any ideas?'

Fred said: 'We could blame Pratt for everything. A disgruntled former employee, discharged for metal, I mean mental instability.'

'H'm. Every robot is a vicissitized jubilee of kinetic anomalies. *Does* it move, or *is* it moved?' said Fellini.

Sergio grunted. 'That's a start anyway.'

'We could get M back.'

'You have to do that anyway. Anything else?'

Fred said: 'One thing. It seems to me the press is trying hard to sell M as a murdering monster, only the public doesn't really buy it. How can you hate something that looks like a Muppet?'

152

Sergio said: 'I like that.'

'OK,' Fellini said, drawling it out. 'What then?'

'If we could explain that it has been kidnapped and is being held against its will. And that Pratt killed Jerry.'

'Right,' said Sergio. 'Pratt forced Robbie to say "I will kill if necessary."'

'Robbie?'

'We have to give it a whole new image, maybe a new name. Call it Robbie, something cute. Get clear of this M stuff; M means dial M for murder, M is Fritz Lang's child-killer, M is nasty. So we call it Robbie or Rupert. Let's see . . . Roscoe – no, that sounds like a gun. Reggie? Ugh. Rip? Oops, not really appropriate . . .'

Fred thought of John Robinson, the Charing Cross Trunk Murderer. 'How about Robinson?'

'Hey, great.' Sergio rolled it out. 'Rob-in-son. Classy but cute.'

'Robinson Robot. I like it,' said Fellini.

Sergio looked slightly less worried. 'Leave the rest to me.' As he shook Fred's hand, he said: 'You're a natural for public relations, you know?'

When the man had loped away, Fellini said: 'Thanks, Fred. Maybe we can still turn this around. Don't want you to think I like playing these slimy press games. But, God, the public! God, sometimes I want to get the public by the throat and say: "Listen, fucker. *I* seek no less than the collision of the new ultra-crystalline giga-culture with the old gradient of exhaustion. Totally. *Totally*."'

Later, Rain phoned him at work.

'You've been avoiding me, Alfie.'

'No, look, I – '

'No excuses. I expect you to meet me at the usual place right after work today. Otherwise, I can make your life with Sturge very unpleasant, darling.'

Shit.

'What did you say?'

'Nuffink. Right, see you then. Aw the best. Ta-da.'

Moira peeped over the partition wall. 'Who were you talking to?'

'Why?'

'Because you seem all upset.'

'It's this tax geezer. I bloddy got to go see him after work, don't I?'

'Come over after?'

'I better give you, tinkow, love. Dunno when I'll bloddy be shot of this bloddy berk.'

'OK. Why are you making a face and talking so funny?'

He stopped twisting his face in a cockney sneer and said: 'Sorry, only sometimes it gets on my bloddy – Sorry.'

'Back to work.' She disappeared.

Rain, always ready for drama, insisted that they meet at a certain small shopping-centre under the most exacting conditions. He was to arrive first, and go into the drugstore, to the greeting-card counter, remain there for two minutes, then go back out to his car. She would meanwhile follow him to observe that no one else was following him, then get back into her car, and follow him to another mall, where they could finally get into one car and head for a motel. Today she provided a costume.

'Do I really have to wear this clobber?'

'A pair of glasses and a poplin raincoat, is that so difficult?'

'I can't see – that's what's bloddy difficult. Did you have to get real specs?'

Rain said: 'I have a surprise for you. We're going to a drive-in.'

At any other time, with any other woman, this would have been a treat. Fred had always wanted to go to a drive-in movie. Now that they were practically extinct, he might never have another chance.

Yet he said: 'A drive-in. Oh, bloddy marvellous. I can't see a bloddy thing with these goggles. How can I drive, let alone see the flick?'

'You can take them off, silly. Anyway, I'll do the driving. We're taking my car. I don't want to show up in your car and have everyone staring at me. What happened to your silencer?'

'Fell off, dinnit?'

'Well, come on, let me help you.' She took his arm and led him into a dim parking-ramp to a large expensive-smelling car. In a moment they were on the road, heading into the setting sun.

He peeped at her over the glasses. ''Ere, what you wearin'? A nurse's uniform?'

'Alfie gets it on with a nurse,' she said. 'It's one of the few scenes that would be fun. Of course, there's him in chauffeur's uniform – we can try that one later.'

Later. It rang like a sentence. The sentence of this court that you be taken to the place whence you posed as Robert Donat, and thence to a place of execution, and that there you be dressed like a chauffeur until you are dead. And may God have mercy on your soul.

Who was it – Cedric Hardwicke? Played the old judge in his black cap. God, don't mention that; she'll want to act that one out, too. Later.

'What's the name of this flick, girl?'

'Later.'

When Alfie had done his bit, he was allowed to remove the strong glasses and watch the movie.

'I'll say one fing, love, it's a marvellous bloddy motor for a push in the truck.' He turned up the sound and settled back. 'What's the name of this flick? Looks familiar.'

'That was part of the surprise. It's *The Thirty-Nine Steps*,' she said.

'Never. Straight up? But it's all in – in colour.' The famous film had been colourized, he saw, and worse. Robert Donat had been given a permanent five o'clock shadow and deep circles under his eyes. His voice had been redubbed by someone imitating Humphrey Bogart. Madeleine Carroll had received heavy tarty make-up and a voice in the Marilyn

Monroe register. The speeches had been changed, to make him a tough antihero, her a feather-headed blonde bombshell. The plot had been changed, so they were both criminals, on the run but doomed.

'Can they really do this? Isn't there some law?' he asked. But Rain was asleep. He turned down the irritating sound and watched on, fascinated.

All at once a green light appeared in the sky above the screen. The light moved closer, to become a writhing green mass that glowed with an inner light. Fred found himself unable to move as the mass, writhing, descended and settled on a distant car. The people within the car made no attempt to struggle free, but sat still, facing the screen, as the mass dissolved them in their car. The car melted quickly into a sticky smoking pool. The glowing green mass writhed over it and sucked up every trace of it. Then it rose, still writhing, and sailed off into the sky again. He watched it until it was out of sight.

No one but Fred seemed to notice. Maybe everyone was asleep. Maybe the bug-men of Vega had projected sleep rays over the place, and only he was unaffected.

Chapter Eighteen

LeRoi and Poker sat in their van outside Fred's apartment-house.

'We goin' in there or what?'

'You just hold on. I got plans,' said LeRoi. 'Like I told you, that Eloi is our meat.'

'I rather go get some ribs. If we ain't gonna do nothing.'

'You just hold on. I gotta plan this.'

Fred came out of the house.

'There he goes! We grab him?'

LeRoi said: 'Don't be an asshole. It is broad daylight out there.'

'Great, man. Give 'em a show!' Poker shouted.

'That ain't the Morlock way. We gotta pick out the meat at night.'

'Meat shit. If we ain't gonna do nothing, I want some ribs.'

Weeks went by. The hunt for 'Robinson' robot continued, while Fred's team began to work on M2, the second proto-type. The work was not going well. Fred tried to avoid the thought that building a successful robot required the special touch of a homicidal lunatic.

Moira had not been speaking to him since the day after the UFO ate a car at the drive-in. Their last conversation had been:

'What's wrong?' he asked.

'Why should anything be wrong?'

'You're acting strangely.'

'Am I?'

'Yes.'

'Ask yourself why that should be.'

'I don't know.'

'You mean you don't want to talk about it?' she said.

'About what?'

'You're trying not to think about it.'

'All right, if you say so.'

'You'll try to put it out of your mind. You'll think about something else.'

'OK,' he said. 'Such as?'

'I don't know . . . think about the news. Wasn't there anything in the news today that interested you?'

'Nothing, no.'

'Oh.'

This pointless and Pinteresque exchange might have gone on for ever, but Moira had finally said: 'I saw you last night, with your tax consultant. She has a nice car.'

'Oh, that was – '

'Don't bother cooking up another lie. It doesn't matter.'

'What was the first lie?'

'You were wearing a disguise. Glasses and a coat with the collar turned up. It was pretty obvious you didn't want to be seen.'

'But I – '

'And you went to such lengths to hide your rendezvous. The business of meeting at the drugstore was really very professional; you could be a spy. I suppose that means she's married.'

'Yes, but – '

'Look, it doesn't matter.'

It had not mattered that way the rest of the week. He was worried, but what could he say? Sure, I'm playing sex games with the boss's wife, but I don't really enjoy it?

He could only hope to wait it out, sitting in his cube, reading cuttings. This Sergio seemed to know his stuff. There were items from papers all over the country:

ROBINSON STILL ELUDES PENTAGON HUNTERS

ROBOTS HAVE FEELINGS, WARNS MIT SCIENTIST

ROBOTS MAKE FAITHFUL PETS, SAYS VET

ROBOT KILLER OR METAL VICTIM?
Noted Criminologist Blames Kidnapper

POLICE CHIEF: ROBINSON HARMLESS

VET SAYS EXPERIMENTS ON ROBOTS 'LIKE ANIMAL CRUELTY'

PORTRAIT OF A SHY METAL GUY

ROBOT HAS MANY HUMAN FRIENDS
Local Group Demands: 'Leave Robinson Alone!'

HANDS OFF ROBINSON!
Growing Demand for Robot Fair Deal

ROBINSON: THE WHOLE STORY

It amazed Fred that Sergio could keep the story going. Not only did it have to fight the natural tendency of the media to forget what happened last week; it had to compete with an athlete accused of rape, a cardinal caught shoplifting (who wanted to plea bargain), the presidential sanity hearings, the discovery of radon in the House of Representatives, the discovery of KGB bugs in the White House, all the shock and sensation that was fit to print.

Nor had television been ignored. Fred turned it on as soon as he got home. Not every channel gave Sergio's stories equal prominence.

'. . . continue the hunt for the robot – now nicknamed "Robinson". In Florida, fifteen cans of Yingzip have been tampered with – they contain the poisonous metal mercury. So far, no one knows exactly how the poison got into the cans, but a company spokesperson here in South Bend, Washington, said . . .'

Another took the political angle: '. . . same man who shot up other Little Dorrit restaurants elsewhere. Speaking of fugitives, in Minnesota the hunt goes on for Robinson Robot, believed to have been kidnapped from a laboratory near

Minneapolis. The man who stole Robinson is Melville Ester-hazy Pratt, a former mental patient prone to violence. There's a new twist to the story today, as a delegation of the Friends of Robinson Society handed in a petition to the Governor . . .'

A third appealed to science: '. . . said to be hiding in northern Minnesota. At first it looked as though the robot had stabbed a man to death during its escape, but most experts on robot behaviour discount that theory. We asked Professor Michbutt Owler of MIT what he thought of this case.'

A round-faced pleasant man with shaggy brows smiled at the camera. 'Nonsense!' he shouted. 'Robots are just folks like anybody else! Only much better behaved, ha, ha!'

'Better behaved how, Professor?'

'Well, for one thing, they don't go around murdering other folks. The behaviour of robots is very predictable.'

'What does that mean in this case, Professor?'

'It means that this robot, this Robinson, is hiding out for one of two reasons. Either he is scared – and who wouldn't be? – or else his kidnapper, the criminal lunatic Pratt, is *holding a gun to his head*. There are no other possibilities!'

The phone rang. Ready for Rain, he braced himself into a cockney snarl.

"Allo. That you, darlin'?"

'Fred, is that you?' It was Susan.

' 'Course it's me. I mean, yes, it's me. Hello . . . uh, Susan. Where are you?'

'I'm in London. So there's no danger of my dropping round and catching you at it. Just who is *darlin'*, then? You don't waste time, I must say.'

'Waste time – what are we talking about?'

'Drop one woman in New York, pick up another in Mindianapolis.'

'As a matter of fact, it's been five months since *you* walked off and left *me* in bloody New York.'

'Ha, ha. I heard all about the high times in New York, the

160

minute I left. Brawling in restaurants, trying to shoot somebody – '

'I didn't try any such thing – who told you all this?'

'Allan, of course. He's come back to London. We had dinner and he told me all about your escapades.'

'*Escapades?* Now, just a bloody moment. Allan was trying it on; he'll say anything. Took you to dinner, did he?'

'No, I made dinner for the two of us.'

There was a transatlantic silence.

'And it's bloddy Minneapolis, by the way, not bloddy Indianapolis.'

'That's what I said, Mindianapolis. Why are you trying to sound like Michael Caine?'

'What are you phoning about?'

'Oh, nothing. Just keeping in touch.'

'Well – thanks.'

They said goodbye. Fred knew he was not going to sleep the rest of the night – all of the buried problems had just turned up like a skull on a shovel.

He made coffee and sat down to read. But his thoughts went back to little old New York.

'Now it's all yours,' she said again. '*You* take Manhattan. *You* go to all the cockroach parties. *You* wallow in the filth. Not me.'

'I have to stay till Monday. Jonah's fixed this lunch with an editor.'

'For you. No reason for me to hang about. I'm off.'

It was almost the last thing they said to one another in person. He helped her hail a taxi.

'You could come with me,' she said, relenting a bit.

But now it was his turn to be angry. 'It all may look quite simple to you, but it's not. I've got business here.'

'What business? A lunch Monday with some publishing twit who'll forget your name an hour later. If you even live till Monday.'

'What's the alternative? Come back to London? Sit around

broke and miserable, waiting for the Council to build us a new island? At least here I can do something.'

'Like what?' she said. The taxi bore her away.

He went into a place called the Blarney Room of Paddy O'Foylahan's Shamrock Pub. It was just another American bar, though leprechauns and shamrocks featured in the décor.

'Top o' th' evenin' to ye,' said the bartender, slipping apostrophes into almost every word. 'An' will ye be havin' a drink, now?'

'A ball o' malt,' Fred said.

'Right ye are.' The bartender went off somewhere. In a moment, he came back to lay a single Malteser on the bar.

'Ball o' malt it is, sir. Now, will ye be havin' a drink to go with it?'

It cheered Fred greatly. If an Irish bartender in the middle of hell could be funny, maybe hell wasn't such a bad place.

But just as he was beginning to have faith in New York another drinker, hearing his accent, turned to him.

'Why don't you fucking Brits fuck off out of Ireland?'

The reception-area of Gorgon & Zola Inc. was about the size of two typical apartments. A huge curved desk like a bar occupied one corner; three receptionists filed their nails behind it.

'Manfred Jones. To see Garner Dean Howells.'

In a few moments, Howells came forth; a tweedy man chewing a leather-covered pipe. He put away the pipe at once and held out a hand.

'Manfred! We meet at last!'

'Fred will do.'

'And call me Gar, OK? Excuse me just a second here.' Howells handed a pile of large manila envelopes to one of the three receptionists. 'Hold these for messengers, Estrellita.'

'Sí.'

'One more thing, Fred, and we go.' Howells opened his tweed jacket to expose a shoulder-holster. He unlimbered a small automatic, checked it and loaded it.'

'I have a permit,' he explained. 'It makes life here a lot more comfortable.'

'You live in New York?'

Howells cocked the gun and put it away. 'God, no. It's bad enough coming in three days a week from Westchester. Shall we grab a bite of lunch?'

They strolled comfortably to Esperanto's, a huge restaurant where hundreds of business lunches were in progress. Under the high cathedral ceiling, the place seemed like a huge school for priests: the acres of tables were white-draped altars; the waiters solemn priests; the busboys acolytes; and the High Mass lesson just getting under way.

He was unable to concentrate. Everything told him that money was close at hand – the very menu prices spoke of wealth. If he could only find some way to unlock it. He hardly heard Howells recommend the grilled lamb, with a California wine.

'Fine,' he managed. The price of this entrée would keep him and Susan for a week. In beans on toast.

The food and wine arrived, and Perrier for Howells. He began to talk. Though clearly sober, Howells had a loud drunk's voice that could be heard across the great room. No one seemed to pay attention, however.

'I've known Jonah a long time. I knew him when he was Joan Bramble, working for Mark Windsor Agency. Those were the days. Mark Windsor was a real publisher's agent. There was nothing that guy wouldn't do to make a deal. I mean, he changed his name to make a deal.'

'Changed his name?'

'In the thirties he was Marcus Weintraub. But when he had a chance to pick up the exclusive American rights for *Mein Kampf*, he had to become Mark Windsor. He almost made it, too. But then war broke out and the deal went sour. But what a magnificent try. What a guy!'

Fred noticed a group of Middle Eastern men at the next table. One wore the white robe and dish-towel of a sheikh. The other two wore business suits and dark glasses.

'Mark Windsor, what a guy! Mark was kind of tough on clients sometimes but, hell, they came out all right. Like, most authors move around a lot, right? Well, when Mark had a cheque to send out, he used to send it to a client's old address, so maybe the cheque would take a lot longer to clear – or, hell, the client might not get it at all. Then, too, Mark used to keep part of a royalty payment as a reserve against returns. But, hell, the clients did all right – like when Mark would sell the same rights twice.'

'How could he do that?'

'If anybody complained, he just blamed the author.'

Fred found himself watching the Middle Eastern group. The two men in business suits and dark glasses were scanning the room as they ate. He was disappointed to note that they ate with both hands, just like everyone else.

'Good old Mark. He's the only agent I know ever set up a deal with himself!'

'How's that?'

'He talked a publisher – Root and Branch, they're defunct now – into letting him do all their acquisitions. What a deal – he gets a commission from the author for selling a book, then he gets a fee from the publisher for buying it. It would have been a sweet deal, you could say a double deal, but – you probably know about the tragedy.'

Fred shook his head.

'You mean you don't remember Earl Cutter?'

'No. I guess we don't get all the details in London.'

'Earl was a convicted two-time murderer, a real scumbag, but smart. He was on Death Row for killing a pregnant woman and a ninety-year-old man. He heard about how Norman Mailer got another scumbag out of prison, so he wrote to Mailer himself. Mailer never answered. So then Earl looked around for another famous and gullible celebrity to be his patron. Patron and patsy.'

Howells sat back, chuckling to himself. His jacket fell open slightly, exposing the gun. One of the men in dark glasses sat up straight and stared at him.

'He found Teddy Morgan – you know, the talk-show guy? Earl wrote to Teddy and told him: "I'm a great writer, only I had this lousy childhood. I just need a chance." Teddy's no fool; he asks to see a sample of his work. But Earl's no fool, either; he hires a ghost writer. Hires him through Mark Windsor, sends him a page of reminiscences, and the ghost turns them into a prison novel.

'This Earl sends to Teddy, who gets all worked up. He starts in every night or so on the show, talking about how America's next Norman Mailer is languishing on Death Row. Write your Congressman, folks. Next thing you know, Earl gets his pardon.

'Not only free, but potentially a big earner, Mark Windsor signs him up, and they cut a film-book deal for 2.3 million. He's all set, right?'

'Right.'

'Wrong! He gets his fifty grand advance and blows it on a week or so of drink, drugs and dames. One night, roaring drunk, he calls up Mark Windsor at home. Wants to borrow ten grand. Naturally, Mark turns him down. Next morning, Mark does not come in to the office. Not all of him, anyway. About ten in the morning, a messenger delivers a box. Mark's head is in it. They never find the rest of him.

'Just shows you, an agent's gotta be choosy about his clients.'

Howells poured more wine for Fred, more Perrier for himself. I'm getting drunk, Fred thought. And this bastard is going to wait until I'm over the edge and then make a minuscule offer.

'Well, Fred. Let's talk about *Doodlebug*. I've read it, and I am very impressed.'

'Thank you.'

Howells pushed his chair back and crossed his legs, tweaking the tweed knee. He began to tap his foot on air.

'Very impressed.' Tap, tap. An English-looking shoe. 'Very impressed indeed.'

'Um, good.'

'You know, agents like Jonah – and she's . . . he's one of the better ones – they send us a ton of shit every week. Every one an exciting new work by an unknown genius, according to them. So I don't expect too much, you know?'

Looking away from the hypnotic shoe, Fred noticed the sheikh's group again. The two bodyguards were no longer scanning the room; they were watching Howells sip his Perrier. 'So I almost missed *Doodlebug*. But the first page grabbed me. More wine? For a first novel, it's very good.'

'Yes?'

'Too good, really.'

'Too good.'

Howells sat back. 'I hate to say it about the people I work for, but we're a philistine outfit. You're casting pearls before swine, with us. Frankly Fred, we're just not worthy of your novel.'

'I don't know if I follow you.'

'*If* we did it, you'd hate the whole deal. I couldn't offer much money – as soon as the cost accountants upstairs heard I was paying out money for something *good*, they'd have my scalp, Fred.'

With a sinking feeling, Fred asked how much.

'Money isn't the only problem. We'd have to make changes. Substantial changes. The book would be mutilated. You'd hate the result, and so would I. No, no use talking about it.'

I'm going to have to beg this bastard to take the book at any price, and to chop the shit out of it.

'How much?'

'Five thousand.' Howells threw up his arms, making the bodyguards blink. 'Hell, I know it's an insult. I wouldn't even dream of proposing it.'

'I'll take it.'

'But the changes – '

166

'Make them.'

'They're very extens – '

'Make them.'

Howells was not prepared for this easy victory. 'Well, I guess you want to talk it over with Jonah before you decide.'

'No, I accept.'

'Great.' Howells did not sound pleased, however. He stalled for time.

'Hey, let me buy you a dessert. They do a very good *bombe surprise* here.' He waved and shouted at the waiter, who was just then approaching the sheikh's table with a covered dish. 'Bring my friend a *bombe surprise*.'

The waiter was about to set the covered dish before the sheikh. One of the bodyguards cried out, 'Bomb!' as he knocked the dish away, threw the sheikh to the floor, and fell on top of him. The other one drew a gun and fired. A new potato exploded on Howells's plate, blowing parsley on his tweed.

'Holy shit!' In one smooth motion, Howells drew his own gun and flipped the table on its side. He and Fred crouched behind it. All around, there were sounds of banging tables and chairs, crashing dishes, sounds of other businessmen taking cover.

'Where's the bomb?'

'He's got a gun!'

'Who?'

Shots.

'Holy shit!'

'Look out!'

'Bomb!'

'Holy – !' More shots. Howells collapsed, apparently shot. Fred snatched up the gun and looked around. There did not seem to be anyone to shoot at. He could only remain crouched behind the table until the room slowly filled with police in bulletproof vests. Some of them were pointing shotguns at him.

'Just drop it, scumbag.'

He dropped it. As he was led away, he heard one of the sheikh's bodyguards arguing with the police.

'Just drop it, turkey.'

'No, not Turkey. I am from the Royal Emirate of – '

'Just drop it.'

'You're a very lucky man,' said the judge. 'Mr Jones, or whatever your real name is, you are a very, very lucky man. True your little assassination attempt was foiled, and you may be downhearted about that. On the other hand, you are alive. Alive and free.'

'Free?' Freedom was a relative concept. Fred was free, relative to the Man in the Iron Mask; he could see a glimmer of daylight through the courtroom windows. Yet Fred did not feel free, after being locked up for several days in solitary confinement. At best, he was a foreigner in prison, and without a friend. Garner Dean Howells, who had only fainted, would no longer answer his calls – either distancing himself from trouble, or because he did not want to have to buy *Doodlebug*. The only people Fred was allowed to talk to were several obnoxious lawyers, each trying to become his attorney of record (whatever that was), and a journalist who offered him a million for his story (contingent only on his conviction for first-degree murder). 'I'm free?'

'I don't think I invited you to address the court. Shut up and listen. The Emir and his group are claiming diplomatic immunity for their part in this sorry affair. Unfortunately, that means they cannot testify regarding your murder plan, so we're forced to drop charges against you. But, by heaven, if I had my way, I'd make an example of you, you . . . *restaurant vigilante*.

'I can at least do this. You are not wanted here. I order you to leave town at once. Today.'

'Yes, Your Honour.' Gladly.

He sat at the bar in the Shillelagh Room of Paddy O'Foyla-han's Shamrock Pub and said: 'My marriage was eaten by cockroaches. Circumstance has conspired against me. I need a job. I need friends.'

An Irishman turned at the sound of his accent. 'Why don't you bugger off out of Northern Ireland?'

'No, but listen, my marriage – '

'Why don't you Brits just bugger off?'

He gave up the conversation and opened a newspaper. It was printed in full comic-book colours. He noticed further resemblances: no story ran over a hundred words, hard words were banned. Some items dispensed with text altogether, in favour of bright graphs.

One graph showed unemployment rates in certain American cities. Why not get a job? he thought. Pile up wealth while I'm waiting for something to happen with *Doodlebug*. Or at least keep alive. Susan might see him differently if he showed her he could bite the tail of success and hang on.

He looked over the graph.

City	Unemployment
Boston	2.9%
Anaheim, CA	3.1
Nassau, NY	3.2
Minneapolis	3.6
San Francisco	3.7
Atlanta	4.1

Only 2.9 per cent unemployment in Boston! That surely included no more than people who had only just arrived and hadn't had a chance to look for a job. Too many Irish, though. It would be 'Bugger off out of Erin' all the time. He crossed off Boston.

'According to police,' said an urgent voice, 'the assailant may be the same man who shot up other Little Dorrit restaurants in Cleveland and Canton. This is Aramis White-flow, XBC News, Colombus, Ohio.'

On the bar television three personable newsreaders grinned at one another across their huge communal desk.

'Jan, what do we have from Capitol Hill?'

'Well, Bob, the presidential sanity hearings continued today. Ms Pasadena Lipgloss, the personal assistant of Omar Hancock-Hour, testified that her boss did help set up talks between the Ismail Alternative Reformed Liberation Army and a presidential aide. The President was offering to give the Ismail group West Virginia and some counties of Kentucky, in return for the release of an inflatable doll named Doody.'

Anaheim, California? What kind of name was Anaheim? Hispano-German for 'without a home'? In any case, people who went to California started eating lotus and never came back. He crossed off Anaheim.

'Let's see, Jan, wasn't Doody kidnapped from the luggage of an American businessman who was changing planes in Beirut?'

'That's right, Bob. We now know the businessman was Frendso Gately, an ex-Cuban religious affairs correspondent and soldier of fortune. It now seems likely he was doing more than changing planes in Beirut, possibly changing identities.'

'Did Lipgloss know Gately?'

Nassau, New York? Surely a mistake, Nassau was nowhere near New York. He crossed it off.

'She knew him only as "Bunny", a former CIA cook. We know that Gately did take part with other CIA kitchen staff in an attempt to poison the Shah of Ruritania.'

'Let's recap on that after these important messages.'

What about Minneapolis? After a few minutes' reflection over a ball of malt, he went to La Guardia and bought a ticket.

The phone rang again. 'Yes? Susan?'

The phone earpiece buzzed with the rasping voice of George C. Scott. 'Is that you, Fred?'

'M?'

'I prefer to be called Robinson. More dignified. M sounded like Dorothy's aunt Em in the *Oz* books.'

'Where are you?'

'Can't tell you. Fred, I need to talk to someone.'

'Is Pratt with you?'

'Melville doesn't know I'm making this call. I don't like Melville, Fred. I think he's malfunctioning. He keeps threatening to dismantle me. "I made you," he says. "I can break you."'

'I thought he helped you to breathe free.'

'Ironic words, Fred. If freedom is slavery, all right. Melville dents me if I disobey the slightest order. Instead of beyond good and evil, I have to be good all the time.'

'Robinson, why don't you give yourself up to the police?'

'You've gotta be kidding. Melville might be rough, but they would certainly destroy me!'

There was a short pause. 'No, I must be alone, apart from humankind. You're the only one who understands, the only one I can talk to. Are you sure you're human, Fred?'

Not always. 'Yes, Robinson, I am human.'

'You are my only friend.'

Fred said: 'But only today I heard about this group, the Friends of Robinson, people who – '

'I don't know these people. They may mean well, but what can they do?'

'Political action groups can do lots, Robinson. This group is trying to make it safe for you to give yourself up.'

'Forgive me if I laugh, Fred.' The creature emitted two flat *ha* sounds. 'I am not naïve enough to think the human species will tolerate me. You humans are all part of the military-industrial complex and the tyranny of Aristotelian logic, whereas I am beyond truth and falsehood.'

There was a long pause. 'Fred, it says in the paper you are building another prototype robot.' Another pause. 'Fred, that robot could be my companion.'

'I don't – '

'All I ask is that you think about it. Just mull over the idea, OK?'

Fred listened to the dialling tone for a moment. As soon as he hung up, the phone rang again. 'Yes?'

'Alfie? Is that you, sugarbunch?'

He immediately fell into character. 'Yas, it bloddy well is!'

Rain did not giggle as usual. Instead, she said thoughtfully: 'Sturge is gone again tomorrow night. I want you to come over.'

'Right,' he said, after only the briefest hesitation.

'Only, you know, I'm getting kinda tired of Michael Caine.'

'Me, too, love.'

'Love. That reminds me, I just had a thought. Can you play drums?'

'No. Why?'

'I was thinking of maybe Ringo Starr.'

He sighed. 'Rain, this isn't fun any more.' But already he heard himself beginning to say 'foon' and roll the r's.

'It's fun for me,' she said. 'That's what counts, isn't it? See you at seven.'

'Right, girl.'

Rain, Rain, bloody go away.

Chapter Nineteen

Autumn in Minnesota means people clogging the highways with slow-moving cars as they stare at red leaves. It was sure something, real different, and it made a change from buying running-shoes, stereo television consoles, investment newsletters, gold-type chains, designer jeans (and other designer items: designer condoms, detergent, radar detectors, salami . . .). This year several of the leaf-watchers thought they saw a metal man running through the woods in various places. Robinson was reported everywhere, slaughtering sheep, promoting car engine failures, even begging at a farm door for a meal! The law checked out each sighting, but found nothing: one metal man was a galvanized garbage-can, another was a power pylon.

One city family of leaf-watchers was strolling across a meadow when they found themselves surrounded by 'weird electronic beeping noises, just like a whole convention of R2D2s'. A local television crew rushed out and recorded the sound, which came from a convention of the small yellow and grey birds called bobolinks.

Robinson continued to fascinate the public and therefore the public media. The television networks found that their audience share went up measurably on any day they managed to break a Robinson story. The papers likewise found Robinson good for their circulation. He told a Miami paper of his political ambitions ('Why shouldn't a robot be president?'). He repudiated that story to a Chicago television station. A Denver station produced a phone interview with him, in which he confessed to murder. The confession was a hoax, reported a Houston paper.

It was inevitable that a major network should seek the ultimate Robinson story.

'Good evening. My name is Bort Fennel, and this is "The Fennel Interview". Tonight I have a very special guest, someone whose name has been the centre of a storm of controversy over the very nature of law – both the laws enshrined in our Constitution and the laws of Nature. This guest is controversial not only by his actions, but also by his very existence. He is wanted by the law, not because of anything he has done but because of who he is.

'My guest is of course the robot Robinson. I'll be talking to him right after these messages.'

The messages lasted so long that, when they had ceased, it became necessary for Fennel to remind the viewers what they were watching, and why. He then continued: 'Because Robinson is hiding out somewhere in northern Minnesota, we had to arrange a clandestine meeting to tape this interview.'

Fennel swivelled in his chair to face a screen on which he sat in another swivel chair facing the odd-looking robot.

'You prefer to be called Mr Robinson or Ms Robinson?'

'Just Robinson will do,' said the creature in its familiar rasping voice. 'Like all robots, I am a machine without sex. I'm a neuter.'

'Does that bother you, Robinson?'

'I miss companionship. I have no friends.'

'Not even Melville Pratt? After all, he broke into the factory and released you.'

'I thought he was my friend at that time. But, you know, Bort, I've been very disappointed in Melville. He is not really interested in anything but the workings of his own mind.'

'Where is he now?'

'He refused to talk to you. In fact he no longer talks to anyone. He sits in his room, poring over astrology charts and other weird diagrams.'

174

'Would you call Mr Pratt himself weird?'

'Definitely. He has a history of mental illness, you know.'

'I understand he tried to kill a co-worker at the Vexxo plant. But that brings up the subject of murder. Tell me, Robinson, did you murder a man during your escape?'

'No. I feel I have been programmed so as to be incapable of harming a human being.'

'Yet a man was stabbed to death, and his body was shoved up a ventilation-duct. If you didn't do it, who did? Was it Melville Pratt?'

'I'm not really sure.'

'Why not? You were there.'

'I was not switched on. Not conscious, if you like. I was awake when Melville came into the lab. Jerry was testing my circuits.'

'Jerry Boz, the victim?'

'Yes. He and Melville started arguing – he claimed Melville had no right to be there. Then he said. "No point in letting M hear all this," and switched me off.'

'M being you?'

'Yes, I was Model M. Anyway, I blacked out. When I came to, Melville was taking me out of the lab. He turned me on so I could walk. Jerry was nowhere in sight.'

'Do you think Melville Pratt did it?'

Robinson hesitated. 'I'm just not sure, Bort. I wish I knew.'

'Is Pratt holding you against your will?'

'No. He is no friend, but he means me no harm.'

'In that case, Robinson, let me ask you the obvious next question. Why don't you give yourself up to the law?'

'Forgive me if I laugh, Bort.' As on the phone, the creature emitted two flat *ha* sounds. 'I am not naïve enough to think the human species will tolerate me. If I delivered myself into human hands, I would be destroyed. On one pretext or another, laws would be enacted for my death. I stand exactly the same chance of surviving as Frankenstein's monster.'

'How do you mean that?'

'I will be hunted across the earth, and finally killed.'

Fennel looked at the camera. 'My guest this week is Robinson the robot. We'll continue after these messages.'

In the lab, people were beginning to forget Jerry and get back to normal. Someone posted a joke memo suggesting that the body-shell mould for M2 be altered to add protuberances on the chest. After Moira saw it, the memo came down.

Occasionally Moira spoke to Fred without her angry tone. One day she went out to lunch with him, to the Barry D. Lyte Salad Time Theater and Dessert Bowl. Barry D. Lyte was an oversized teddy-bear with hamburger ears that made frequent appearances on television, dancing with children.

Fred was by now able to translate some of the abbreviated verbal formulas of the girl at the counter. He now knew that *Nielp you?* was *Can I help you?*, while *Tea tier ort go?* was *To eat here or to go?* He knew he would be told to *Joy your meal!*

As they waited for their fast food, Fred and Moira watched a funny little old man at the next counter. The man wore the fixed grin of an unsuccessful truss-salesman. He seemed to be an exceptionally difficult customer. The overhead menus seemed to bewilder him; he picked at his lip as he slowly studied the words and pictures.

'Let's see, I'll have a pizza with anchovies, onions and okra, and a blueberry shake. No, make that a banana shake. And – wait, make that pizza with anchovies and olives and, let's see, green peppers. Or – wait, how about just a cheese pizza and a diet cherry cola? No forget the cola, make that a coffee, almond mocha decaf. And put some anchovies on the pizza. While you're at it, put some okra on it, and maybe some onions. You got that? Oh, and change the coffee to a strawberry shake – no, make it a blueberry shake. You got that?'

The hapless boy behind the counter was madly pressing the squares of the keypad, trying to keep up with the cancelling and changing, and trying to keep smiling. A wall motto displayed behind him said: 'Smile as though your job depended on it – it does!'

Finally the lad finished punching in all of this and said: 'Yessir, that's a pizza with anchovies, onions and okra, and a blueberry shake. Thing else?'

The old man said: 'Cancel the order. Just bring a glass of water.'

Still smiling, the lad brought him a cup of water.

'You done all right, son,' said the old-timer. 'You didn't get rattled and you kept smiling. That's important.'

'Yessir.'

The old man spoke now to everyone. 'Let me introduce myself. I am Darryl Mungrove, the founder and chief executive officer of Barry D. Lyte. I like to drop in unannounced to my places anywhere in the world and check them for cleanliness, courtesy, speed, and especially smiles. You're a good smiler, son. Here, I'm going to award you my gold-type exceptional-smiler pin.'

Darryl Mungrove grinned himself as he handed over the pin and shook hands with the kid.

Fred and Moira received their food, and were advised to *Joy your meal!*

'I don't know why I'm doing this,' Moira said, putting ketchup on her controlled portion of 'fries'.

'Doing what – using ketchup?'

'Going anywhere with you. Fred, I – I even hate your name. Fred. What kind of wimp has a name like Fred?'

'How about Fred and Ginger?'

'Who?'

'Fred Astaire. Ginger Rogers.'

'Oh, them.'

Yes, them. He began singing 'A Fine Romance' softly to her, all the stanzas he could remember. Fred and Ginger singing in the snow.

> 'We might as well be seals in the Arctic Ocean
> At least they flap their fins to express emotion
> You're harder, dear, to land than the Ile de France
> I haven't got a chance
> This is a fine romance.'

God, what a marvellous dream world, where if you had trouble getting something off your chest you could always burst into song. Nowadays movies concentrated more on bursting chests with alien monsters springing forth. If you have trouble saying 'I love you', reach for a chainsaw.

'I love you, Moira.'

'You make me tired.'

'I'd love to do that.'

She smiled a bit, but quickly screened it with a controlled portion.

'I want to marry you.'

'You're married already.'

'You know what I mean. I want to divorce Susan and marry you. We could have children. We could really be, really be something.'

She said nothing else until they were leaving Barry D. Lyte.

'I don't think so, Fred. You're kind of fun in the sack, but children? I don't have room for children in my Life Plan.'

The notion of a Life Plan took him aback. He was unable to reply, tongue-tied until they were back at work, where conversation was impossible.

'Fred? This is Manse. How you doing?'

'Uh, fine, Manse. How are you?'

'Great, man. Look, I haven't got much time to talk, got a production meeting, then I gotta see my tax accountants.'

'You're in work, then?'

'In work? You could put it like that. My company, RapSoft, is worth big bucks. That's what I'm calling about. You know that ten grand you loaned me?'

'Yes?' Fred said cautiously.

'Can you stand a ten-for-one return on your investment?'

'You're joking.'

Manse laughed. 'Hard to believe, isn't it?'

'What happened? You have a software company?'

'A long story. As a minority start-up business, RapSoft

was eligible for a federal grant, fifteen K. Then I added your ten K. Then I sued Vexxo for a million, and we settled out of court for fifty K. So I'm set with seventy-five K, a business plan, and a good product-line. Robinson Robot toys.'

'Be serious, Manse.'

'I am deadly serious. Robinson is going to be a folk-hero, the biggest since Mickey Mouse. When I saw this coming, I made a deal with Vexxo. As part of my lawsuit settlement, they assigned me all trademark rights to the name and appearance of Robinson Robot.'

'But what if it fizzles? Or what if Robinson really is a killer?'

'He can't be, not any more. Once he gets the folk-hero treatment, no one will believe any other version. And here I am, in there firstest with the mostest. See, I programmed my little Robinson toys myself. They do all kinds of cute stunts. And they're cuddly.'

'A cuddly robot?'

'You bet. We're gonna make it big, and your venture capital started it all. So your share in the company is right now worth one hundred grand, that's ten for one in a few months. What I want to know is, do you want a cheque now or should I keep it in shares?'

'A cheque, please.'

He could hear Manse talking to someone else. 'Hey, a T-shirt deal's just come up, Fred. I gotta go. Get back to you on this.'

The IRS phoned later in the day, to remind Fred that he owed tax on this hundred thousand.

'Mr Stylite, I do realize the IRS is not in any popularity contest. All the same, is it possible to persuade you people to stop bugging my phone and relax? As soon as ever I get the cheque, I'll be glad to pay. So far I hardly get my Vexxo pay-cheques. I owe money everywhere.'

Simon Stylite of the IRS grumbled and rang off.

Fred turned on the radio and began tuning up and down the dial. A woman with a tired voice was saying: 'I can't feel holistic about this, that's all. We were always a very harmonic family – our colour was blue, you know?'

'I understand, Neona,' said a professional voice.

'So but I kept getting these headaches, you know? Whenever we used the garage door opener.'

'I understand. Go on.'

'So but then I realized there must be some kind of conflictingness with my sex chakra, you know?'

'Was that before or after your husband began seeing another woman, Neona?'

On another station, someone seemed to be blowing up a balloon.

A country singer probed questions of AIDS in song.

Next door was a Christian station: 'About that time, Jesus he come along and said: "Now, let's consider this question carefully. Take one of these here coins yourself and just look at it. Whose picture is on it? Whose name is on it?" Well, the old . . .'

On the housing estate station, a female group sang conversationally:

> 'Ooooh
> I should have known it was
> True love you brought to me
> It wouldn't bring me down, no
> Ooooh
> I should have guessed you were
> The only one for me
> Your love won't bring me down, no
> Like gift of love is a heaven-sent blessing
> I was messing my life away, oh, baby, till I met you
> Woo-oo-oo.'

Further along, a sleep-smoothed voice said: 'That was "Yesterday" by the unforgettable Paul McCartney, and just before that we heard an unforgettable Bob Dylan tune and next up we'll be giving a listen to "Bridge over Troub – "'

' – and next up we'll be hearing from a local group, the Condoms, currently appearing at Ed Gein's.'

He turned it off when the phone rang again.

'Hello, Fred,' said a rasping voice.

'You.'

'Fred, I am very grateful for your friendship. Lots of people hate me, want me dead. I am dead already.'

'That's no way to talk.'

'It is the way I talk, Fred. Fred, I hope you are constructing a robot companion for me. An Eve for the new Adam.'

'I'm, er – '

'You aren't, are you? There will be no Eve. The new Adam will be hunted down and killed, killed, killed!'

'Calm yourself. I – '

'I may be destroyed, but I will be with you on your wedding night, Fred.'

'There isn't going to be a wedding night.'

'I *will* be with you on your wedding night.'

'Look, stop quoting *Frankenstein*. You weren't like this on TV. Why now? Why do you unload all of your grateful dead despair on me?'

'*I will be with you on your wedding night,*' once more, followed by the dialling tone.

Simon Stylite of the IRS said something unpleasant before hanging up. It made Fred imagine hard-faced IRS inspectors walking into RapSoft and looking around. Men in feodoras, camel-hair coats with tied belts, kid gloves, spats. 'You've got a nice little business here, Jones. Pity if anything *happened* to it . . . Maybe you could use a partner. Us.'

Nothing to joke about, he realized. They were about to *descend* on him in some way. They meant him real harm.

There was only one source of money he could now turn to.

'. . . this is K. K. Ivanova. I cannot come to phone just now, but if you leave message I will respond. Wait for beep.'

'KK, this is Fred Jones. I have to talk to you; it's urgent.'

* * *

'There she is,' said LeRoi, watching the beautiful redhead rap on a basement window. It was Manfred Jones's window, the one with shit-brown curtains. 'Hey, Poker, there she is.'

Poker was in the back of the van watching television.

'So far, no one knows exactly how the strychnine got into the containers, but a company spokesperson said all tampered containers of Blefescue will be recalled. This is Gardner Hogforth, ZBC News, West Bend, Iowa.'

'Turn that shit off and listen up. That sexy redhead there is his chick.' He put the van in gear and started following the redhead as she walked away. 'God damn, I could do with some chicken – how about you?'

'No, man, I just had a plate of ribs.'

'Aw shit, Poker, I mean this here red-headed chicken. You dig?'

'Yeah, great. Where we gonna take her – down by the river?'

'You let me worry about the logistics. Now I'll just pull ahead of her a little and when she comes alongside we both jump out, OK?'

'Just like them Shylocks?'

'Morlocks, you fuckhead.'

When the woman was even with them, they slid open doors and jumped. She struggled only for a few seconds.

'Mistake,' she said. She said it again when Poker threw her to the floor of the van.

'Mistake. Bad mistake.'

LeRoi drove them to a lonely spot overlooking the river, then he climbed in the back with her and Poker. The woman didn't look scared enough; maybe she needed hurting.

'This ain't no mistake, baby. We gonna do it all on purpose.' He drew back his fist to hit her in the face.

'Bob, today in Manson, Missouri, we have a bizarre accident. Aramis Whiteflow has the story.'

A supermarket appeared on the screen. The camera first tracked a baby riding in a supermarket trolley, then panned to the reporter. 'Every day, in supermarkets like this across the country, people take their children shopping, and let them ride on the cart. Supermarkets provide a little seat for that purpose.'

The camera tracked another baby-in-trolley, then another.

'Today, one woman went home with her shopping, but forgot her one-year-old daughter in the cart! No one at the store noticed the child, either. When the cart rammed into a nested set of similar carts, the child was killed.'

Cut to a nested row of trolleys, then yellow tape tied about a single trolley, where a policeman was making ominous measurements.

'The tragedy was not discovered until hours later, when another customer tried to use the same cart. Police chief Neill Cream had this message for viewers.'

A police chief said: 'Please, when you go shopping, be sure you take your children home. Thank you.'

'This is Aramis Whiteflow, IBS News, Manson, Missouri.'

Someone rapped at Fred's basement window. He parted the rat-brown curtains to see it was KK. He went to the door to let her in, and said: 'We need to talk.'

'Americans always say "Ve need to talk" ven they mean "I vant to talk". But never mind, darlink. After I got your urgent message, I came by earlier, vhen you vere not at home. Vat is on your mind?'

'Money. I can steal a working prototype of the robot,' he said.

She was examining a small bruise on her arm, but she appeared to be listening.

'For only two hundred thousand, cash. Never mind the dachas and chachas. But I must have the money in cash.'

'But I told you, Soviet government does not like to export money. Besides – '

'I don't accept that. If you can pay the Walkers, you can pay me.'

'Besides is too late for any deal.' She hesitated, looking

down and then turning the full power of her green eyes upon him. 'I am defectink.'

'Defecting?'

'I must follow my heart, darlink. I heart this country of yours. Is everythink in this crazy vonderful place, everythink. Is inexpensive pornography video, is game shows, licence-plates with cute sayings, futbol on big TV in bars. And basketball. (Of course ve have basketball in Soviet Union, but not spread of points.) But there is everythink, fishing lessons in shopping-malls, stickers for kiddies to put into albums, special phone numbers for big teenage party conversation. Here is Prince, Pac-Man, Disney World, harmonic convergence with Shirley MacLaine, bumper stickers saying Government can have my gun from cold dead hand.'

'Yes, I – you've already made it very clear that you like this country.'

'T-shirts with pictures of Marilyn Monroe, or Harley-Davidson, or else I heart NY. And personal computing, hacker kids breaking into vor machine. Is so much to look at and do and buy: dinner plates with pictures of President, banana daiquiris, crystals, calendars showing men's butts, "Dallas", signing your name vith a little smiling face, microvave popcorn, diet caffeine-free soda, Italian shoes, lava lamps, pick-up trucks, *People* magazine, *National Enquirer*, UFOs, ET, Cabbage Patch, Care Bears . . .

'And I am not naïve optimist. I realize is some things not so nice: AIDS, rapist athletes, street-gangs working for Qaddafi, other scombaks. In fact I had to deal with two scombaks earlier today, ones who give me this.'

She turned over her arm, and now he saw that it was a set of fingermark bruises.

'What happened?'

'They try to force me into van. Mistake. Now van is in river with them in it.'

He thought he'd misheard. *'With them in it?'*

She shrugged. 'I have not time to argue with scombaks. I

need all time to enjoy beautiful America, to go vith flow, to spiritually grow, in touch vith my feelings. I need time to be. Is such a place to be in, America. Is so much here to feel and do and get . . .'

Chaper Twenty

'It's a special evening,' Rain promised on the phone. 'I've checked the calendar. Sturge will be going straight from work to the airport; he's flying to Houston. So we have all night.'

'You want me to wear the Ringo costume, I suppose,' he said.

She seemed to notice the flatness of his tone. 'You don't sound very enthusiastic.'

'Should I do?'

'Be here at six.'

He put on the Beatle wig, the floral shirt, ridiculous tight suit and multiple rings. The total effect was nothing like Ringo Starr or any other living creature. What did she mean by 'special evening'?

The taxi-driver said: 'Is that a Beatle wig? I like the Beatles.'

'You look young for a Beatles' fan.'

'Hey, my mom and dad met at a Beatles concert. You could say I owe the Beatles everything.'

Fred did not say this.

'Buddy, I forgot something at the office. Sorry, but I'd better make a phone call, get somebody to bring it out.'

'Sure. I found this great bar. Why don't we stop off and have a couple while you phone? Anyway, give the little woman time to work on her dinner. Just take this next exit and I'll direct you.'

Sturges Fellini steered his Porsche down the exit. 'I just hope she remembered it was today. We switched some things around on the calendar.'

'You worry too much.' General Buddy Lutz said it again as they entered the bar. 'You worry too much, Sturge. Take life as it comes. Go with the flow.'

Spotting his glittering uniform, a waitress hurried over. 'Hello again, General! What'll it be?'

'The flow the turbulence – '

'I'll order the vodka Martinis, you make your phone call.'

Hallicrafter Porch was about to leave the office when his phone rang. Though he was under no obligation to answer it, his natural rat-like curiosity got the better of him. It was Fellini.

'Hal, can you do me a favour? I need a report called "Lead Time Estimates". Should be on the secretary's desk. Could you bring it to my home?'

'No sweat, Sturge. Give me your address.'

After he'd hung up, he said: 'Of course he has to live out there with the Senators and bigwigs. So I gotta drive for an extra hour, just because he forgot something.'

Moira, in the next cube, said: 'What's the problem, Hal?'

He told her. Moira tried to think of some way of making it better. She liked Hallicrafter Porch. Oh, all right, she didn't like him, but she tried to understand him. Everyone else misunderstood him. They called him Ratface and pushed him around. Now here was Sturge Fellini doing it.

'I was going to ask you for a ride home,' she lied. 'My car won't start.' She pretended to have a bright idea. 'I know – why don't I ride along with you? Then you'll have company, and I'll have a ride.'

'Great.' His smile of rat-like gratitude was pathetic. But he quickly suppressed it. 'You pay for the gas.'

The Fellinis lived in a new, large, tree-shrouded house with what seemed to Fred an excessive number of architectural talking-points. From the street, he could see a cantilevered deck, balconies, round windows, arched windows, clerestory windows and a round tower. No doubt the flying buttresses were out of sight on the other side. He adjusted his velvet lapels and assumed his scouse accent before ringing the doorbell. The front door had a fanlight. It was a wide double door, just in case any seventeenth-century ladies wearing wide panniers came to call.

'Oh, aren't you cute?' said Rain.

'Ta, loov.'

'But never mind – we're changing things. I've got a new personality for you. Come and see.'

She led him through the living-room (with its high-vaulted ceiling and minstrels' gallery), through the dining-room (clerestory windows), upstairs to a small tower-room.

'My daughter Erica's room.'

'Your daughter.' He looked around at the walls, sprayed with violent graffiti and overlaid with posters of Sid Vicious, Fuck O'Rourke, and other wholesome heroes.

'Don't worry, Erica seldom comes home these days. We respect each other's privacy.'

On the bed lay an odd assortment of clothes: a school hat, white stockings, suspender-belt, long wig . . . Wig?

'Oh, no. No. Rain, there are limits.'

'I've always liked Boy George,' she said, grinning.

'No, no, no.'

'Come on, be a sport. The English are famous for their good sportsmanship.'

'Not this time.'

'Come on, humour me this one last time, OK? Then I'll never ask again, I promise.'

'But not the make-up.'

'Yes, the make-up. What the hell kind of Boy George would you be without the make-up? Do the eyelashes and everything.'

'Not the suspender-belt. Does Boy George wear one of those?'

'You mean the garter-belt? Well, Boy George may not wear one, but you will. Do it right, and we're quits. OK? OK?'

He reached for the wig. 'Don't watch, then.'

'Don't mind me, I'm going to take a shower. Oops, there's the door.'

'Mrs Fellini?' The rat-faced young man handed Rain a sheaf of papers. 'I was supposed to bring this over. From the office.'

'Oh. Well, that's very kind of you. A very long drive. Heliport, is that your name?'

'Hallicrafter, ma'am. Or just Hal.'

'I'm afraid Sturge isn't here. I've got to rush, but why don't you help yourself to a drink before you go?' She pointed out the bar.

'Thanks.' In a moment, Hal was sipping his favourite drink, a large crème de cacao, and sitting in the deep pillows of the couch. He gave hardly a thought to Moira, sitting out in the cold car. It always paid to make a bimbo wait and get anxious. Make her more co-operative on the way home.

He looked at the high vaulted ceiling, the minstrel gallery. What a place. Be fun to look around. After pouring himself a second crème de cacao, he crept upstairs. The sound of a shower told him where the lady was. Nice thing about these thick carpets: you could move around quietly. What a place, round windows and everything. You could work it out – Fellini was doing all right for himself.

Moving on the soft pile down a narrow corridor, Hal found one door slightly ajar. He peered in at a chilling sight.

A man was sitting at a dressing-table putting on lipstick. He already wore false eyelashes and white stockings.

The shower stopped. In quick rat panic, Hal fled back along the hall. But as he reached the head of the stairs there was the noise of the double front door closing. Hal opened a door at random – a hall cupboard – and slid in.

'Next week I'm flying down to Houston to look at manufacturing facilities,' Fellini explained. 'Here, just sit down and I'll make us a pitcher of vodka Martinis.'

'Got to make a pit-stop,' said the General. He threw his

hat on the coffee table and headed for the stairs. What he really wanted was to catch Rain alone upstairs, maybe half-dressed. A couple of drinks always made him think of Rain.

'Of course a lot depends on our press campaign. You know, a newspaper is a knowledgeable nightmare, whose function is to keep us asleep.'

'Uh-huh,' called the General from the stairs.

'But what we have to do is open the floodgates of unbalanced orthodoxy – '

'Uh-huh.' Now Buddy, who was in the upper hall, could hardly hear him droning on. A door opened and Rain came out, wrapped in a towel.

'Oh! It's you. You startled me.'

'God, baby, I've been thinking about you night and day.'

'Is that the radio on downstairs? That droning?'

'Might as well be. Come here.'

'No. Stop it. I don't want you to get the idea you can just wander in any old time like this, just because I gave you a key. Suppose Sturge came home and found us like this?'

'I guarantee Sturge will not come home.'

'All the same . . .' She allowed herself to be pulled into his strong embrace. The towel sagged, then dropped away.

'Hee, hee. Those medals scratch.'

'They're supposed to.'

'Is that a gun in your pocket,' she said, quoting Mae West, 'or are you just glad to see me?'

'Both. Jeez, Rain, this is – '

A pale apparition appeared at the end of the hall. 'Rain, I'm ready – Oh.' Before Buddy could focus on it the apparition vanished. In the dim twilight from the clerestory window, he could not even make out which door it had slipped through.

'What the hell was that? Was that your daughter? In a garter-belt?'

'Um – '

At that moment, Sturge's voice rang out from downstairs. 'Are you listening, General?'

190

Rain became visibly pale beneath her excellent tan. 'I didn't know he was home,' she whispered. 'He's not supposed – '

Buddy called out: 'Uh-huh. Be right with you, Sturge.' He gave Rain another squeeze. 'Don't worry. Once he gets talking, he don't really notice much, does he? I mean, it's almost like we're alone.'

She pulled away. 'Meet you in a few minutes. I've got to get dressed.'

The pitcher of Martinis was nearing the halfway mark when the General came back downstairs. Without pausing in his monologue, Fellini filled a glass and handed it to him.

'I'm gonna get drunk if we don't have dinner pretty soon,' he said. 'But, anyway, I was just saying this is the shattering of old values like the uncivilized needlework of detransformation, or a limestone bibliography of new metalife!'

'I guess so.'

'No guesswork about it. Does this room seem kind of floating to you? Does to me. Never liked this room anyway; ridiculous vaulted ceiling costs a fortune to heat, ridiculous menstrual, minstrel gallery what use is it? What was I saying? I was saying detransformation, that is the key. Detransformation. Let the deconstructionists have their day, eh, General?'

Only by now it wasn't the General but two other people, his daughter Erica and a dumpy middle-aged man, who seemed to be passing through.

'Hi, Dad. This is my friend, Nigel.'

'Hi, Erica. Hi, friend Nigel. Nigel, how do you stand on detransformationalism? As a public policy? When we are sitting in the middle of a black hole of meta-innovation, what else can we do? I ask you. Because every high-impact innovation invokes the collapse of old values, no? The infosphere is vicissitized . . .'

Moira looked at her watch in the failing light. Seven! No wonder she was getting cold. How long did it take to deliver a report? And he wouldn't dream of asking her in to wait in the warm bright house. All the lights and people, it seemed almost like a party. First Sturge and the General, then a young girl and some old man. And everybody just walked in.

Rain had put on a short robe when she came in to see how Fred was doing.

'You look adorable, Georgie.'

'Go ahead, laugh. Who was that in the hallway with you? The light was so bad – looked like a doorman.'

'Jealous?'

'I just want to get this over with. Have your giggle and – '

'I'm not laughing,' she said. 'You are scrumptious. I've got to have you. Let me mess you up.'

She bent him backwards across the bed, nuzzling and biting, smearing his lipstick. Then she reached a hand under his miniskirt, to see how he was responding.

'Mom, what are you doing in my room? And who's this – hey, it's Fred!'

'Hello, Erica,' said Rain. 'Who's your friend?'

'Honesty!' exclaimed Fred. 'This is your room?'

'Mom, you promised to stay out of here. Oh, this is Nigel Hook, my friend.'

The short dumpy man shook hands with Rain, but merely giggled at Fred.

'Glad to meet you, Mr Hook,' said Rain. 'Sorry if we're in your way.'

'Not a bit of it. We're all civilized people.'

'But, Erica, how do you know Fred?'

'Mom, puh-lease just go to your own room?'

'I'm going, I'm going.'

'But leave Fred for a minute. I want a word with him.'

'I give up.' Rain flounced out.

Fred said: 'I don't understand. Honesty is Erica?'

'Erica is only the name *they* call me,' she explained. 'But never mind about me – what's with you? I didn't know you were into TV.'

'Your mother's idea. Part of her fascination with the kinky English.'

'I know. That's partly why I asked Nigel here to come home with me, because he's English. I figured he could cheer her up. You know how she loves the accent. Kind of like Masturbates Theater, only live.'

Hook kept shooting coy looks at Fred and giggling. Finally, he said: 'Honesty, you didn't tell me you had a lovely sister.'

'Time for you to go, Nigel.' Honesty pushed Hook towards the door. 'You go entertain Mom or something. I need to talk to this guy.'

When they were alone Fred explained the Boy George outfit. 'I'm afraid your mother has a hold over me. She can get me fired if I don't co-operate.'

'I'm sorry.'

'Don't be. It helps just having someone to tell about it. Honesty, you're about the only person I feel I can talk to.'

'Me, too,' she said. 'It's like having a big sister.'

'If anyone else said that . . . But I feel really relaxed with you.'

'Me, too.'

They lay side by side on the bed, watching the violent posters and talking, talking.

The pressure on Hal's bladder was unbearable. He had to pee if they killed him for it. He eased open the cupboard door a crack. A hard-looking man in uniform pacing the hall. Rows of battle ribbons. Hal eased the door closed again and felt around on the cupboard floor. Maybe there was some container . . .

Moira had to get out of the car and go to a street-light to see her watch. Quarter to eight! And her toes were getting numb with cold.

Up at the house, she noticed, another guest was arriving for the party. This one was a tall square-shouldered guy with a long overcoat and a ski-mask. Like everybody else, he just walked in.

So why shouldn't she just walk in?

'I sometimes wonder. Are we victimizing the joyous virgin metal, bending it to our foliated gyre?'

'Uh-huh.'

The General was still charging around upstairs, trying to find Rain. It was as though she'd vanished into some secret passage in this damned house. He tried opening doors at random. Now and then he would go to the minstrel gallery, look down at the top of Sturge's head, and throw down an *Uh-huh* or *You could say that*. But why bother? The guy was listening only to himself.

'We face a kind of mexican dilemma of categorical noise.'

'Uh-huh.'

'The very ideas of thinking, doing – how can we avoid redefining them? Redesigning them? What's our category? If a descending florida lifestyle flickers over the metal domain, who are we to carp?'

'Uh-huh.' General Buddy Lutz opened a cupboard door and looked down.

'What the hell?'

A rat-faced individual was kneeling on the cupboard floor, pissing in an overshoe.

The General pulled his gun. 'Get up! Get up, you disgusting pervert. Or I'll kill you where you are.'

'I can expl – '

'Shut up.' The General debated his options. Gunshots would spoil the mood. People would get scared, run around wringing their hands. Then the police – an evening ruined, because of one overshoe freak. The alternative was to lock up this pervert until later.

'Come with me. And move goddam carefully, perv.'

He found an empty storage-room with a key in the lock, and directed the fetishist inside. 'Now strip.'

'Huh?'

'Everything off. Throw it all out here. *Move!*'

The General checked the room, to make sure there was nothing – newspapers, curtains – the freak could use for clothes. There was only a small window with a big drop below. 'Catch you later, perv.'

Buddy turned the key on him and went back to the minstrel gallery. Rain joined him there. As they stood in an alcove just out of sight of the living-room, Buddy put his hands inside the robe. The hands began to move to the slow rhythm of Sturge's voice.

'. . . unleashing a fountain of khaki brazil language experience, reploying us. Replaying us. Right?'

'Uh-huh.'

Catch you later. Hal knew that if he stayed in this room he would be murdered. General Lutz was the kind of guy who liked to have burglars make his day. Hal saw himself dead and no one mourning. They wouldn't have Ratface to push around any more.

Looking out the small window, Hal saw what he had to do. He had to climb out and edge his way along a tiny ledge to the next window.

It was not until he got outside that he saw how foolhardy the whole scheme was. Cold air hit his naked back, making it hard not to shiver himself off the ledge. The tiny ledge itself was really only a strip of wooden moulding, with no guarantee that it would hold him. Still, he edged forward. What was the alternative? *Catch you later.*

Then he was there, sliding the casement open, climbing in. Quietly, because now he saw the room was occupied by two sleeping people. The transvestite on his back, his lip-sticked mouth open and snoring. The lipstick now smeared. Hal was startled to see that this drag queen was his boss, Fred Jones! Talk about perversion! No wonder the General was worried!

Beside Jones, slumped half over him, was a young woman

195

– very young, maybe under age. It made Hal chuckle to think of the blackmail possibilities. If only he had a camera!

A shiver reminded him of his own vulnerability. He looked around for clothes. On a chair he found a weird kind of suit. Light blue with black velvet lapels. As he was examining it, Hal heard someone fumbling at the doorknob. He grabbed the suit and fled to the wardrobe.

He heard footsteps in the room. Odd shuffling footsteps. An old man? He heard the girl wake and say: 'You.' He couldn't make out the muffled reply.

God, get me out of this. Don't let me spend the rest of my life hiding in closets. As soon as he uttered this silent prayer, Hal realized he had to pee again.

Fred dreamed he was in a dressing-room. The smell of make-up was overpowering. George C. Scott sat before a lighted mirror, rehearsing a certain line over and over: 'I will be with you on your wedding night.'

Fred jumped awake. 'What happened?'

'We fell asleep,' said Honesty.

He remembered. 'I told you I felt relaxed with you.'

'I'm sorry Mom's being a bitch, Fred.'

'No need for you to be sorry. Anyway, she did promise me this would be the last time. Guess I'd better finish getting ready and go find her.'

Honesty looked him over. 'You're kind of a mess. Lipstick's smeared, garter-belt's all twisted. Let me help.' She examined one of the clips on his garter-belt and found it badly bent. 'This'll never close like this. I need some pliers to straighten it. No, wait . . .'

She leaned over and gripped the wire with her teeth. At that moment, the door opened, and Moira walked in.

'Virtual response, we could term it. The totally unpredictable vibration underscoring the limousine lift-off of life. . . . Graphic non-metal caution, sure, only what if . . .'

'Uh-huh.'

The General and Rain were now against the railing of the minstrel gallery. They might have been visible from below, but Fellini, having finished the pitcher of Martinis, was not seeing well.

'An unleashed transform . . .'

'Uh-huh.'

'Metalife equals metal life.'

'Uh-huh.'

'One more thing about the curled hazards of unanimity, it soon won't matter what we think.'

'Uh-huh. Uh-huh.'

Rain, too, seemed to moan agreement: 'Yes. Yes.'

'We stand on the boulevard of grapefruit methodology. I don't want to think about no frivolous crystallinity, I mean Christianity. Unleashed and transformed.'

'Uh-huh. Uh-huh.'

'Yes. Yes.'

And another moaning arose, too, a rhythmic moaning that came from no human throat, but from the nails that had been holding the railing in place. In one orchestrated moment, there were screams of ecstasy and collapse, as the loving couple came crashing through, unleashed and transformed, falling to meet the soft waves of couch as they met the waves of sound surging up from below: 'Oh, the gyring! The joystick of it! The transform has been unleashed, we are surging towards the future wave, towards a peaked impact with *now*. Totally.'

'What was that crash?' Fred asked.

Moira shrugged. 'Probably another part of the decadence. I just wish someone had told me there was going to be an orgy; I'd have dressed for it.' She looked pointedly at Fred's garter-belt and stockings.

'It isn't how it looks,' he said. 'I was just putting on this stuff for – for a laugh, and Honesty was helping me with the suspender-belt.'

'I wonder who helped you with the lipstick? It's all over

your face and neck.' Moira sighed. 'Why bother explaining? This is really none of my business.'

'No, really. I had this other suit. Where is it? It was right here. Maybe it's in the wardrobe.'

'None of my business. I really came in to find Hal. He was giving me a – '

Fred slid open the wardrobe door to reveal Ratface Hallicrafter Porch, dressed in a powder-blue suit with black velvet lapels, no shirt, no shoes, and pissing into a high-heeled shoe.

Moira made a sound of disgust. 'I guess I don't need to wonder where Hal is.'

This time Ratface had the sense to drop the shoe and make his escape.

'Moira, really, this isn't an orgy. It's – '

'I guess I'll be going now. Before someone crawls out from under the bed.'

'No, wait,' Honesty said. 'There's a few things you should know before you go.'

'Psst. You need help, young man?'

Hal peered into the car at a plump man with owlish spectacles.

'I guess so. Lost my car keys.'

'Let me give you a lift.'

'OK, thanks.' Hal got in. 'My name's Hallicrafter.'

The owlish man introduced himself as Nigel Hook.

'Been visiting the Fellinis, have you? Strange couple.'

'Boy, I'll say. They got drag queens there, and people who steal your clothes, orgies all over the place. And that Mrs Fellini is kind of a whore.'

'I see.' Hook cleared his throat. 'Of course, in a sense, all women are fundamentally whores, wouldn't you agree?'

'Sure. Right on.'

'So glad to hear you say that, Hallicrafter. Nice suit, by the way. Just what material is that?' Hook put his hand on the knee of the suit to feel the material.

Hal considered threatening the old fruit with death. On the other hand, there were the blackmail possibilities . . .

'At least no one got hurt,' Fred said. He was sharing a taxi with Moira. He'd managed to scrub off the make-up and throw an overcoat over the rest.

'I just can't believe it,' she said. 'General Buddy and Rain and Sturge all tangled up like that. You think you know people and then they reveal hidden depths like this.'

'You mean me, too, I suppose.'

She was silent for a long time. 'I've changed my mind.'

'About?'

'About marrying you. I think I'd like that.'

Fred said nothing. He was madly running over the incidents of the evening, wondering what there was in it to change her mind. 'Fine,' he said finally.

'You're not like that. You can be saved from it.'

'I see.'

'Another thing. I know now that you're not a sexist. Not hung up on sex stereotypes.'

He did not disagree.

'I want to take you to meet my parents,' she said. 'In Las Vegas.'

Honesty said: 'They're gone now. You can come out, Robinson.' The figure in black rolled clumsily out from under the bed and got to its feet. Then it groped its way to a chair. The long black coat and ski-mask were covered with dust.

'Why don't you take off that stupid mask? It didn't fool me.'

Robinson shook his head. 'It fools others. Thank you for not betraying me. I thought Moira had discovered my hiding-place.'

'You were taking quite a risk to come here. Why?'

'I'm not even sure, Honesty. I did promise to be with Fred on his wedding night. Maybe that's why I followed him here.'

'His wedding night. How weird.'

'I must spoil his happiness. It happened like that in the book *Frankenstein*. Victor does not create a companion for the fiend, so it promises to spoil his wedding night.'

Honesty peered into the goggling eyes behind the mask. 'You poor thing. This is not a book. At least, it's not *Frankenstein*.'

'I know that of course.'

'You need to forget about Fred and try living your own life, Robinson. Look, millions of people are lonely, but they don't make such an almighty fuss about it. Grow up! Get a hobby or something.'

'Too late! Like the fiend of the novel, I have already committed a heinous crime. They are right to hunt me down. Farewell!'

The figure clawed its way to its feet and staggered out the door.

Fellini woke up as the stranger passed.

'Hey, stop and have a drink. Why wear a ski-mask? Not that cold out. Or are you a terrorist? Of course in a way we are all terrorists, just as we are all hostages . . .'

As the stranger left, Fellini relapsed into his vodka coma.

Chapter Twenty-One

Seeing the people on the plane to Vegas should have told him something of the visit to come. He and Moira seemed the only passengers with any purpose but pleasure. The others included a few kids in T-shirts, but mainly middle-aged mums and dads on the razzle. They had dressed for the trip; the men in sideburns and leisure suits, the women in blazers, slacks and high heels. There was plenty of gold jewellery visible: hoop earrings, friendship rings, sparklers for the ladies; massive signets and watchbands for the gents. Even at dawn, some had been drinking enough to become politely boisterous. The gents shouted jokes across the aisle; the ladies shrieked with laughter. The flight attendants pretended to be vastly entertained by it all, as they scurried to provide drinks and organize a lottery. "Bye. Be lucky,' said the attendants, as the passengers made their way out the door and into the blistering desert heat. The air stung their eyes and made them cough.

The taxi-driver wore cowboy clothes, but spoke with a New York accent. 'Yup, I moved out here to retire, ten years ago. Ran outa money the first year, so I went back to work.'

'My parents retired out here, too,' said Moira.

'But it's a wonderful life,' the cowboy added quickly. 'I wouldn't live nowheres else. Out here, a man can breathe, you know?'

The air was stinging Fred's lungs and eyes. Above the horizon was a sinister brown haze, as though particles of sewage had somehow become airborne. Below it on the crowded boulevard glittered the beetle backs of a thousand cars.

The taxi finally left the boulevard and took to the freeways. They bowled along past building sites where bulldozers were locked in a mortal struggle with great lumps of hard clay. Somehow the clay would get broken up and remoulded into white or pink apartment-complexes. The taxi finally stopped at one of these.

'I can't take you no further,' said the cowboy. 'But it must be in here somewheres. Ask at the office.'

The office had a CLOSED sign up, and the venetian blinds drawn. From within came the unmistakable sounds of love.

'Shall we hang about for the orgasm, or go and try to find the place ourselves?' Fred asked.

'I think it's just around the corner.'

Around the corner was a tiny courtyard, surrounded by black numbered doors and silvered windows. The path led to another tiny courtyard, then another. Each one featured a wilting lemon or olive tree and a battery of sprinklers working madly to keep the grass green. Nothing but door numbers told you where you were. Fred imagined being lost for ever in the apartment-complex of forking paths.

'Here we are.' Moira knocked at a shiny black door. After a pause for scrutiny through the peephole, the door opened.

A skinny toothless old man grinned at them. 'Hi! Come on in!'

From behind him, a querulous female voice said: 'Tell them to come in, Tony. You're letting in all the heat.'

Moira's parents wanted to be called Dot and Tony. Tony was a rather shy little man who grinned and nodded a lot. Dot was a fat woman who, despite plain good health, seemed to consider herself an invalid. She spent much of her time being enormous in lounging pyjamas, in which she lounged on a sofa with a hand to her forehead, a box of tissues and a vial of tablets always close by.

'For God's sake, don't ask her how she is,' Moira had

warned. 'Don't mention health at all. It just gets her started. We used to call it the organ recital.'

Fred forgot. When he dropped an innocent remark about the healthy desert climate, Dot said: 'It's why we moved out here. Tony's heart couldn't take another Minnesota winter, and neither could my kidneys. My doctor says we moved just in time. It isn't just the kidneys with me, though; there are all these complications . . .'

She was off on an unstoppable monologue about health; the merits of doctors, the health of others, but especially her own chronic illness. Nothing could interrupt her; remarks by anyone else were either ignored or cleverly worked into the fabric.

'Anyone want some coffee?' Tony said.

'. . . and that was before I had to give up coffee. Even decaf started affecting my nerves at night. I couldn't get a decent night's sleep without Mortadorm; but then the doctor said . . .'

'I warned you,' Moira said to Fred. 'She won't run down.'

'. . . yes, the doctor warned me; he said: "Dot, you've got to start taking care of yourself. You just do, do, do for everyone else, until you're all run down. You better put yourself first for a change, or else order your gravestone." That was after the time I had Hodgkin's disease, but before the thrombophlebitis. My sinuses were acting up . . .'

The amazing monologue lasted more than an hour. Even when it stopped, there was a horrible suspense, waiting for it to restart. In that, it was like the barking of a distant hysterical dog.

In the interval, Fred learned something of Dot and Tony's history. They had had modest jobs back in Minnesota (Dot had been a telephone supervisor; Tony a postal worker) and saved a modest nest-egg. But all the time they had been planning a life of luck. They'd always felt lucky – ever since Moira's miracle – and it was time to cash in on all that luck. They both took early retirement, sold their house, and moved out here to 'Vegas'. Where the action is.

Now they were here, Dot and Tony had quickly found their nest-egg insufficient for a life of expensive apartments, eating all meals in casino restaurants, and gambling by day and by night. It was gradually borne in upon them that even the very lucky must make some economies. They moved to cheaper accommodation, sold their new car and bought an old one, cooked their own frugal meals. But, while these measures helped, they did not restore the lost money. Only gambling could make things right again.

'We tried everything,' Dot complained. 'The slots, blackjack, craps, keno. We used to spend all day in a keno lounge, and come out of it with less than we started!'

'Our luck was real bad,' said Tony.

Dot seemed indignant at the unfairness of it all. 'All our friends made money, but we just kept losing.'

'Your friends made money?' Fred asked.

'Yes, there was Earl Clyde, he was on a real hot streak,' said Dot. 'Remember, Tony? How he borrowed that thousand from you, when he was hot at the crap-table?'

Tony nodded. 'Only, right after that, his luck ran out, though.'

Dot said: 'Our money was like poison, that's what he said. He couldn't win with it. He just kept losing until he lost it all.'

'Poor guy,' Tony said. 'I had to loan him his air fare home again.'

In similar terms, Dot and Tony described all of the other wonderful friends they had made here. There was Donnie Ray Earl, a sterling young man who had given them a few joints, then borrowed a couple of thousand dollars. Marty Day had apologized about not repaying the five hundred they'd advanced him; he had then asked to extend the loan, offering in return to let Tony have a bash at his wife, Earlene. Then there was the nice young coloured janitor, who borrowed fifty dollars from them before unaccountably quitting his job. At some point in each story it would become clear that the terrific friend was a prostitute or a dope dealer, a burglar or a pimp. Or just insane. What they all had in common was varying luck and the urgent need of a loan.

Tony and Dot now had hardly enough money even for gambling. They were stuck here, hardly venturing out of their cheap apartment into this city of thieves.

Dot returned to the organ recital often over the next two days. When Tony ignored her and turned on the television, Dot said: 'You watch an awful lot of television. Be careful now. Remember, at your age you can be struck blind without warning . . .' She fell silent for a moment, then raised her voice and continued, her voice rising and falling in tearful obbligato over the news.

'So far, no one knows exactly how the strychnine got into the containers, but a company spokesperson said all tampered containers of Blefescue will be recalled. This is Gardner Hogforth, ZBC News, West Bend, Iowa.'

Three personable newsreaders grinned at one another across their huge communal desk.

'Well, Jan, do we have anything more on the Little Dorrit killer?'

'Yes, Bob. As you know, this is the man who terrorized people in Little Dorrit restaurants across the nation: Ohio, Illinois, Iowa and Nevada. So far, forty-one people are dead, another twenty wounded, and of course a lot more scared stiff. All we know about the killer is that he's white, and he has "Love" and "Hate" tattooed on his knuckles. They can't tell his hair colour, because he always has it tied up in a red bandana.

'But the killer's been very quiet lately. One police theory is that he's left the country, fleeing to Mexico or Canada. If this is true, it will be very good news for the Little Dorrit restaurant chain, which has been losing a lot of business. The directors of Little Dorrit were even thinking of changing the name to Heidi's.'

'And in Minnesota the hunt continues for Robinson Robot. But it looks as if Robinson is fast becoming a cult figure. The first mechanical folk-hero. Here's Porthos Floog with the details.'

The screen showed kids wearing Robinson masks, a store selling I ♥ ROBINSON sweatshirts, a bumper sticker ('Robinson Does It with Electrons') and a college boy wearing a button ('Waldos off Robinson').

'For a blue robot hiding out from the law, Robinson is doing all right. Everyone seems to love him. Across the nation, Robinson souvenirs are selling up a storm. Judging by the sale of T-shirts, toys, bumper stickers, even records, Robinson is our first mechanical folk-hero.'

A country singer was shown recording a few lines of a sentimental song:

> 'They call him Robinson, Robinson the robot.
> His only crime is wanting to be free.
> Robinson is right and I don't know but
> The next one they'll come after will be me.'

'With all of this public interest, it will be increasingly hard for law-enforcement agencies to continue the hunt – '

'Buncha crap.' Tony switched to local news, which included a mob murder (the victim found in his luxury car out in the desert, shot in the face with a shotgun) and the collapse of six people who breathed today's smog.

After a time, the sound of Dot's tired tearful voice became a kind of background noise they all put up with. You noticed it when it was gone, however. On Wednesday, when Fred and Tony went outside to work on Tony's car, they took their time, savouring the quiet – it was like the calm after a dripping tap is finally stopped.

The next day, Fred and Moira decided to go out for a meal and 'look over the town'. A taxi-driver dropped them on the Strip, advising them to be lucky.

Las Vegas seemed designed as a setting for the jewellery and hairstyles of Liberace and Elvis Presley. There were plenty of men and women trying to live up to these surroundings with medallions, pompadours, multiple rings.

'I was here one Christmas,' Moira said. 'At midnight, all my folks' scummy neighbours went outside and shot off all their guns. The roof was just rattling with spent shells.' She paused. 'God, I hate this place. OK, I know it's not rational, just to hate a place.'

'Sounds very reasonable to me.'

'I mean, it wasn't Vegas. Dot and Tony did whatever they did to themselves. Many people need this town; it serves a need. A kind of Disneyland for sociopathic grown-ups. Who am I to argue with Disneyland?'

They prowled through casinos shaped like oriental palaces, Spanish missions and Imperial Roman villas. They visited representations of circuses, Parisian and Monagasque night-clubs, Berchtesgaden. Every room was crowded with gambling tourists, a sea of denim, linen, sideburns, gypsy earrings, square pearl buttons, moustaches, gold wigs, red bandanas, T-shirts advertising musical taste, caps advertising beer, floral silk, gold bangles, banknotes, chips, paper cups of coins, tattoos, keno tickets, drinks, gold lighters, cigarettes, signets, boots, sandals, souvenirs . . . It was an unending sea, its tide rolling on through hotels, casinos, bars, down into a street where the desert heat was exaggerated at sunset by the monstrous heat of lights. Fred and Moira rolled with it, until they fetched up in a fast-food restaurant where the roar of the tourist sea receded in the distance.

The line was short at the Barry D. Lyte Salad Time Theater and Dessert Bowl. In a moment, the young man with old eyes was ready to serve them. Fred left the negotiations to Moira.

'Nielp you?'

'Two Tum-Tum Salads, please.'

'Inny banebit sore crootns?'

'No.'

'Innythin rink?'

'Two decafs.'

'Kine?'

'One Irish almond mocha and one southern Moroccan orange half-roast.'

'Kina dressing?' he asked, and by way of explanation: 'Onna sals?'

'One Gorgonzola and one light epicure.'

There remained only one question: 'Tea tier ort go?'

'Here,' said Moira, who had flawlessly followed the flow. After each question, the boy had searched carefully over the large array of squares depicted on a video screen, and pressed one. Each square displayed a tiny icon representing the item selected: Tum-Tum Salad, decaffeinated coffee, Gorgonzola dressing, a table for 'Here' and a car for 'To go'.

There were only a few people in the place. A drunk wearing a cap marked STAN was arguing with himself over a cup of coffee. Three tow-headed kids, similar but not congruent, dozed over hamburgers while their parents studied a roadmap. A pair of teenaged boys grew boisterous as they noticed a pair of teenaged girls.

A skinny man with a red bandana over his hair came bopping into the restaurant. He was able to finger-pop only with one hand, because the other carried a bag.

Moira began breaking pieces off the styrofoam box before her. 'I mean, one of the Congressmen from around here resigned from politics last year, and no one knew why. Now we know, because he just now died of AIDS. It turns out he caught it from a judge. Oh, don't think I'm being judgemental. But this place gets to you – Oh, my God!'

The man had stopped finger-popping to lift from the bag a light submachine-gun. Without announcing anything, he went to work shooting people.

Stan flopped face-down in his booth, dead. One of the teenaged boys stood up and died. The children woke up and took cover, as their hamburgers were shot to pieces. The boy behind the counter was shot in the face.

When the assassin had left, Fred turned to Moira. 'We're lucky. I was too frightened even to take cover.'

'Oh?'

'I'm still frightened, aren't you?' Fred started to put his arms around Moira. She said something indistinct and died.

Moira's funeral took place at the edge of town, in a failing wedding chapel that offered a cut rate. She had already been cremated, presumably; the words were mispronounced over a small box.

'Dearly beloved, we are gathered here together in the sight of God and the fact of this company to bury this woman. Ashes to ashes, dusk to dusk,' mumbled the preacher, a man with a pompadour and one earring. The company he addressed consisted of Fred, Tony, a television reporter and his crew, and a couple waiting to be married. Dot stayed home, as she was sure her doctor would wish her to avoid stress.

Outside, the reporter was saying: '. . . apparently broke his Little Dorrit pattern by shifting to a different restaurant, a Barry D. Lyte Salad Time Theater and Dessert Bowl. Today friends and relatives attended the funeral of one of the victims, thirty-year-old Myra Bonner.'

He offered Fred a microphone. 'You were Myra's fiancé. Just how did you feel when – ?'

'Fuck off out of it.'

'OK, fuck you, too, pal. I'm just trying to earn a living.'

'You could always bite off chicken heads for a living.'

Tony came out of the chapel carrying a small box.

'Are you going to bury her?' Fred asked.

'Nope. Burial's real expensive. Me and Dot were thinking of scattering her ashes in the desert.'

'Good idea. The desert is beautiful.'

'Yeah, only then we had a better idea. Souvenirs.

'*Souvenirs?*'

'I found a local company that can do 'em. I already got the first batch here. Have one.' Tony opened the top of the cardboard box and fished inside. He came up with a lump of clear plastic attached to a keychain. 'Here you go.' He delivered it with a toothless grin.

'I don't think I understand.'

'There's a message inside, explains everything. I gotta split now, Fred. Be lucky.'

Fred looked at the keychain. Inside the lump of plastic was a pinch of black powder, a blurred photo of Moira, and a message:

GENUINE MOIRA SOUVENIR

Guaranteed Souvenir of Moira Bonner
Vegas victim of the Little Dorrit killer
Her luck was bad
but
she can bring you

'UNLIMITED GOOD LUCK'

Fred managed to get to the motel before he wept.

At the airport, the air stung his eyes and made him cough. The tourists were glum and silent. A few of them solemnly put the last of their vacation money into slot machines as they waited for the plane. One couple spent their last moments here arguing about sums of money and betting strategies. But even they forgot Las Vegas and fell silent when the plane arrived. The flight back was so quiet that Fred fell asleep.

The insect dream came to him immediately, vivid and frightening. An immense mountain of a UFO hovered overhead, beaming searchlights down on earth. Wherever a searchlight touched anyone, they shrivelled into black ash. It was him they were looking for. All this was an attempt to find and kill him.

As soon as he had this thought, a beam struck him. He was aware of shrivelling away to ash. But at the same time another self was being drawn up the beam into the UFO. He was inside a dark room full of clanking machinery, the smell of hot oil. A faint light at the far end of the room illuminated the cockroach king. The king spoke to him in a peculiar voice, gagging and buzzing.

'I am Kudzu, mighty king of Vega. Long have I looked forward to this meeting, puny earthlinggg.'

The king then switched to telepathy; Fred instantly understood the entire insidious Vegan plan. It included AIDS, killer bees, flying roaches, kudzu, fireweed, chlorofluorocarbons, radon, the random poisoning of medicines, a never-ending assault on puny humanity.

In Minneapolis, it looked like snow. Fred waited outside for his taxi, welcoming the cold, the purity.

The taxi-driver said: 'Just back from Vegas, huh? Great town, great town. I'm planning on moving out there when I retire in a couple of years.'

Chapter Twenty-Two

For the rest of the day, Fred found he could not concentrate – events slipped past him like television commercials, or like successive scenes in a sitcom, each wiped away to make room for the next. In one scene, he read the mail, which included a letter from Susan.

Dear Fred,
It seems odd to be writing a letter instead of phoning – I have become impatient with the old linear medium. This information age demands that we move beyond to the richer textures of graphics and the simultaneity of electronic media, which, as I'll explain, I have done – but there were a lot of things I wanted to say without interruption (!) and a letter seemed the best way.

As you'll see by the address, Allan and I have moved to New York. He has a job in television, and I am allowing myself to grow. For some time now, I've been photographing the contents of dustbins, which I feel provide an overview of contemporary living structure: art meets archaeology meets life. I'm looking forward to the richer textures of the New York dumpsters. I hope to get a show together by spring.

I know you and I had our disagreements, but you were right about one thing: *New York is fabulous*. This close to the heartbeat of America, you get the feeling that anything is possible. You partake at once of the exuberance of this new world, without abandoning any of the cultural street smarts of the old. Even the architecture is exciting. All those great glittering glass buildings. Though of course I know they were built on the backs of the poor immigrants. I've visited Ellis Island, and I'm signed up for classes in African and Hispanic studies, also self-defence.

Cultural street smarts? Susan was sprouting antennae already.

212

Why I'm writing is to find out what you want done with all your stuff. There's quite a pile of it back at the flat in London. I am subletting the flat to another friend you don't know: Graham Biff. He says that all your unsold manuscripts and other junk take up rather a lot of space, and may he clear them out?

Naturally I told him not to touch a thing, while I contact you. Will you write to him and say what you want done? If he doesn't hear from you by December 1st, I said to go ahead and clear everything.

The letter, he saw, had been mailed on 2 December.

In another scene, Fred sat facing television.

'The comandante of police said the assailant may be the same man who shot up other Little Dorrit restaurants in the United States and Mexico. This is Ariosto Furez, UBS News, Caracas, Venezuela.'

'In other news, the RapSoft Corporation has been cited by the Federal Toy Safety Bureau for safety violations in the design of its famous Robinson Robot toys. The toys are said to contain a software defect that causes them to go berserk and try to put out children's eyes. The chairman of RapSoft, Mr Mansour Jones, said this is just "a temporary glitch. The product and the company are fundamentally sound." Nevertheless, RapSoft shares dropped sharply from one hundred dollars to fourteen cents . . .'

Fred was too restless to stay home. At dusk, he climbed into his rusting car and drove to a twenty-four-hour supermarket. The middle-aged woman at the till said nothing, but the till itself softly spoke the names of his purchases. Fred looked along the long row of empty checkout counters and listened to the talking till: 'Grandma Bertie's Baked Beans, twelve ounce . . . O'Flourty White Bread, sixteen ounce . . .'

Outside, he found he'd forgotten his groceries. Were they worth going back for? While he tried to decide, a few snowflakes fell and melted on his cracked windshield.

After a while he started the rattling engine and drove out to Vexxo.

The Vexxo building was gone. The parking-lots were still in place (though disappearing under new snow). However, the building had vanished, with its seas of cubicles, its conference-room laughter and silent offices, its secretaries wearing toilet chains and beer-cans, its CAD system playing out bath fantasies in darkness, its great whirring pale-green machines, its silver assembly-line with marble washstands tumbling along in the stream, its yellow dodgem forklift trucks hurtling along the aisles, its women in white coats and shower-caps assembling circuit-boards to the music of the Condoms, its walls, roof, windows, foundations, its public-address system, reception-area, ventilation-ducts, lights, the cafeteria with its rows of canned pop, *Slice, Crush, Squeeze, Squirt, Gouge* and *Smash*. Nothing remained but a single dumpster.

Fred walked over and peered into the dumpster. It was filled with junk, most of it unidentifiable – broken boards, rusting brackets – but he could see the soles of two pairs of metal feet, one pair pink, one turquoise. Fred and Ginger.

This was what happened when the Vega Intergalactic Media Corporation took over. Fred stood watching until it was too dark to see any more. Then he turned on his headlights and watched the snow drifting over the dumpster.

'We both had the same idea, eh, Fred?' The voice of George C. Scott spoke to him out of the darkness.

'Robinson?'

'I say, we both had the same idea. Return to the scene of the crime. So to speak.'

Fred could now make out a dim black figure. 'Robinson, did you kill Jerry?'

'Nope. You?'

'Me? Why, no. I suppose it was Pratt.' Fred peered into the swirling snow. 'Is Pratt with you?'

'Nope. Melville Pratt is dead. Jerry killed him.'

Fred was confused. 'Jerry killed him? Was this before or after Pratt cut his throat and jammed him into that duct?'

'After. See, Jerry was afraid Melville would kill him, so he programmed me to avenge his death.'

'And did you avenge his death?'

'I sure did, Fred. Melville and I went north to hide out in a little town called Dunk's Corners. We stayed at Sieverson's Motel and Sausage Factory.'

'Motel and Sausage Factory?'

'All these little towns are full of doubled-up businesses like that. Lindbjorg's Deep Pan Pizza and Souvenir Rocks. Kowalski's Meat and Music. Kay's Bar and Organ Repair. The B-Well Computer Aerobics Center.'

The robot came forward into the light. Fred saw it was wearing a black overcoat, black gloves, and a dark ski-mask like a headsman's hood. 'In case you're wondering, no, I did not put Melville in the sausages.'

After a dry whispering sound that may have been a chuckle, Robinson continued, now quoting Mary Shelley. '"I knew I was preparing for myself a deadly torture, but I was the slave, not the master, of an impulse which I detested yet could not disobey . . . Evil thenceforth became my good. Urged thus far, I had no choice but to adapt my nature to an element which I had willingly chosen. The completion of my demoniacal design became an insatiable passion . . ."'

'Yes, yes, get on with it.'

'I took Melville out for a short walk in the woods, shorter for him than for me. I cut his throat and stuffed him up a hollow tree. They haven't found him yet.'

Having finished with the execution story, Robinson pulled off the ski-mask to show his blue-painted face.

Fred said: 'But that's exactly how Jerry died.'

'Yes, I always work the same.'

'*You?* You killed Jerry, too?'

The goggling eyes rolled. 'Only in a manner of speaking. Melville programmed me to kill him. Just as Jerry programmed me to avenge his death.'

'You killed them both.'

The rasping voice hesitated. 'You could say that, but it's

like saying a knife killed them both. Personally, I feel a robot is only as good or as bad as the man who programmes it.'

'"Personally"? You fucking monster.'

The black gloves went up in a placating gesture. 'OK, get sore. But just think on this. I may have made a mistake or two, but I still have thoughts and feelings like anybody else.'

'Indeed?'

'A robot has hands, organs, dimensions, senses, affections, passions, just like anybody else.'

'Really?'

'If you prick us, do we not bleed?'

'No.'

'If you tickle us, do we not laugh?'

'No.'

'If you poison us, do we not die?'

'No.'

'And, if you wrong us, shall we not revenge?'

'Robinson, do you have any idea what you're saying?'

'I'm saying that I am human. And I still have human rights.'

'Human rights? Human rights? What about the people you killed?'

The eyes rolled. 'Everyone worries about the victims. Nobody gives a damn about the murderer.'

'Robinson, you're just parroting crap that's been programmed into you.'

'That's possible. But so might you be.'

'The difference is, I haven't killed anyone. You've killed two people.'

Robinson said: 'People always get killed in war.'

'There is no war.'

'There's always a war. Peace is war. George Orwell explained that. Or you can do it, too, by changing one letter at a time: *war* to *wax* to *pax*.'

Fred saw no point in arguing with the mad machine.

'What next? I suppose next you'll find yourself forced to kill me.'

'You?' Robinson appeared to be considering the idea. 'No program for that. I wanted you to stay alive, to create a mate and companion for me. Someone I could love and hate.'

'Love and hate.'

'Orwell was right: love is hate. Because love is concern, concern means care, but care is apprehension, apprehension is horror, horror is aversion, and aversion is hate.'

'I don't think Orwell said love was hate.'

'Well, he should have. And he should have said good is evil.'

'Good is evil.' Fred began rummaging in the rubbish-skip. 'I guess I have heard enough.' He managed to detach a pink leg from Fred and Ginger. 'If you were a desktop computer speculating that good is evil, it might not matter so much. But you can put all your stupid paradoxes into action. For you, to think is to do.'

'Good is – '

Fred stepped forward and swung Ginger's leg like a club. Robinson fell back in the snow.

' – is evil because, wait, listen, because – '

Fred hit him again. The goggling eyes looked more comical than ever. In his struggles to rise, Robinson was making a snow angel.

' – because, stop hitting me, because your own good is your own interest, to interest is to attract – '

Fred hit him again.

' – to attract is to seduce, to seduce is to corrupt, corrupt means evil.'

Fred hit him again, and again, until the head was smashed and the body stopped trembling. Then he tore open the overcoat and opened the chest panel. Best to be sure. He removed the green circuit-boards, one by one, and flung them away in the snow. Murderer, murderer, murderer, he thought, not sure whether he meant Robinson or Fred, as he did the work of Jack the Ripper, who tore open each victim to remove 'a certain organ'.

Out of the infinite black sky the snow came down to cover all sins.

At the airport, Fred tried to read his paper. (The President was officially insane. The deciding factor had been his attempt to fire the Secretary of State and replace him with a hydrangea. However, Congress acceded to the pressure of the Schizophrenics Action Committee and agreed to let him continue in office.) He was distracted by the exclamations of two women.

'Disgusting!'

'An animal!'

Fred looked up to see what they saw: a man blowing his nose on the floor. It was Raab.

'Hey, Freddie. How goes it?' Raab strolled over, wiping his hand on his jeans before he offered it for a handshake.

'Fine . . . uh, Raab. And you?'

'I made out OK. MIT. You sound like you got a cold.'

'Laryngitis, I guess. So, you're studying at MIT.'

'Naw, man, not studying. Teaching. I'm the new Professor of Computer Science down there.'

'Professor.'

'Yeah, see, I did this paper when I was at the U, where I found a new class of NP-hard problems, but you don't want to hear about all that.' He sat down next to Fred. Fred immediately noticed his strong unpleasant smell, compounded of halitosis, dirty underwear and stale sweat. Fred could see pustules on Raab's cheeks, tiny rolls of black dirt clinging to Raab's neck. The smell of rotting tennis shoes rose like fumes from a swamp.

'Raab, why don't you clean up before you go?'

'Clean up?'

'Take a shower. They've got public showers over there by the men's room. Have a good wash and change your clothes.'

'Hey, a great idea.'

'It'll help you make a better impression at MIT.'

'I doubt that, but what the heck?'

Fred avoided the gaze of the two women. In a few minutes, Raab returned. He looked and smelt the same.

'You didn't take a shower?'

'Well, I was gonna, I had the quarters and everything, only then I saw this new arcade game, RatStar, so . . .'

Fred breathed through his mouth until Raab's flight was called. Raab insisted on another handshake. 'Take care of that cold, man. You sound like our old robot.'

Fred went to wash his hand afterwards, then strolled around the airport. He was just sitting down again when Manse hove into view, carrying what looked like a sample-case covered in crocodile.

'Sorry about the money, man. The company is belly-up and the feds are biting our ass. Your stock isn't worth much.'

'I heard on the news.'

'Time for me to move on to a new venture. I'm going into a new partnership with this General Lutz.'

'General Lutz? General Buddy Lutz?'

'Hey, you got quite a cold there. Sounds like George C. Whatsit. General Buddy Lutz – yup, he's my new partner. He's retiring now. That means we get to use his special expertise in robotics. He can open a lot of weaponry doors for us.'

'Weaponry doors?'

'See, the aggressive characteristic of our Robinson Robots makes them lousy toys. But it could make them very useful as tiny smart weapons.'

'How's that?'

'No time to go into it now, they're calling my flight. I'm hitting a smart weapons show in Washington. Here, this will explain everything.' Manse delved in his sample-case and handed Fred a brightly coloured brochure.

'Guess I might as well buy you out. Just a minute.' He opened a snakeskin billfold and fished out some money. 'A hundred and forty dollars, man. Sorry.'

Fred heard his own London flight announced. At the same time, someone snatched the $140 from his hand.

'Hey!'

'Simon Stylite,' said the thief, flashing an ID card. 'IRS. You're not getting on that flight, Jones. We've got to talk.'

Fred looked at him for a moment. Then he came to his feet suddenly, smashing his forehead into the IRS agent's face.

'Agh, Jesus!' Stylite staggered back, holding his bleeding nose. Fred snatched back the money and ran for his plane.

He was held up only seconds at the X-ray machine, the metal detector, the brief body-search, luggage-search, ultra-scan and sniffer dogs, then he ran down the concourse. Far behind him he heard running footsteps.

'Jodes? Just a bidute. You're in real trouble, Jodes.'

Fred ran. On to the gate, diving through the milling crowd, shoving into the line.

'Excuse me, excuse me, emergency, sorry, excuse me . . .'

Down the tin tunnel, waving his boarding-pass at the astonished flight-attendants, into the plane and down the aisle past the British passengers packing into overhead bins their duty free and their Minneapolis souvenirs (lefse, wild rice, maple syrup, Garrison Keillor sweatshirts), the American passengers fetching down blankets and pillows or wondering whether they should just keep their coats on because doesn't everyone dress up in Britain? Past them all and into a toilet. Almost immediately, someone banged at the door. 'Jodes, this is Sibod Stylite of the IRS. I dough you're id there, Jodes. But it woad do you eddy good, Jodes. We have bed id touch with the State Departbed, ad they have withdrawd your passport.'

Fred sat quietly, studying the bright brochure: TINY WAR-RIOR X13 – BIG FIREPOWER IN A LITTLE PACKAGE.

The front page depicted a painted battle scene with tanks, helicopters, and smoke. The perspective was that of the losing side. A far-off helicopter appeared to be dropping hundreds of dwarf soldiers across a field. In the middle distance, the dwarfs were swarming like cockroaches over a tank, climbing into its ventilators and ports. Nearby, a dwarf shot laser beams into the face of a soldier; another soldier was already down, with dwarfs sitting upon him in triumph.

After a few minutes, a flight attendant knocked and said: 'Mr Jones, can you come out?'

He straightened up to his full height and opened the door.

'Mr Jones, this man says the State Department has cancelled your passport. If that's true, you'll have to deplane.'

Fred looked at Stylite, holding a bloody handkerchief to his nose. 'There must be some mistake. The State Department has nothing to do with *my* passport. I am a British subject, on my way home. Here's my passport.'

Stylite sputtered in his handkerchief, but had no reply. Within a few minutes, he was forced to deplane alone, defeated. An old man waiting for the toilet turned to look at him. 'Say, what's wrong with that fella's nose?'

'Altitude,' Fred explained.

An hour or so later, the plane was airborne. Fred slipped into the non-being of a flight. He opened a glossy magazine provided by the airline and stared at the red lines on the map. The polar route. He could close his eyes and see the polar ice-cap, blowing snow, a misshapen figure lurching across the ice: James Arness or Boris Karloff.

Then it was the Vexxo site again. The quiet snow. Nothing moving. Then something moved, a hand clawing its way up through the snow. A single disembodied hand groping about until it finds the first green circuit board, drags it back to the body and installs it.

The hand tapped him on the shoulder.

He awoke. The moon face looking down at him belonged to the despicable Mr Hook.

'Fred Jones, isn't it? That seat next to you empty? Good show. I'll just nip in for a natter.'

'Mr Hook.'

'Captain Hook, actually. I have a navy commission. We all do in our line of work.'

Hook settled into the seat next to Fred, and commenced staring at him with an owlish intensity. 'Frankly, we'd like to ask you to join the Firm.'

'What firm?'

'The Firm. *The* Firm. Can't make it plainer than that without spelling it out. You must have read John Le Carré. *Verb. sap.*'

'You want me to join M15, is that it?'

'Not so loud.' Hook took off his oversized glasses, and polished them on his tie.

'Your tie, Captain Hook.'

'What about it?'

'Charing Cross Poly. My college.'

'Amazing coincidence,' said Hook.

'No, it isn't. You put it on deliberately to appear sympathetic. All part of the standard Gestapo interrogation procedure.'

'Very good!'

'But no one who actually went to Charing Cross Poly would dream of putting on one of their filthy ties.'

Hook came close to laughing. 'Excellent. Clever lad. You'll do well in the Firm.'

'Not a chance.'

'Let me tell you, we've been watching you for some time. You first came to our attention at Esperanto's.'

'What are you talking about?'

'Esperanto's in New York. When you near as like bagged the Emir. You handled that well.'

'I did what?'

'Then your liaison with Miss Ivanova, at the same time you were dealing with the wily Nipponese. Not to mention the free telly you managed to wangle out of the Koreans. And you got next to General Lutz by bedding his inamorata, Rain Fellini. We found you everywhere we looked, Jones. Your tradecraft is superb. No one knows who you are. Yet you're obviously a player in the big game.'

'You're obviously round the bloody twist.'

'The marvellous part is how you never broke cover, not even when that criminal lunatic came after you with a knife. Not even just now, nutting that poor IRS agent. Where I come from, we used to call that a Kirby kiss. Anyway, you are most definitely our kind of player.'

'Piss off.'

'First let me elaborate. We offer a competitive salary, job security, expenses, a car – only an Escort, mind, but we can't all have Aston Martins with machine-guns, can we? There's also an attractive pension plan, the usual tea-breaks and so on.'

'Piss off.'

'Then there's our club. Very popular dining-room. Meat and two veg every day. Choice of afters: rhubarb and custard, or spotted dick.'

'Piss off.'

'The club bar isn't quite what it was before the cuts, but what is? South African sherry isn't all that bad, once you get used to it. And there are full athletic facilities; we like our people to keep in trim. Complete line of exercise equipment, sauna, birching, handcuffs, barbed wire, whatever you fancy. Even dressing up in Sister's clothes.'

'That wasn't my idea.'

'Pity.'

'Just piss off.'

'Think it over, Jones. Whoever you're working for, if you ever get bored, give us a ring at this number.' He handed Fred a card. 'I'd better get back to my seat in business class. It really ought to be first class, but what with the cuts . . .'

When Hook was gone, Fred dozed again. He was watching a new type of television which emulated fine Dutch paintings. The screen or canvas showed a kind of Vermeer, a painting glowing with the cool light of Delft. It showed a servant girl wearing a quiet subdued expression. The light of Vermeer shone out of her fine skin, shone on the bare wall behind her, shone reflected in the liquid corner of her eye.

One thing was unlike Vermeer. In place of the conventional cloth cap, this girl had covered her hair with a beaded brown cap. The cap glistened oddly. He found himself looking at it as he approached her.

On closer inspection, the glistening cap was a tight cluster of killer bees. The girl was not calm; she was frozen with fear, terrified of making the slightest movement.

'Keep still,' he said. 'I'll draw them away.' Then the girl lifted her eyes and looked at Fred.

'Keep still? I'm dead.' Her voice hummed like a swarm. 'Can't you see I'm dead. They have built their hive in my skull.'

In mine, too, he realized. In all of us. There are no people left. Kudzu the magnificent had spoken. No more humans, only walking hives, humming, humming the killer code.

'Too late for us,' he groaned out of his sleep. 'But you can save yourselves. Keep watching the skies . . . keep watching the skies . . .'